Dear Reader,

One of the things that I've learnt from your letters (and do *please* keep them coming in – I'm always delighted to hear from you all!) is how much you enjoy the variety of *Scarlet* characters and storylines. That's why choosing the month's books is always such an exciting challenge for me. Will readers prefer the ups and downs of married life to a story about a single woman finding happiness? What about books featuring children?

This month all of these themes appear. The heroines of Clare Benedict's *A Bitter Inheritance* and Margaret Callaghan's *Wilde Affair* are both, in their very different ways, prepared to make sacrifices for the sake of a child's happiness. *The Second Wife*, by Angela Arney, highlights the problems involved when two single parents fall in love and decide to combine family forces. In *Harte's Gold*, by Jane Toombs, the no-nonsense single heroine faces a different sort of family problem: how to protect her susceptible grandmother from being conned when a film company rents their ranch and she has her doubts about the attractive leading man.

Whatever your taste in romantic reading I hope that you enjoy this month's *Scarlet* selections.

Till next month,

Sally Cooper

SALLY COOPER,
Editor-in-Chief – *Scarlet*

About the Author

Jane Toombs is a registered nurse and well-known as the author of many romances, both historical and contemporary. She has twice been a finalist in the prestigious Romance Writers of America published writers' contest. *Harte's Gold* is Jane's first book for *Scarlet*.

In her spare time reading remains Jane's consuming interest, as it has been all her life. She likes to travel and has particularly enjoyed visiting the British Isles and Canada. She also knits, sails, and plays the occasional hand of bridge as well as gardening, 'which is mostly dealing with weeds!'

Other *Scarlet* titles available this month:

THE SECOND WIFE – Angela Arney
A BITTER INHERITANCE – Clare Benedict
WILDE AFFAIR – Maragret Callaghan

JANE TOOMBS

HARTE'S GOLD

Enquiries to:
Robinson Publishing Ltd
7 Kensington Church Court
London W8 4SP

First published in the UK by Scarlet, 1997

A copy of the British Library Cataloguing in
Publication data is available from the British Library

ISBN 1-85487-860-3

Printed and bound in the EC

10 9 8 7 6 5 4 3 2 1

CHAPTER 1

Carole Harte wheeled her black mare so her back was to the clouds darkening the northern sky and reined in at the crest of the hill.

'We need the rain, Sombrita,' she said.

The mare's ears twitched and she raised and lowered her head as though nodding agreement.

Carole smiled at Sombrita's response. Sometimes she was almost positive the horse understood her. Her smile faded almost as soon as it began. Yes, rain would be welcome, but it was only a stopgap. Unfortunately, the other needs of the ranch couldn't be solved so easily.

She brushed away a strand of raven hair blown across her face by the freshening breeze and gazed at the valley below, the land golden in the September sunlight.

Ezra Harte, her twice great-grandfather, a gold-seeking Forty-niner, had settled on this land instead of merely staking a mining claim and Hartes had flourished here in California's San Joaquin Valley ever since. He'd found no

1

gold but, a farmer to the marrow of his bones, had established a successful ranch after buying an old, abandoned Californio ranchero.

Except for her grandmother, Carole was the only Harte left and she, like her grandfather and father, had inherited the Harte love of the land. After her father died, she'd made a vow to keep Harte's Way in the family no matter what.

The question was, how? Where was the money to come from? When she was a child she'd believed the old story of stolen gold hidden on Harte land by Californio bandits and had searched diligently, finding nothing. Her father used to tease her, saying the only gold around was in her 'California' eyes. 'Unless you count the groves and the grass,' he'd always added.

She glanced to the right where orange trees sidled up terraced hills, the silver blades of the wind machines on their tall towers glinting above them. No gold to be seen at the moment – the fruit was as green as the leaves on the navels and the Valencias weren't yet in bloom. The orange trees would welcome the rain.

To her left the golden grass of the Sierra foothills was dotted with grazing Herefords. From the time she was big enough to sit a horse, she'd ridden over the ranch with her father, learning to love the land as he did. The last three years she'd ridden alone and she still missed him.

Carole turned to glance at the Sierra peaks

rising to the east, knowing the coming storm would add to their perpetual caps of snow. Like her father, she never tired of coming to this rise where, in every direction, the view was breathtaking. Though she'd tried more than once to persuade her grandmother to ride here with her, Theda Harte never had.

It wasn't that Theda didn't love beauty – the problem was she loathed horses. And she'd never been interested in ranching.

A plume of dust caught Carole's eye – a car speeding east on the county road. A white sports car she didn't recognize, possibly a Jag. A knight in a shining white Jaguar? She grimaced at the errant thought. She had no need – or time – for knights, even if they still existed. And especially not if they drove Jags.

Could the car be headed for the ranch house? Carole shook her head – Theda hadn't mentioned expecting company. A cloud blotted out the sun, darkening the day and she glanced over her shoulder, seeing she'd have to hurry to outrun the rain.

Clucking Sombrita into motion, Carole let the mare pick her way down the hill before urging her into a lope. When they came to a narrow road running north and south, Sombrita veered on to the gravel, aware without needing Carole's guidance that it was easier to cross the stream via a bridge than to push through the giant reeds called tules.

They rounded the curve leading to the bridge and Sombrita snorted, dancing to one side as an oncoming truck braked, air whooshing. Carole pulled the mare on to the grassy verge, staring in surprise at the large semi and the caravan of smaller trucks and trailers that had stopped behind the semi. After a few more miles this road dead-ended – where on earth could they be going?

'Hey!' The driver of the semi, a burly gray-haired man with a red rose tattooed on his upper arm, leaned from the window. 'You on the horse. How the hell do I get to a ranch called Harte's Way?'

Carole gaped at him for a moment before gathering her wits. 'Why do you want to go there?' she demanded.

'I was told to, lady. You know the way or not?'

'There must be a mistake. I'm Carole Harte and I –'

'I don't give the orders, I just do the driving. No mistake, Harte's Way's what I was told.'

Confused, Carole told him he'd missed the right road. 'You'll have to turn around and go back to R18,' she said. 'But I don't believe –'

'R18,' the driver repeated, scowling. 'It ain't no picnic to turn this rig around but if I gotta, I gotta.' With a quick wave of thanks to Carole, he shifted gears and started off.

She remained where she was, watching the truck roll past, catching her breath when she saw the logo on the side of the trailer behind the cab. A golden sun rose over a blue line and across the sun black letters proclaimed 'Horizon'.

Horizon was a film company.

Theda!

Carole urged Sombrita into a gallop, past the line of trucks, across the bridge and off the road to ride between rows of orange trees. What had her grandmother gotten them into this time? Carole wondered as the mare raced from the grove into a field. Theda had never forgotten her days as a Hollywood starlet in the mid-forties.

'If I hadn't married your grandfather,' Theda liked to say, 'I might have become famous. A star. I can act, you know, it wasn't just my looks.'

In her sixties now, Theda was still attractive. Carole was sure her grandmother must be the youngest-looking and prettiest woman of her age in the entire state. Sometimes, though, she wished Theda wouldn't use quite so much makeup and would let her hair return to its natural shade.

'I'd rather not find out that my hair's turned gray,' Theda had protested when Carole last suggested it. 'Staying a blonde is much more fun.'

Theda kept in touch with a few old friends from her Hollywood days – most of them with their hands held out. Or so it seemed to Carole. She had no right to tell her grandmother what to

5

do with her money from her trust fund, but it hurt to see what she thought of as deadbeats given what was so desperately needed to keep the ranch afloat.

'Carole, dear, they're down on their luck,' Theda always said. 'They'll repay me when they can. Any one of them would do the same for me if I needed help. I know you'll keep the ranch running. Your father always said you were the best foreman he ever had.'

Yet Daddy had left Harte's Way to Theda, not to her. She didn't begrudge her grandmother the inheritance or the money from Theda's trust fund. But now the ranch was in trouble and Carole couldn't bear to think of the possibility of losing Harte's Way. Taking her father's advice, she'd never discussed financial difficulties with her grandmother and she didn't intend to start now. She'd find another way to raise the money – there must be one.

The film company trucks were surely here because of some scheme of her grandmother's. Unfortunately, Theda's plans had never yet proved financially successful and Carole only hoped it wasn't too late to stop this one.

A drop of rain splashed on her cheek, then another and another. The sky grew darker and the rain slanted down in earnest so she crouched lower on Sombrita, feeling her hair cling wetly to her neck as the mare galloped on.

They approached the house from the rear. It

wasn't the original ranch house – that was an old adobe hacienda a half-mile away. This house, built by her great-grandfather, was a rambling two-story structure with large verandahs and a cupola in front. She loved every Victorian inch of it. Carole pulled up by the stable and José limped from the barn to meet her as she slid off Sombrita.

'You go inside,' he ordered, reaching for the reins. 'I take her, you *vamos*!'

'*Gracias*, José, I *am* in a hurry.' She ran across the back verandah and pushed open the French door to the music room. Skirting the baby grand piano, she heard her grandmother's high tinkling laugh coming from across the hall.

'Theda,' she cried, bursting into the living room, 'why is that film company sending trucks here? What have you –?' Her words trailed off when she saw her grandmother wasn't alone. A man rose from a fawn velvet chair to face her. Carole caught her breath.

His hair, raven-black as her own, curled low on his neck. His eyes, staring at her from his lean, tanned face, were dark, too, almost black. He blinked and she saw him take a deep breath, apparently disconcerted by her sudden appearance.

Tall, on the slim side with wide shoulders, he wasn't conventionally handsome, but something in his steady gaze made the blood pound in her temples. She was suddenly conscious of her

7

dripping hair and her old, rather disreputable work clothes.

'Carole, dear, this is Jerrold Telford.' Theda said the name as though she should recognize it. 'He'll be playing Joaquin Murieta. Jerrold, this is my granddaughter. We named her Carole with an *e*, you know.'

Carole acknowledged the introduction with a brief nod and immediately turned to her grandmother. 'Playing?' she echoed, pushing back her wet and tangled hair. 'What do you mean?'

'Why I'm certain I told you Horizon would be filming *Bandido* here on the ranch. Didn't I?'

Carole shook her head, well aware her grandmother knew the possibility of the film being shot at Harte's Way had never been mentioned between them until this moment. No doubt because Theda realized Carole would argue against the plan.

'In any case,' Theda went on, 'Jerrold is the male lead. The star.'

Carole had never heard of Jerrold Telford. What kind of a company would cast an unknown as its star? Could this all be an elaborate scheme to con her grandmother into parting with money?

'It's a pleasure to meet you, Ms Harte,' Jerrold said, startling Carole into looking at him again.

Hearing his English accent, she wondered how long it had taken him to perfect it. No doubt he was a phony like that so-called Hungarian count who tried to con her grandmother two years ago by courting her. Jerrold was considerably younger, of course – he couldn't be much over thirty – and was better looking.

His natural suede jacket and tan pants hadn't come off a rack, that much was certain. How well they became him, with the white silk shirt emphasizing his dark virility. No wonder he'd been able to charm her grandmother; he was the most attractive man she'd ever seen. How could any woman resist him?

Her grandmother might not be able to, but *she* definitely could! Carole clenched her hands into fists, wishing she were strong enough to throw him out bodily.

Theda rose from the powder-blue love seat that matched the color of her eyes, crossed the room and put her hand on her granddaughter's arm. 'Dear,' she said, 'you really should change out of those wet clothes.'

At five-eight, Carole was six inches taller than her grandmother. Theda was tiny and exquisite and always beautifully dressed. By contrast Carole felt more disheveled than ever – she knew her hair straggled dankly, that her faded jeans were torn and that her father's tattered old windbreaker was too big for her.

'I'm not moving until I know exactly what's going on,' she muttered, all too conscious of her ungraciousness. Though she knew she was right,

9

she didn't like upsetting her grandmother. She'd been taught to be polite to guests and up until now she'd tried her best, even with the phony count. But Jerrold, she felt, was an exception to that rule.

'Perhaps we could discuss the script another time, Theda.' Jerrold smiled, his teeth white against his tan, a smile guaranteed to start butterflies fluttering in female stomachs – Carole's included.

How dare he make her feel this way? She knew very well she was totally unappealing at the moment, windblown and wet and wearing old clothes. She quelled the impulse to push at her hair again, assuring herself it made no difference what he thought of her. She would *not* be taken in by him, no matter how much voltage he tried to turn on.

'I'd hoped you'd have dinner with us, Jerrold,' Theda said. 'Do at least wait until the rain stops.'

He inclined his head. 'How thoughtful of you, *Tia* Bella. Another time I'd be delighted.' He flicked a glance at the window where the slanting rain sent rivulets streaming down the glass. 'It'll be right – my grandmother always insisted a spot of rain never melted anyone. Good day.'

Jerrold nodded at Carole and turned to walk into the hall. She was so furious she couldn't speak. *Tia* Bella? How dare he call her grandmother his beautiful aunt? Theda began to flutter after him but Carole intercepted her, saying that she'd see him out.

He stopped in the entry to look down at her. She knew he must be well over six feet for her head barely came to his shoulder. Their eyes locked and the dark intentness of his gaze made her breath quicken. She never dreamed any man could have so much animal magnetism and she involuntarily moved back a step, shifting her gaze downward hastily along to his feet. Jerrold, she saw, wore desert boots of rough leather, exactly matching his suede jacket. He was too perfect to be true.

Suddenly she found her voice. 'I've never seen you in a film,' she challenged, though not quite looking at him. 'I've never heard of Jerrold Telford.'

'I'm not surprised.' To her consternation he touched her arm. 'I make no claim to fame.'

A tingle ran through her as though his fingers contained an electrical charge. Momentarily trapped by his dark gaze, she thought she saw an answering flicker in his eyes. Belatedly, she jerked her arm away.

Jerrold raised an eyebrow. When she didn't say anything more he opened the door. 'Good day, Ms Harte,' he murmured.

Carole watched him run down the steps to the *porte-cochère* and saw him slide into the open-top white car – a Jag, she'd been right. With some satisfaction she realized that with the top down he was going to get as soaking wet as she was.

Before she closed the door a rumbling drew her gaze along the drive and she saw the semi heading toward the house. Jerrold spun out of the circular front drive and waved at the trucks, gesturing off to the left toward the dirt road leading to the old hacienda.

'No!' she said aloud as the caravan followed the Jag down the road. She drew back and slammed the door. 'Theda!' she cried, running into the living room. 'You couldn't have told them they could use the hacienda!'

'You must change into dry clothes, dear. Those wet things will give you a chill.'

Carole took a deep breath and let it out slowly. She loved her grandmother; she'd never shouted at Theda in her life. Though she'd been tempted. Especially now.

'I'm staying right here until I find out exactly what we're in for,' she said. 'Just what arrangement did you make with Horizon *and* Jerrold Telford?'

'I saw no reason why they couldn't use the hacienda. They'll set it up as their headquarters besides filming scenes in the courtyard.'

'But what about my basket-making studio? What about Sawa?'

Theda smiled. 'Not to worry. I told Jerrold nothing must be touched and he said the director, Herwin Holden, is a fanatic for authenticity

12

and, since the baskets are genuine, they'll probably use them in the filming. And Sawa is bound to be thrilled by what's going on.'

Carole shook her head. If she had anything to say about it, nothing would be going on. She didn't want them at the hacienda and intended to stop them from setting up there if she could. Taking a deep breath, she said, 'Maybe you ought to begin at the beginning.'

Theda blinked. 'I thought I mentioned Horizon to you a few weeks ago. I certainly meant to. You know I wouldn't go behind your back.'

'I don't recall any such conversation.'

'I distinctly remember saying to you that Horizon was planning to film a period drama set in old California. Spanish California. About the Ghost of Sonora, Joaquin Murieta.'

Carole dredged up a dim memory of Theda mentioning something of the sort. 'You may have talked about the movie, but you didn't tell me it had anything to do with us. I can't believe you'd agree to let Horizon film the picture on the ranch.'

'But Harte's Way is perfect, dear. Even to the hacienda.'

Carole threw up her hands. 'They'll disrupt everything. No ranch work will get done because all the hands will be too busy watching the filming. And neither Sawa nor I will be able to use the studio at the hacienda. Oh, Theda, why didn't you talk it over with me first?'

13

Her grandmother sighed. 'Because you get so riled-up, that's why. I do hate to see you worry. When you worry you frown and that makes lines on your forehead. You're too young for worry lines.'

Despite herself, Carole smiled. Lines on her forehead were the least of her worries.

Theda brightened immediately. 'Isn't Jerrold Telford the handsomest man? A hunk, I believe is today's word. He's a star, you know, a famous actor. I really think he resembles Tyrone Power a bit. Of course, I never actually knew Ty personally, but Jerrold has that same darkness, that intense, smoldering masculinity.' She closed her eyes, a hand over her heart.

To Carole, Tyrone Power was an old-time actor she'd seen once or twice in a late movie on TV, leaping around dramatically in the lines of a sailing ship. And hadn't be been a bullfighter in one?

'I'll admit I've heard of Tyrone Power,' she said, 'but not Jerrold Telford, hunk or not. Though from what I've seen of him, I can believe he'd make a perfect *bandido*; he's certainly the type.'

Theda's eyes popped open. 'I realize you don't keep up with what's going on in the movie business, but I'm sure you know Horizon is a bona-fide film company. One of the smaller ones, to be sure, but they've made some excellent pictures. You remember *Pale Moon* – I distinctly recall you saying that you liked it.'

Carole *had* enjoyed that film. 'Okay, I'll agree Horizon is legit. But I still don't think it's a good idea to have them filming at Harte's Way.' She touched her grandmother's arm pleadingly. 'You must see how disruptive it will be to have them here. There have to be dozens of ranches in California just as appropriate for the filming.'

'Actually, no. Mr Holder chose Harte's Way because of our legend about the bandit gold. This location, he's convinced, will help publicize the film and, of course, he's right.'

'What on earth does that moldy old story have to do with anything? It's not even true. There's no ghost gold any more than there are ghosts.'

'We don't know that for sure, dear. Just because no one's ever found the gold doesn't mean it isn't hidden somewhere about. And who knows about ghosts for sure? Just because we've never seen one doesn't mean they don't exist. In any case, what better publicity could Mr Holder ask for than to film *Bandido* on a ranch with a mysterious legend of stolen bandit gold?'

'I can see his point,' Carole admitted reluctantly. 'But I'm not sure I understand yours. If only you'd mentioned this before the trucks descended on us, I wouldn't have to ask them to turn around and leave.'

Theda clasped her hands in front of her, avoiding Carole's eyes. 'I'm afraid you can't do that, dear. It's too late.'

Carole's heart sank. 'Why?'

15

'They've already leased the property, including the hacienda. You'll just have to put up with the Horizon crew for the next ten weeks or so.' Her artless gaze finally met Carole's, the blue eyes glinting with an emotion Carole couldn't quite believe was amusement. 'And with *bandido* Jerrold Telford as well.'

Carole stared at her grandmother in consternation. Ignoring the gibe about Jerrold, she focused on the dismaying fact that there already was a signed contract. 'You didn't,' she said.

Theda blinked. 'You're annoyed with me, I can tell.' Tears filled her eyes and she turned away, hurrying from the room.

Carole started after her, then stopped. It hurt her to see her grandmother cry, especially when she was the cause. Theda always made her feel guilty when she questioned or commented on her grandmother's actions which she tried not to do unless she feared either Theda or the ranch would suffer. All she wanted was what was best for both her grandmother and Harte's Way, but Theda never seemed to understand that.

She bit her lip, hesitating, then decided it might be best to let Theda be for a few minutes. Besides, she really did need to change out of her wet clothes.

In her room, Carole draped the sodden clothes over the shower door in her bath while reflecting on how dearly she loved her grandmother. She hated to upset her but, at the same time, how could she allow anyone to take advantage of Theda? And that seemed to her to be exactly what this film company had done. Along with Jerrold Telford. *Bandido*, indeed.

After slipping into brown cords and a gold-knit shirt, she stood frowning at herself in the mirror as she blew her hair dry. Noting the forehead lines her grandmother had warned about, she abandoned the frown but not her displeasure at her mirror image.

Her skin color, a constant tan from spending so much time outdoors, complemented her amber eyes. But her face, framed by shoulder-length black hair curling slightly at the ends, looked bland, lacking focus.

Muted peach lipglow touched lightly to her mouth helped some. She supposed she should use makeup more often – Theda was constantly reminding her – but there seemed little point in doing so. Not when her days were spent over-seeing the grove and the cattle hands, checking the irrigation system and all the other endless supervision necessary to keep the ranch running. 'You pay José to do all that,' Theda had chided more than once. The truth was it took both her and José to run Harte's Way, though lately their best efforts hadn't been enough to allow her to break even.

Dismissing the bleak financial present for the moment, she cocked her head to study the effect of the lip gloss. Better, yes, but something more was needed. She unearthed a container of gold-brown eyeshadow, applied it carefully and studied the results. Theda was right about the magic of makeup. No doubt about it, her face was definitely more vivid. More interesting.

Leaving her room, Carole went in search of her grandmother, finding her exactly where she expected to, in her 'memory room', as Theda called it. The pale-blue walls were covered with framed, autographed pictures of movie stars from Hollywood's golden age.

'Good luck from one blonde to another, Marilyn Monroe,' one read.

'To Theda Standish, a swell gal on her way up, Clark Gable,' the bold script on another said.

Theda had prevailed on her daughter-in-law to name baby Carole for Ms Lombard, who'd been Gable's wife and an actress Theda had greatly admired. Carole touched her dark hair, so very different from Lombard's blondness. Sometimes she wondered if Theda was disappointed in how she had turned out. She certainly was no Carole Lombard. But then she really didn't want to be, either.

She'd watched enough old movies to recognize that Clark Gable had an indefinable magnetism that came across even on the screen. Finding herself wondering if Jerrold Telford's undeniable charm would show up as well on film as Gable's, she shook her head. Why waste time thinking about him?

Her grandmother insisted she had to put up with Jerrold until *Bandido* was finished, but actually she didn't. If she couldn't avoid having the movie made at Harte's Way, she could at least avoid its star. Her top priority would be to to stay out of Jerrold Telford's path.

With luck, they'd not meet face to face again.

CHAPTER 2

In her memory room, Theda reclined on an ivory brocade *chaise longue* with an open scrapbook on her lap. No longer crying, she looked up and smiled sadly when Carole crossed to her and sat on the floor beside the chaise.

'I'm sorry,' she said to her grandmother. 'I didn't mean to upset you.'

Theda sighed. 'Sometimes I think your father raised you to be too independent. Of course I'm responsible, too. How tragic that poor Eleanor died so young and you only seven. Naturally you were affected by your mother's loss. I did try my best to take her place but I'm not certain how well I succeeded.'

Carole reached up and took her hand, pressing it to her cheek. 'Whatever I am, you're not to blame. You've been a wonderful grandmother. You still are. I was just trying to protect you.'

'Admirable, I'm sure, dear, but I don't need protecting. Though I do have to admit I was at fault in not discussing the matter with you ahead of time. My only excuse is that I desperately wanted Horizon to film *Bandido* here. It's been so long since I've had anything to do with making a movie.' Theda freed her hand and pointed to a *Los Angles Times* clipping pasted in the album she held. 'The last picture I was in.'

Carole glanced at the newspaper photo of young Theda. She'd read the review many times before: 'Ingenue Theda Standish considerably enlivens an otherwise routine romantic triangle.'

She smiled at her grandmother. 'No wonder Grandpa Lyle fell in love with you – you must have been the prettiest starlet in Hollywood.'

Theda closed the album, set it aside and rested her hand on Carole's shoulder. 'I should have remembered how important your studio in the hacienda is to you. I just didn't think and I'm sorry.'

Reminded that the trucks must be at the hacienda by now, Carole sprang to her feet. 'I'd better hurry over there,' she said. 'Sawa won't know what's going on with all those people descending on her.'

Theda gazed critically at Carole. 'You look much better, but do wear the beige raincoat – not that ghastly poncho you usually put on when it's raining.'

Carole flushed, knowing her grandmother had noticed the makeup and had decided it was for Jerrold Telford.

Isn't she right? Carole asked herself. You knew you'd be going to the hacienda and you certainly didn't use lip gloss and eyeshadow to impress the truck driver with the rose tattoo. In your mind, at least, you've already broken your vow never to meet Jerrold face to face again.

The beige coat was water-repellent, not water-proof like the poncho, so she was likely to get wet all over again, but she did as her grandmother suggested. Glancing in the hall mirror, she was pleased to note how the belted coat accented her small waist.

This is ridiculous, she decided. Why am I taking such pains to look my best for a man I don't like or trust? She started to unbelt the coat, determined to put on the poncho after all, then shrugged, changing her mind. Why make such a big deal out of this? All she meant to do was find Sawa and reassure her, then remove her equipment from the studio, if that seemed necessary. She probably wouldn't even see Jerrold Telford, which suited her just fine.

Sawa was the widow of Grandfather Lyle's foreman. She was a Miwok, a descendent of Native Americans who'd lived in the Sierra foothills long before the coming of either the Spaniards or the Americans. As well as being an old friend, Sawa was teaching Carole to make Miwok baskets from willow and tule fiber and for several years now they'd worked together in the studio at the hacienda.

But the studio meant far more to Carole than a place to weave baskets. She retreated there when she needed to be alone; it was her place to be private, just as the memory room was Theda's. Horizon and Jerrold Telford were trespassing on her privacy.

'Carole,' Theda called.

Carole paused, one hand on the doorknob, waiting while her grandmother drifted into the entry.

'You will be tactful, I hope,' Theda said, 'Jerrold really is a star. He's a very talented young man.'

Carole's lips tightened. 'Very,' she muttered.

'Oh, I admit he's not as well known in this country as he soon will be, but in Australia –'

'You mean Horizon is casting an unknown Australian as Joaquin Murieta? The lead of *Bandido*?'

'Australians have made some wonderful pictures in the past few years. And we've borrowed their talented actors before – take a look at Mel Gibson. Why not Jerrold Telford?'

Carole shrugged. 'I won't argue. Just as long as you haven't put any of your trust fund into this picture. You haven't, have you?'

Theda bristled. 'And what if I had? At sixty some-odd I've lived long enough to know what I'm doing.'

'I don't mean to tell you what to do.' Carole paused, trying to find the right words. How could she protect her grandmother without hurting her feelings? It seemed an impossible task. 'You must try not to live in the past. Recognize that Hollywood has changed, the entire film industry has changed.' She essayed a smile. 'They don't even have such things as starlets these days.'

'You sound just like your father,' Theda snapped. 'I may not be a starlet any more, but you're not Frank Harte, either – you're his daughter and there's no reason to parrot him. I said you were independent and so you are, but you tend to take on your father's opinions as your own. Think for yourself! I'll admit you do a wonderful job running the ranch, but in some ways you're younger than your twenty-five years. I've had forty more years of experience than you and I know what I'm doing, whether you believe me or not.'

Carole had never seen her grandmother so stirred up. Since she'd already upset her, she might as well go for broke. '*Did* you give Jerrold Telford any money?' she demanded.

'Certainly not! Why on earth would I offer him money he doesn't need?'

'How about the Horizon people?' Carole persisted.

'Nor have I given one cent to Horizon. They paid me. I told you they leased the ranch for ten weeks. I'll show you the contract.'

'I'm sorry,' Carole said as she followed her

24

grandmother into the room that had always been the study. 'I don't mean to try to interfere in your life but . . .' She stopped there, having been already scolded for trying to protect Theda.

Neither she nor her grandmother had changed the study since Frank Harte's death three years ago, though they both used the big mahogany desk. Theda opened a drawer, reached in, pulled out a sheaf of papers and thrust them at her granddaughter.

Carole scanned the legalese, re-reading some of the sections. When she finished, she tossed the papers on the desk and looked at Theda.

'Yes, they're paying you, but it's no more than a token fee. You might as well have let them come here free of charge.'

Theda clasped her hands in front of her, managing to look like naughty child afraid of being chastised. 'Well, in addition to the fee, I *was* promised a small role in the picture.'

It took Carole a moment to find words. 'Theda! Don't you realize you're letting these people use you?'

Theda shook her head. 'Oh, no, you're quite mistaken, dear. Actually, I'm using them.'

Seething with anger, Carole sped along along the dirt road lined with olive trees, mud churning under the pickup's tires. She could imagine how Jerrold must have fawned over her grandmother, charming her into signing the lease agreement.

Theda hadn't been in front of a camera for what — forty-some some years? Not after Lyle Harte had swept her off her feet and into marriage. Their son, Carole's father Frank, had been born in their second year of marriage and Theda settled down to be a mother as well as a wife. Later, when Frank's wife died young, she'd had to raise Carole.

Perhaps her grandmother had been forced to put any acting ambitions she still entertained on hold while she raised her granddaughter, but surely she didn't expect to go back to such a demanding profession after all these years. How could Theda possibly think she could handle a movie role now, so many years after she'd been a starlet?

As Carole understood the forties, in those days the starlets were acquired more for their looks that any acting ability. Young Theda Standish had been pretty enough, but had she ever been able to act? Carole had no idea and she feared the worst.

She cringed at the idea that her grandmother's performance would prove to be embarrassing for everyone. The thought of Theda's possible humiliation made Carole's stomach clench. She couldn't bear to have her grandmother hurt.

I ought to throw them all off the ranch, lease or no lease, she raged.

The rain had lessened to a drizzle as she parked by the trucks unloading beyond the hacienda. She noticed trailers were being set up on the flat expanse of land to the south of the hacienda. The trailers must be living quarters for the cast and the other Horizon people, she decided as she walked quickly to the low adobe building whose two wings enfolded a courtyard.

In the courtyard, Sawa stood under the dubious shelter of a huge fig tree, talking to a tall man. Though his back was to her, Carole recognized Jerrold Telford.

'Why not?' Sawa was saying as Carole approached. Neither noticed her. 'I don't care if you take my picture when I make baskets. All the better if you pay me.'

'You can count on it.'

Sawa grinned up at him. 'I will.'

First he'd cozened her grandmother. Now Sawa. Carole seethed with anger.

'That's an interesting gold coin you're wearing,' Jerrold said to Sawa. 'Mind if I take a closer look at it?'

In answer, Sawa lifted the coin she'd strung on a thong around her neck. 'My husband gave me this,' she told him. 'Long time ago, when we marry.'

'Spanish, isn't it?' he said.

Sawa nodded.

From the corner of her eye, Carole noticed a man slip behind the thick bole of the fig tree. Before she could decide whether or not they might have an eavesdropper – after all, he could just be passing by – she was distracted by Jerrold's words.

'Any connection with the ghost gold I've heard about?' he asked Sawa.

The old woman took a step back, closing her hand around the coin she wore, muttering, 'The ghosts keep their gold.'

That put him in his place, Carole told herself. Good for Sawa. He had no business in bringing up the subject in the first place.

'You're certainly a star at one thing, Mr Telford,' she snapped. 'And that's exploitation.'

He whirled to face her. Sawa flicked her a glance, then shuffled away toward the entrance to the studio.

Jerrold lifted an eyebrow, saying nothing as he studied Carole's face.

'You took advantage of my grandmother,' she said, 'and now you're working on Sawa. I want you to leave the ranch people alone. They're not actors. And I don't like you quizzing Sawa about that old legend.'

His eyebrow climbed higher. 'Don't you ever let people make decisions for themselves? Both your grandmother and Sawa are intelligent adults quite capable of telling me to buzz off if they don't like what I suggest. What's wrong with my asking Sawa a question? If she doesn't want to answer, obviously she won't. And I see nothing wrong with giving her a bit part in the film. She's perfect for the role of the old Indian woman and I think she'll enjoy seeing herself on the screen. Most people do.'

Carole glared at him. He was everything she'd learned to mistrust. The foreign sports-car-personality boy, hollow under his cultivated charm. Jerrold Telford might be from Australia, but she'd seen his type often enough. More than one had driven up from LA to visit her grandmother, most often not merely out of the goodness of their hearts.

Why did he look at her so intently? He'd done the same when he first saw her, almost as though he knew her from somewhere. He didn't. It was undoubtedly one of his ploys, the dark, magnetic gaze.

His eyes *were* magnetic, that was the trouble; his gaze held hers so that she couldn't look away. She saw danger smoldering in those sable eyes, a hidden fire that might flare up at any time and consume her. If she let it.

Something almost tangible spun between them, a tenuous thread binding them together. Carole couldn't breathe and the blood pounded in her ears, but still she couldn't look away. Did he feel what she did? Her lips parted and she drew a ragged breath.

Her anger dissipated, crowded out by the burgeoning growth of desire. She wanted to him to touch her, longed to feel his fingers caress her cheek, move gently over her face . . .

No, she thought desperately. No, this can't go on. I can't allow myself to be trapped. 'You're staring at me,' she blurted out.

'Am I?' He placed a hand on her arm and involuntarily she glanced at his square, blunt-fingered hand. Strong. Capable.

'Let's call a truce,' he suggested.

She wanted to shake off his hand while at the same time she wished he'd draw her closer.

'Fraternize with the enemy?' she asked, attempting a light tone, hoping he couldn't tell how shaken she was.

'I don't want to be your enemy,' he said.

From the corner of her eye, Carole noticed Sawa emerging from the hacienda carrying several finished baskets and was reminded of her reason for coming here. She was being evicted from her studio and Jerrold was responsible.

'I don't think we'll ever be friends,' she said coolly.

He dropped his hand. 'We have ten weeks, more or less, to find out.'

Ten weeks. The words echoed in her mind. Ten weeks and he'd be gone, she'd be rid of him. It wasn't a long time – seventy days, to be exact. Why didn't the thought make her happy?

'Please don't invite *me* to be in your film,' she said. 'I'm no actress.'

He smiled that devastating smile. 'No, I don't believe you are.'

Carole wasn't certain how to take his words.

Did he find her transparent? Did he realize the extent of her response to him? She flushed, conscious of behaving like a moonstruck teenager.

'You're the first Californian woman I've met whom I'd like to know better,' he said softly.

She felt a quick rush of pleasure. In spite of everything – her worry about Theda and the chaos caused by the filming – Carole realized there was nothing she'd rather do than to spend time with Jerrold.

She couldn't, of course. Wouldn't. Even if she trusted him enough to believe he meant what he said, they were nothing alike, they had nothing in common. He was an actor, accustomed to glamor and fame, a man of bright lights and cities. She, on the other hand, hated crowds and was truly happy only on the ranch. She had to admit she was drawn to his powerful masculinity, but it wouldn't do at all to become involved with him. Not in any way.

Still, he'd be around – almost underfoot, you might say – for ten weeks. 'I imagine we'll run into each other now and then,' she said carefully. 'Since I ride over the ranch every day we can hardly avoid it.'

His eyebrow climbed again. She found it so easy to go on looking at him. She could understand the reason he'd become an Australian film star; he must have captivated every woman in that country.

Well, she was one woman who wasn't going to be lured into Jerrold Telford's web of charm.

'Do you know your eyes are the exact shade of the Tanami Desert when the sand is first lit by the morning sun?' Jerrold asked. 'The color of molten gold.'

She blinked. 'I – I don't even know where Tanami Desert is. Australia?'

'You've never been to Australia?'

Carole shook her head.

'Someday I'd like to show you Tanami. And the rest of the country.'

Easy words, she told herself. Empty words. But her heart speeded as she pictured herself crossing the Pacific with Jerrold, imagined the two of them journeying across the Australian continent. Together . . .

'Maybe you'll show me over the ranch sometime,' he went on. 'I'd like that.'

Would he really? She had difficulty with the concept. 'Oh, I imagine you'll see quite a bit of the property while you're filming,' she countered.

'That's not what I mean. I'd like you to ride with me over your land.'

He'd phrased it so oddly that she frowned, not quite understanding what he meant or his motive for saying such a thing. She decided not to pursue it, but for a moment a mental picture of Jerrold standing atop her favorite hill gripped her.

The slam of a car door made her jump. At the same time she heard the sputter, then the muted roar of what sounded like a dirt bike starting up and moving off. Glancing toward the road, she saw a maroon Mercedes parked by her pickup. The dirt bike was nowhere in sight.

She'd been so enmeshed by Jerrold she hadn't even heard the car arrive. Thank heaven something had broken the web he'd woven about her.

A woman strolled into the courtyard, her blonde hair glistening. She wore dark wine jeans and a brilliant pink silk shirt. No coat. Carole was surprised to see the rain had stopped.

'Hello there!' the woman called. 'Here I am at long last.'

She was gorgeous. The thin silk revealed opulent breasts and the wine jeans clung to the voluptuous curve of her hips. Her lips matched the pink blouse and silver eye makeup enhanced the blue of her eyes. With a start, Carole realized she was looking at Marla Thurlow, the star of *Pale Moon*.

Marla stopped in front of Jerrold. 'Oh, my,' she said. 'You looked fantastic on the screen but in the flesh you're truly *mucho macho*. What fun it's going to be working together. I've been dying to meet you.'

Jerrold clasped the hands she held out to him. 'You're Marla,' he said. 'My pleasure.' He bowed slightly over her hands.

Marla sighed. 'If that's the Australian manner, I like it.' She leaned forward and stood on her toes. 'Here's a sample of the American way.' She kissed him full on the lips.

Carole clenched her teeth. Marla had totally ignored her, but she didn't care about that. What she did mind was how Jerrold smiled down at the blonde actress as Marla stepped back. As far as either of them were concerned, Carole Harte might as well not exist. So much for Tanami eyes, along with all his other meaningless words.

She turned abruptly and walked quickly into the hacienda and her studio. Standing among the basketry supplies, dried reeds coiling about her feet, she was forced to recognize the emotion that made her want to strike out at Marla Thurlow.

She was inexplicably, infuriatingly, unreasonably jealous. Of a man she scarcely knew . . . and certainly didn't trust.

How could she trust him? She was sure he'd swayed Theda into signing the lease with Horizon. And what about his question to Sawa? Sawa had worn that coin on its thong around her neck for as long as Carole had known her. Was Jerrold suggesting Sawa's husband, by giving her an old coin, had access to the legendary gold? The thought distracted Carole from her fixation on Jerrold.

Actually, the idea of discussing the ghost gold with Sawa had never occurred to her. Not that she believed Sawa's long-dead husband had discovered where it was. If he had, he'd certainly have told Grandpa Lyle because the two men were long-time friends. And her grandfather, while indulging her childish interest in searching for the bandit cache, had never given her any reason to think he knew its location. Or even that he believed the cache existed.

Her father had always pooh-poohed the entire notion of hidden gold, saying, 'The only gold on the ranch is in the oranges, Carole girl, so see you take good care of the groves.'

Still, what harm would there be in mentioning the ghost gold to Sawa? She didn't expect Sawa to offer anything new but, on the other hand, what if . . . ?

Harte's Way badly needed money to survive. Allowing the filming of *Bandido* on the ranch offered no more than a pittance. More of a hindrance than a help, really. Especially since she'd have to cope with Jerrold Telford for the next ten weeks.

'Oh, there you are.' Marla's voice startled Carole. 'You must be a Harte. I'm sorry we didn't get a chance to shake hands.' The actress advanced into the studio and looked around. 'Fascinating. Do you actually make Indian baskets?'

'I'm learning,' Carole said shortly.

'From a real live Native American?'

Carole nodded.

'I'd love to meet her. Baskets have always

interested me.' Marla picked up a partially finished one and studied it.

'I'm sure you will meet her, since Sawa is evidently to have a bit part in the movie.'

'Marvelous. I understand Theda Harte will also be working with us. Is that you?'

'I'm Carole. Theda's my grandmother. Actually, I have no acting ambitions.'

Marla set down the basket and looked at her. 'How strange. Most people can't wait to get in front of a camera. But I'm sure you have your reasons. Have you met Jerrold? Oh, but of course you have. He was talking to you when I drove up. A dream walking, as they used to say in the old days.'

'We've met.'

Apparently reacting to the tartness of her tone, Marla said, 'You don't want to be an actress and you're not susceptible to hunks either?' She chuckled. 'Oh, honey, I can't believe that.'

Carole smiled, reluctantly responding to what she realized was meant to be friendly teasing. 'Even my grandmother calls him a hunk so I guess I'll have to concede the point,' she said. Be gracious, she urged herself. You have nothing against this woman.

'I'm glad to have the chance to meet you,' she confessed. 'I enjoyed your acting in *Pale Moon*.'

Marla beamed. 'Thank you. Compliments from a woman, and a contemporary at that, are important to me.' She glanced toward the door. 'I must find my trailer before I collapse. Would you believe I've been up since six this morning?'

Tempted to comment that she was up at six or before every morning, Carole bit her tongue. 'See you around,' she said instead as, with a wave of her hand, Marla left the studio.

How, Carole asked herself as she got into her pickup, could she ever hope to compete with perfection? Because Marla was about as close to that state as any woman ever reached. And she was friendly, besides. At least when she wasn't distracted by men she considered hunks.

Carole had no intention of even trying to compete. What for, when she didn't want the prize if she did win? If you could consider him a prize. For her, he wouldn't be. To her, Jerrold Telford represented nothing but bad news.

She should be grateful for Marla's arrival because now he had someone else to practice his magnetism on, a much more willing subject than she'd be, if Marla's attitude was any clue.

I can relax, he's out of my hair for the ten weeks, Carole told herself as she stopped the pickup at the house. I may have to put up with the filming but he won't be a problem any longer and I'm happy about that, I really am. Happy and relieved. She marched purposefully into the house.

'My,' Theda said when she entered the living room, 'whatever happened to make you look so

37

glum? One would swear you'd lost your last friend.'

'I'm fine,' Carole insisted and immediately changed the subject. 'You didn't tell me Marla Thurlow was in *Bandido*. I just met her. She's gorgeous and, actually, quite pleasant.'

Theda slanted her a knowing look. 'I see,' she said.

About to take Theda on, Carole decided to let it go. When it came to innuendo she was no match for her grandmother. Glum, my eye. Relieved was the word of choice.

'Never mind, dear,' Theda said. 'Remember, he saw you first.'

38

CHAPTER 3

The film company lent a holiday atmosphere to the Harte ranch that Carole could do little to counter. With José's help, she did her best to see that their regular ranch hands finished the necessary work, but the part-time workers were harder to corral.

She hesitated to dismiss any, feeling it wasn't fair for a man or woman to lose a job because he or she was caught up in the excitement of watching the filming of *Bandido*.

Because it *was* exciting. Even though Carole did her best to ignore the Horizon people, she couldn't help being conscious of them. Especially after a helicopter flew in during the second day of filming and landed in a field near the hacienda. The 'copter whirred daily over the ranch with, she presumed, cameras taking shots from the air.

On the fifth day, Carole saddled Sombrita early, telling herself she needed to inspect the irrigation outlets used to water the lemon grove behind the hacienda before the day's shooting began.

Since the crew's arrival, she'd changed her habit of tossing on the first clothes she set hand to – never mind how old or faded. Today she chose a pair of rust twill jodhpurs that Theda had bought her several years before. They were like new for she'd never worn them. They fit very well and, since she was slim, the flare at the thigh was flattering, making Carole wonder why she'd never bothered to don them until now.

The morning was cool so she put a rust-colored leather vest over her white-knit turtleneck shirt. Her boots, scuffed and comfortable, were custom-made of handtooled leather. Heaven only knew when she'd be able to afford a new pair.

Though in a hurry she'd taken time to gloss her lips. If she did happen to run across any of the film crew, Carole was determined not to be caught at a disadvantage a second time. Not that she was trying to compete with Marla Thurlow – how could she? As for Jerrold, she didn't expect to talk to him again. Or want to, she told herself firmly.

José came limping toward Carole as she swung on to Sombrita. 'You ride early,' he observed.

'I have to check the valves by the lemon grove,' she told him.

'You check them two weeks ago.'

'I thought I'd take a look at them again.' She felt uncomfortably defensive.

José shrugged. He was a contemporary of her father and the two men had been life-long friends. After his car accident fifteen years ago, Jose came to the ranch as an odd-jobs man, working his way up to assisting her father as overseer – as he did now for Carole. She thought of José as the uncle she'd never had.

Waving goodbye to José, she urged Sombrita into a trot. She glanced back and, seeing José's knowing grin, wished she hadn't. No doubt he thought she was using the valves as an excuse to ride near the hacienda.

Was she? The water valves had been in perfect working order two weeks ago, just as José said. On the other hand, she'd started early to avoid running into the film crew and, after all, she had to begin her re-check of the irrigation equipment somewhere, didn't she? Why not at the lemon grove?

José was off base in his suspicions.

She rode along the road to the hacienda, glancing at the olive trees to either side. They'd need pruning soon, but the silvery gray-green of their foliage was so soothing to her eyes that she always hated to have them cut back.

Olives came originally from the warm lands bordering the Mediterranean, from Italy,

Greece and the Holy Land. Did they grow in Australia? She'd looked in an atlas and found that the Tanami Desert was in the center of the continent. What grew in an Australian desert? she wondered. Sage brush? Manzanita? Or strange, exotic plants and animals – like the exotic man who came from that country.

Carole shook her head. She wasn't likely to visit Australia so what difference did it make?

Abruptly she turned Sombrita and rode between two olive trees, leaving the road, skirting the edge of the lemon grove, heading away from the hacienda. Who was she trying to fool? She'd been hoping to see Jerrold again – the valves were a flimsy excuse, just as José had guessed.

The worst of it was she'd tried to fool herself with the valve excuse, attempting to conceal her real purpose. Not from José; he'd seen through her. The only one in the dark had been Carole Harte. She'd never before lied to herself and she was determined not to let it happen again. Nor did she intend to go near the hacienda this morning now that she knew her real reason.

Changing her agenda, she decided to visit Sawa's cabin, have coffee with her old friend and then ride south to look over the cattle grazing near the boundary of Harte's Way. There she'd be as far away from the hacienda as she could get.

Carole took a deep breath of the cool morning

air. The day was clear, the Sierra peaks mauve and pale blue tipped with white against the deep blue of the sky. A mocking bird swooped past her to perch on a branch, its protesting squawk imitating a blue jay's call.

Urging Sombrita up a rise, Carole passed the last of the orange trees and reached the crest where she reined in and looked down. She gasped.

A magnificent palomino galloped into the field below her, blond mane and tail flying. His rider, dressed entirely in black, seemed one with the horse as they raced along in a flowing rhythm. The sun glinted from silver ornaments on the horse's saddle and bridle and from the silver decorations on the rider's jacket and pants.

To the right of the palomino, a roan burst from a copse of live oaks. Its rider was a woman, her blonde hair streaming behind her. Three horsemen galloped from the oaks and thundered after the woman.

The man on the palomino wheeled his mount, veering to intercept the woman, and Carole belatedly realized he was Jerrold Telford and that she was watching a scene from *Bandido*.

A moment later a truck, camera mounted on top, drove from the trees and followed Jerrold across the field.

The blonde must be Marla. As Carole watched in fascination, Marla's horse stumbled and the actress catapulted over its head to

43

somersault on to the ground. By the time Marla rose and looked dazedly about her, her horse had recovered and was racing on without her. Her three pursuers were dangerously near.

The palomino pounded toward Marla and, as Jerrold passed her, he leaned from the saddle, caught her about the waist and swept her onto his horse. Carol's mouth opened in amazement. It was the most skillful exhibition of horsemanship she'd ever seen.

Her heart beat faster as she imagined herself in Marla's place, Jerrold's arm holding her close, his face inches away . . .

Stop it! she warned herself. Don't indulge in fantasy. Isn't the movie make-believe enough?

Carole watched as Jerrold's horse galloped on ahead of the pursuers. The palomino plunged into a stand of sycamores bordering a stream and was lost to her view. After the three horsemen and the camera truck followed the palomino, there was nothing below Carole except the empty field.

No wonder the ranch workers couldn't resist the filming, Carole thought as she struggled to bring herself back to reality. When she was certain the actors weren't going to reappear, she guided the mare down the hill on her way to Sawa's cabin at the far side of the live oaks.

Carole had almost reached the trees when she heard hoofs pounding behind her. Turning, she saw the palomino closing in. When Jerrold waved and called her name, she brought Sombrita to a halt.

'I saw you on the hill,' he said.

Carole smiled, surprised that he'd noticed her, pleased that he'd ridden after her.

'You're a fantastic rider,' she said, adding, 'and Marla's good, too.' Fair was fair, after all.

'Marla? You mean on the roan? That wasn't Marla. Ina Jacobsen, she's a stunt woman, played her part. Ina's as good on a horse as any jillaroo in the Northern Territory.'

Carole remembered the Tanami Desert was in that part of Australia. 'What's a jillaroo?' she asked.

'What you'd call a cowgirl here in the States. Unless the official title is now cowperson. A jillaroo is a woman who works with cattle, who looks after them.'

'Is that where you live, in the Northern Territory?'

He frowned and shook his head. 'Not now.'

The silver on his Californio costume glittered in the sunlight, dazzling her. At least she tried to tell herself it was the silver and not Jerrold. Black became him, making him look like the man he portrayed – Joaquin Murieta, an arrogant Spanish don turned *bandido*.

'I grew up on a cattle ranch in the Northern Territory,' he said. 'As a boy I worked as a ringer, a cowboy.'

'I never saw anything to equal the way you swept the stunt woman on to your horse.'

'Thanks. Our director – you haven't yet met Herwin Holden – had his doubts about letting me do the stunt, but he gave in when Ina said she was willing to take a chance on me.'

No wonder, Carole told herself. He sat the palomino as though he owned the world, as though he was capable of any imaginable feat of horsemanship.

Jerrold patted the palomino's neck. 'Without these trained horses neither Ina nor I would have looked as good. It's incredible how smart they are.'

Trained horses or not, it took daring and skill to do what she'd seen him do. Carole was pleasantly surprised by his modesty.

'Herwin's really interested in this Harte's Way legend of stolen gold,' he said. 'He's asked me to look into it for him.'

Was that why he questioned Sawa? Not willing to be drawn into a lengthy discussion of the bandit gold, she waved a dismissive hand. 'Legend is the operative word.'

'No truth to it?'

She laughed. 'Well, *I*'ve never found any gold, hidden or otherwise. A reference to "ghost gold" does appear in old family records, but there's no indication anyone really believed the story even way back when.'

'Ghost gold. You can be sure Herwin'll use

that phrase to the max. He wants to believe in the legend, you know.'

'Legends are free for the taking. He's welcome to it. You don't sound much like Paul Hogan,' she commented, changing the subject. 'I mean, in his movies he uses all sorts of colorful Australian phrases.'

'I was trained out of Aussieisms,' he said. 'A few creep in from time to time, especially if I lose my temper, but the parts I've played in the past called for the King's English and it's gotten to be second nature.'

'And now you're supposed to be a Californio.'

He shrugged. 'Quite a switch. But accents aren't too difficult to pick up after you've been trained to subdue your own. With luck I won't sound like an Aussie faking the King's – or maybe it's considered the Queen's now – English with a phony Spanish accent.'

Disarmed by his friendly sharing, she said impulsively, 'If you don't have other plans, please join us for dinner tonight.'

'I'd like to. Or as they say down under, *goodo*.' He smiled at her.

She still wasn't accustomed to that smile and her heart began to gallop like a runaway horse. 'Seven?' she managed to say before digging in her heels, urging Sombrita on, away from Jerrold. Why did he affect her so intensely? She hoped he hadn't noticed her breathlessness.

The less she had to do with Jerrold the better. What on earth had possessed her to invite him to dinner? He was fast lane freeway, she was country-road slow. Rich Erskine was more her speed. He might not thrill her, but Rich was a Valley rancher and therefore she and he had a lot in common.

Carole grimaced, recalling the last time Rich had taken her to dinner. June. A soft summer evening, a full moon, the sweet scent of orange blossoms – and what had Rich talked about? Nematodes preying on the roots of orange trees. Romantic, Rich wasn't.

Well, she'd be extra careful not to allow Jerrold to fluster her this evening – she'd be calm, cool and collected. Casual. Theda would be happy to see Jerrold; she'd let her grand-mother monopolize him while she stayed in the background.

Sawa's log cabin sat among a stand of syca-mores that bordered a tiny creek. Though this was Harte property, Grandfather Lyle had willed Sawa and her husband a life tenancy to the cabin and the land it was built on. The old woman's pet crow flapped up from the roof of the cabin, cawing as Carole approached.

'Blackie's better than a watchdog and a lot less trouble,' Sawa would say. 'Cheaper, too. He finds his own food. Never bites anyone and he only poops on people he don't like.'

By the time Carol tethered Sombrita, Sawa

stood in the open doorway. 'I dreamed you were coming,' she said. 'In my dream you wanted to talk about the ghost gold.'

Taken aback, Carole stared at her.

'I see I dreamed true,' Sawa said, moving aside so Carole could enter the cabin.

'At the hacienda the other evening, I heard Jerrold Telford asking you questions about your gold coin,' Carole said defensively. 'It made me realize I'd never asked you about the old legend.'

'You didn't,' Sawa agreed, gesturing toward a kitchen chair, 'but those movie men, they're asking everyone. I keep out of their way.'

'I noticed you've put your coin under your shirt where it can't be seen.'

Sawa nodded. 'I promise my husband I wear his gift till I die but for now I hide it, like the gold is hidden. The ghosts, they don't like no one talking about their gold.'

'Then you do believe in the old story.'

'Depends on how it's told. Joaquin Murieta and his bandits had nothing to do with the gold.'

'Do you know who did?' Carole asked, kicking herself because she'd never asked Sawa before.

'Told you the ghosts don't like talk. You know about the snakes. We can't tell certain of our stories except in the winter 'cause the snakes will hear and come to bite us. When it's cold the snakes sleep and then they don't hear and it's safe. But the ghosts, they don't ever sleep.'

49

'Miwok ghosts?' Carole persisted, intrigued by Sawa's evasiveness.

Sawa shook her head. 'Other people's ghosts. Just as evil, though. Ghosts always want to do harm.'

Hazarding a guess, Carole said, 'If the gold is in Spanish coins like the one you wear, they must be Spanish ghosts.'

Sawa clutched the front of her shirt, holding the coin through the cloth. 'I don't tell no one about how he got my gift, only you. My husband, he don't find this. He say one day a whirlwind come along and pick him up so he lose his way in the dark swirl. He's in a bad place, try to grab here, there, can't find anything solid. The darkness finally spit him out with my coin in his hand, he don't know how, don't know where it come from. Don't want to know, either of us.'

Though Sawa had spoken the last words with finality, Carole ventured one more question. 'Did he say where he was when the whirlwind caught him?'

Sawa turned away from her without answering. 'I fix coffee,' she said with finality. 'Then we talk about baskets.'

Later, riding home, Carole dissected what Sawa had told her and came to the conclusion that what she'd heard was the truth as the old woman saw it, but she didn't believe Sawa had told her all she knew. Could the ghost gold actually be a real cache, hidden somewhere on the property? But where? Harte's Way was a big spread and other people besides the child she'd once been had searched and found nothing.

Sighing, Sara concluded that if Sawa's husband really had been trapped in a violent whirlwind, the wind itself could have picked up the coin from miles away, outside the boundaries of the ranch. She'd be a fool to pin her hopes on finding gold to relieve the ranch's financial problems.

That evening, she still wasn't ready by five to seven. She'd chosen a V-neck silk dress of pale apricot with clean and simple lines. With it she wore a braided silk belt in a darker shade of the color, her sandals matching the belt. The ensemble had been a gift from her grandmother several years ago and Theda was going to be horrified to see Carole wearing it now. Fashion was important to Theda and the dress, though becoming, was far from the latest style or color.

Carole lifted an antique enameled locket on a heavy gold chain from a satin-lined box and fastened it around her neck. The locket had been her great-grandmother's and inside there was a picture of a solemn young man. Her great-grandfather.

She took extra pains with her make-up but, as she studied the results in her mirror, she thought of Marla with her skin as fair and pale as bone china. Looking at her own tan, she scowled, dissatisfied with what she saw. She reached for her usual light floral cologne, then, shaking her head, she picked up a small vial of French perfume instead, a gift she'd never opened until now, and delicately touched the stopper to her wrists.

By the time Carole came into the living-room, Jerrold was already seated and talking to Theda. As he rose, her gaze flicked over his dark blue pants and his pale blue pullover, open at the neck, and came to a halt when she saw the hostile look in his dark eyes. She blinked, taken aback, but then he smiled and greeted her and she decided she must have been mistaken.

Theda dominated the conversation at the dinner table, her heart-shaped face animated as she talked excitedly of the film. Carole had to admit her grandmother looked younger than she had in years.

'Carole and I agree you're *the* perfect choice for Joaquin Murieta,' Theda told Jerrold. 'How astute of Herwin to see it. Of course he's a fine director. His *Pale Moon* was *my* choice for the Academy Award.'

'I've always admired Herwin's work,' Jerrold agreed.

'My role as *Tia* Bella may be small but I love the part,' Theda went on. 'She's a pivotal character, changing everyone while at the same time not realizing the effect she has on others.'

Jerrold nodded.

He was too polite to say so but Carole wondered if her grandmother wasn't overemphasizing her role in the picture. She feared Theda would overact and make her performance a disaster.

Maybe they'd even edit her part from the finished picture. Theda would be crushed if they did. She'd be equally hurt if the director she so much admired humiliated her in front of the crew by criticizing her performance.

Carole narrowed her eyes, trying to see her tiny, vivacious grandmother with her fluffy blonde hair as a left-on-the-shelf Spanish spinster. No, it was impossible to imagine. Yet she knew nothing would prevent Theda from going on with the role. Carole would never be able to convince her she could be heading for disaster.

'I've done nothing but chatter all evening,' Theda said when Lollie, the maid, brought in the plum wine. 'You were the one, Carole, who invited Jerrold to dinner and you've scarcely had a chance to say a word. Shame on me.'

'I was only echoing your earlier invitation,' Carole put in hastily.

Her grandmother smiled. 'Just the same, I do believe I'll forgo the wine and retire to take another look at my lines. I intend to be letter perfect.'

When Carole and Jerrold were left alone at the table, Carole felt suddenly shy. She turned the stem of the wine glass between her fingers, staring down at the dark amber liquid.

'You took off so quickly this morning,' Jerrold said, 'I didn't get a chance to say you ride as though you were born in the saddle. The mare's a beauty – Arabian?'

'Yes, her dam was Misty, a California champion. My father bought Sombrita for me shortly before he died.'

'He was an excellent judge of horses. As my father once was.'

Carole stared at him, uncertain of what he meant. 'It's not a skill you lose,' she said mildly.

'My father has other interests now.' Jerrold's clipped tone closed the subject.

'I learned everything I know about horses from my father,' Carole said after a pause. 'And about cattle and oranges and ranching. We rode the land together and he taught me all he knew.' Tears pricked her eyes and she blinked them back. How she missed her father.

'This is beautiful country,' Jerrold said softly. 'Harte's Way is all a ranch should be.'

'I do my best to keep it up. Not just for Grandmother and me, but because I'm a Harte and the land has been ours for generations.'

Seeing Lollie, hovering in the archway, waiting to clear the table, Carole pushed back her

54

chair. About to lead the way into the living room, she paused.

'If you're interested in horses, we might walk to the corral,' she told him. 'We have a chestnut gelding I'd like to show you.'

After Jerrold admired the chestnut, it seemed natural to stroll on past the corral along a path winding among the tall pines planted by the first Harte to settle in the Valley. Beyond the stand of pines the reflection of the half-moon shimmered palely from the water of El Dorado Creek.

'The stream's low,' Jerrold said.

'We're lucky to have any water in it at all in September.'

'Quite like Australia, only there we have entire years when the streams stay dry. Australian weather's inscrutable and often cruel but God, how I miss it, dry creeks and all.'

His words showed another side of Jerrold, one Carole was more at ease with. He almost seemed like a friend. Maybe they had a few things in common, after all.

As she did with Rich Erskine?

'What do you know about nematodes?' she asked mischievously.

'Nothing. A new rock group?'

Carole laughed. 'Not even close. Nematodes are tiny worms that infest the soil among orange tree roots and damage the trees so that they die from the top down. We call it spreading decline – it's one of the banes of citrus growers.'

He clasped her hand, halting her. 'This is too perfect a night to waste on nematodes.'

His clasp was warm, his voice deep and low. As his hand enfolded hers Carole felt that her entire being was as entrapped as her hand. Excitement quivered through her. Jerrold was no longer like an old friend, he was a stranger, the dark knight in the white Jag she both wanted and feared.

She breathed in the scent of pine mingled with damp earth, a smell she knew as well as she knew her name. Everything around her was familiar, everything except this man who held her hand captive and fired her desire as no man had ever done before.

A man who'd leave in less than ten weeks. Leave here. Leave her.

His face drew closer, his dark eyes shadowed. If she had any sense she'd pull her hand free and run.

He smelled clean and fresh, like the outdoors, like the orange groves after a rain. His fingers stroked her cheek and traced the curved outline of her mouth. Her lips trembled, her knees sagged. She couldn't breathe.

His fingers left her face and his arms closed about her, drawing her to him, crushing her against his body as his lips came down on hers. His kiss wasn't gentle – it didn't ask, it demanded.

Carole found herself clinging to him, her mind

in a whirl, the rest of her quivering in eager response. Her lips parted and his tongue invaded her mouth. He tasted of plum wine and something dark and male that was more intoxicating than any wine. She wasn't totally inexperienced, but his kiss stirred passions she'd never felt before.

When his hands slid over the curve of her hips, molding her closer to him, she lost all sense of time and place. There was no one in the world except herself and Jerrold. Nothing existed outside their embrace.

An owl called four times from the pines, the mournful cry penetrating her dreamy cocoon of desire, reminding her Jerrold *was* a dream, he was as make-believe as the film he starred in, and if she stayed in his arms she'd be lost forever, she'd never find her way back to reality.

But the force of her need was too compelling for her to break free; she could only moan softly as his lips trailed down to the V of her dress.

Then he thrust her away, so suddenly that she staggered. 'Even the same damn perfume,' he growled, stepping back. 'I ought to have my head examined.'

Bewildered and hurt, Carole hadn't a clue as to what he meant.

'Since this is your turf, I'm sure you can find your way home,' he said, his tone chill. 'Goodnight.' He turned on his heel.

Hands pressed to her burning cheeks, Carole

watched him disappear into the darkness. Perfume? The French scent she'd used for the first time tonight? What had that to do with anything? Was he disgusted with her because she'd responded so ardently?

She'd never been so humiliated in her life!

CHAPTER 4

After a night of tossing and turning, Carole rose the next morning as angry at herself as at Jerrold. If their paths crossed at Theda's party for the film crew, she'd be polite but cool and distant. She'd never again give him the chance to hurt her. She must have been out of her mind to let him kiss her in the first place.

Driving the pickup into Hubbard's Corners, the nearest town, to buy needed supplies, she turned up the volume of the radio, hoping loud music would keep her from dwelling on what had happened the night before. The plaintive country-western songs of heartbreak and betrayal blasting in her ears only reinforced her misery.

In the feed store she ran into Rich Erskine with, as usual, an ancient Stetson jammed over his blond hair. His smile of greeting and his clear blue gaze reassured her that he was the same old dependable Rich, a man who might not excite her but who would never deliberately wound her.

'I hear tell those film folks you got at the ranch are something else,' he said.

'You'll be able to see for yourself soon,' she told him, 'since my grandmother's planning a party for them. You're on her invitation list.'

He grinned, obviously pleased. 'Hey, all right. You can count on me being there.'

'You wouldn't be so happy about it if they were on your property distracting your hands so the work doesn't get done.'

'The novelty'll wear off.' He stepped closer and lowered his voice. 'Speaking of movies, how about taking in one with me this weekend down in Bakersfield?'

'I can't, I'm too busy.' She spoke without thinking, accustomed to turning Rich down. She liked him but there was no spark between them as far as she was concerned and she feared Rich wanted more from her than a casual friendship, more than she could or would give him.

'You haven't been out with me since June,' he complained. 'You shouldn't be working that hard. Everyone needs time off. If you don't want to go to a movie, how about us taking that jaunt up to the sequoias like we were always going to?'

Carole hesitated. She loved the mountains and she certainly could use a day away from the ranch. Away from Jerrold. 'I'll think it over and let you know,' she promised finally.

'I won't let you forget,' he warned.

* * *

Driving back to the ranch, she wondered why she'd always easily fended off kisses from Rich – a friend she liked and trusted – only to fall into Jerrold's arms the moment he touched her?

Never again! She'd said those words before about Jerrold and failed to hold to them, but this time she meant to stand firm. Would stand firm. Absolutely.

The two men were about the same age and, in his own way, Rich was also good looking. He was a successful rancher, capable, strong, and amiable. Dependable. Predictable. And yet . . .

She sighed and flicked on the radio. 'I gave away my heart,' a woman's voice sang, 'to the wrong man, to an up-and-gone man . . .'

At least my heart's intact, Carole assured herself, turning down the volume. And I only have to put up with Jerrold being on the ranch for a few more weeks, then he'll be up and gone forever.

As soon as she let herself into the house through the back door and stepped into the kitchen, she heard a man's voice and froze. Jerrold? After a moment she decided she was wrong and relaxed. Theda must have an unexpected guest.

Lollie, who'd been rummaging in the refrigerator, straightened and closed the door, a carton of milk in her hands.

'You're back in time for lunch,' the middle-aged maid said. 'Gonna be kind of fancy on account of he's staying.'

'One of the film crew?' Carole asked, trying to decide if she wanted to to sit through lunch with whoever 'he' was. Maybe the director?

Lollie shook her head. 'Not exactly one of them film people, but close. He's Mr Telford's pa. Drove up about an hour ago.'

Jerrold's father? The man who used to be a good judge of horses? Carole's curiosity was piqued. Glancing down at her cords and shirt, she wondered if she ought to change and shook her head. She was presentable enough – after all, this was a working ranch. Besides, why should she worry about the impression she might make on Jerrold's father? He had nothing to do with her.

Her mind made up, she strolled into the living room.

'There you are, dear,' Theda said. She fluttered her fingers at the man who'd stood at Carole's entrance. 'This is Calvin Telford, Jerrold's father. Calvin, my granddaughter Carole.'

Carole held out her hand, looking into hazel eyes totally unlike Jerrold's. His father was several inches shorter and definitely stockier than Jerrold, but there *was* a family resemblance. Calvin Telford, who must be in his sixties, was still an attractive man. His brown hair glinted with silver strands and, like his son, he had a charming smile. He was casually but expensively dressed. She guessed him to be not so many years younger than her grandmother.

'You don't take after your grandmum,' he said, assessing her as he shook her hand. 'Got your own style, though. Theda tells me you run this ranch. Doing a bloody good job, you are.'

Carole eyed him in surprise. He certainly was different from Jerrold. She liked his directness – it reminded her of her father – but she'd learned the hard way not to trust one Telford so she had no intention of letting down her guard with this one. 'I'm a Harte,' she said at last. 'Harte's Way is important to me.'

He nodded, as though that was to be expected. 'Ranching's a tough job and one you never get away from. Thanks to Jerrold that perishing life's behind me.'

Theda beamed at Calvin. 'Exactly my sentiments. I keep trying to convince Carole there's more to living than riding around on a horse all day making certain cattle aren't dropping dead or orange trees shriveling up.'

'You'll never get *me* aboard a horse again,' Calvin said.

'We agree perfectly,' Theda assured him.

Lollie, standing in the archway, cleared her throat loudly. 'Lunch is served,' she announced.

Carole didn't see eye to eye with Calvin about ranching; he seemed to have something against it. By the time they finished eating, though, she had to admit she was warming to him. Clearly her grandmother was as well.

'I'm delighted you arrived in time to attend the party I'm planning for the Horizon people,' Theda told him as they sat around the table over coffee.

'Wouldn't want to miss it,' he said, 'but my staying at the location depends on Jerrold.'

Theda's puzzled frown cleared after a moment. 'Oh, I see – you mean there may not be room for you in the trailers. Heavens, Calvin, you'll stay here, of course. We've loads of room and I'll quite enjoy having a man in the house again.'

'Most kind of you, but I couldn't think of putting you out.'

'Nonsense.' Theda slanted him her most charming smile. 'I won't take no for an answer.'

Carole was taken aback to see that Theda was actually batting her eyelashes at Calvin. And he seemed to be lapping it up. She watched him cover her grandmother's hand with his own and press it briefly. Theda's color heightened. Her grandmother blushing? Unbelievable! Theda had never behaved this way with any of her old-days Hollywood male friends. Or with the phony Hungarian count, for that matter.

'If you'll excuse me?' Carole said, pushing back her chair.

Both Calvin and Theda started slightly as

though they'd forgotten she shared the table with them.

Deep in thought, Carole walked to the corral. She wasn't altogether sure she approved of her grandmother's flirtatious attitude toward Calvin. Naturally he'd be attracted to Theda – he might be a few years younger, but her grandmother was a very pretty woman.

Don't play dog-in-the-manger, she chastised herself. Theda's been a widow for ten years, she has every right to be interested in Calvin if she so chooses.

He wasn't some suave, persuasive con man, he was a forthright Australian ex-rancher. What harm would it do for Theda to amuse herself by flirting with Calvin for the short time *Bandido* was being filmed?

Actually, Carole rather liked Calvin Telford. She was surprised to find Sombrita wasn't waiting for her at the gate, but a glance toward the far end of the corral showed her why. José and Jerrold stood outside the fence, Jerrold absently patting the mare through the bars as he listened to whatever José was saying.

He even fascinates Sombrita, she thought bitterly as she considered taking the coward's way out by ducking back into the stable to avoid facing Jerrold. Before she made up her mind, José hailed her.

She waved in response and both men started in her direction. Sombrita, left alone, trotted across the corral to greet her. Carole opened the gate, let the mare through, and led her into the stable to saddle her. She was damned if she meant to stand around waiting for Jerrold. She didn't look up even when she heard his voice.

'José says you've been running the ranch for the last three years.'

She tightened the cinch. 'I believe I told you much the same thing.'

'I underestimated you. Sorry.'

Did he mean he thought she'd lied to him? Anger stiffened her spine as she straightened and turned to face him. He didn't look sorry, he looked as annoyed as she felt. She didn't understand why *he* should he be annoyed when she was the one who'd been rejected last night.

'Doesn't Australia have any women ranchers?' she demanded.

He waved his hand, dismissing the question. 'That's beside the point.'

Unwilling to be drawn into an argument, she shrugged and turned back to Sombrita, finished the saddling and swung on to the mare's back. Jerrold blocked her exit.

'If you don't mind?' she said coldly.

He didn't move. 'I'd like to ride with you and take a look at the entire spread.'

Despite her resolve, her heart leaped as she pictured them riding together. But she was determined not to give way. 'Why?' she asked.

'From your father I got the impression both of you were happy to leave ranching behind.'

He scowled. 'My father? Where in hell did you meet my father?'

'He had lunch with Grandmother and me.'

'The bloody conniving bastard,' he muttered.

Carole stared at him, shocked. What a way to speak of his own father!

Without another word, Jerrold whirled and marched from the stable, heading, she noticed, for the ranch house. Did he mean to order Calvin off the premises? But why? She hesitated, wondering if she should go back to the house. Calvin, though, had seemed perfectly able to take care of himself and it really was none of her business.

As she rode out of the stable, she saw José standing by the corral gate and reined in the mare.

'I noticed you talking to Mr Telford,' she said, striving to sound casual.

'He ask a lot of questions about the ranch. Seem like he know cows, he know horses, but he don't know oranges.' José smiled. 'He ask about you, too. I tell him Señorita Carole is the best foreman in the Valley. Why not? She go four years to college to learn and her papa teach her what those college professors don't know.'

Carole smiled back at him. 'Plus what I'm still learning from *Tio* José. Sometimes I think you ought to be a *profesor*.'

José laughed, then shook his head. 'What I

know don't come from books.' He bent and picked up a handful of dirt, letting it trickle through his fingers. 'I learn from this.' He dusted his hands, wiped them on his jeans and squinted up at Carole.

'We talk about Joaquin Murieta, about the dangerous *bandidos* in the old days,' he said slowly. 'He say maybe some of them hide gold around here – who can know?' José shrugged. 'In that movie he's Joaquin but Señor Telford, he's no bad *hombre*.'

So he'd gotten to José, too, Carole thought. Was she the only one who didn't trust Jerrold? 'So he was asking about the ghost gold?'

José chuckled. 'I tell him how you search and search all over the ranch for that gold when you a *muchachita* and he laugh and say, "Determined even then, I see."'

Carole smiled ruefully. 'Maybe I gave up too soon. We could use a windfall right now, that's for sure. Do you think there's any truth in that old legend, José?'

'Me, I say like Señor Telford – who can know?'

As she rode off, it crossed Carole's mind that everyone seemed to be asking questions about the ghost gold. What would be next? The film crew out with pickaxes and spades, digging for the legendary gold? She wished them luck – the Valley adobe soil could be all but impenetrable.

★ ★ ★

By the night of the party, the moon had waxed to three-quarters full and its silvery light added the final touch to Theda's carefully planned evening. For as far back as Carole could remember, her grandmother's parties had always been special. Tonight's looked to be no exception.

The evening was mild enough so the patio could be used and small round tables covered with bright gold cloths dotted the brick paving. Candles flickered in iron-and-glass containers. Some of the guests were seated at the tables but most drifted about, forming and reforming small groups.

Carole had unearthed a long blue dress from the back of her closet, one with a low sweetheart neckline. She couldn't recall when she'd last worn it or why but the dress still fit, so she decided to wear it and, after taking some care with her makeup, was pleased with what she saw in the mirror. Theda's nod of approval warmed her.

All the Hartes' neighbors were present at the party, plus Jerrold, the entire film crew and a few of Theda's old friends from LA. Also Calvin Telford.

'I think it's a shame,' Theda had confided in Carole, 'how cold Jerrold is to his father. The poor man doesn't complain, but I can see how it hurts him. I simply can't understand Jerrold's attitude. He tried to hide it from me, but I could tell he was terribly cross when he discovered I'd invited Calvin to stay with us. It's as though he doesn't want his father anywhere near him.'

Carole had been a bit disturbed when her grandmother put Calvin in what used to be the master bedroom. No one had used it since her father died. But, as her father would say, that was no reason to leave it empty; rooms were meant to be used. Besides, the more Carole saw of Calvin, the better she liked him – which was more than she could say for Jerrold. It couldn't be that he was ashamed of his father – Calvin might speak bluntly, but he certainly behaved like a gentleman. He was downright courtly with Theda. Even José liked him.

'He call me mate,' José had told Carole. 'He say in his country mate mean *compadre*, mean *amigo*.'

So far this evening, Carole had managed to avoid Jerrold and she hoped she could continue to do so. He'd come in with the director, Herwin Holden, and Marla Thurlow. Marla had quickly been surrounded by admiring local males while the women gravitated to Jerrold. Herwin, fifty-ish and balding, was presently deep in conversation with Theda.

'A ripper night, Carole girl,' Calvin said, appearing at her side with two glasses of champagne. He handed her one. 'Join the celebration.'

She smiled. 'Just what are we celebrating?'

'You're too young and pretty to need a reason and I'm too old and wise to try to think up one.'

'I'm not much of a drinker.' But she sipped the sparkling wine.

'Thought I'd pegged your young man but it looks like I could be wrong.' Calvin gestured toward the group around Marla. Rich was the one being favored by her attention at the moment. 'That sort of do bother you?'

Carole shook her head. 'Rich isn't "my young man." Actually, I don't have anyone special.'

'So you think.' Calvin lowered his voice. 'There's someone watching every move you make. He's clever, nobody's caught him at it except me. He's never been able to hide a perishing thing from his old man.'

He couldn't mean Jerrold! Carole stared at Calvin, at a loss for words. She hadn't noticed Jerrold so much as glance at her.

Calvin nodded conspiratorially. 'Don't let on I put you wise.'

Before Carole could decide how to answer, Theda came up to them and laid her hand on Calvin's arm. 'My friend from the golden days is just dying to meet you,' she told him. Smiling at both him and Carole, she added, 'I'm sorry to drag off the most interesting man at the party – please do excuse us, dear.'

Theda was acting positively seductive, Carole thought as she watched them walk away. It had always amused her that her grandmother had been named for Theda Bara, a vamp from the silent movie days, because she believed no one in the world was less vampish than her grandmother. Calvin had certainly brought out a side of Theda that Carole had never before seen.

'I don't much like the looks of that.' Jerrold spoke from slightly behind her, causing her to almost drop her champagne.

She didn't turn to look at him, but his nearness set her pulses racing. She downed most of her drink in an effort to drown her involuntary reaction to him before saying, 'If you mean my grandmother and your father, they're both adults.'

'It's far from a good idea. In fact, it's a bloody rotten one.'

Stung by what she saw as criticism of her grandmother's behavior, Carole set her glass down and swung around to face him. 'Why don't you mind your own business?'

'What he does *is* my business. And I won't have him cosying up to Theda. Look at her – she's eating it up.'

How dared he? Carole felt her hands balling into fists. If she were a man she'd sock him in the jaw.

Her expression must have broadcasted her fury because Jerrold held up his hand. 'Don't get your blood up, I'll handle everything in good time.'

She didn't have a chance to reply before he

groaned, grasped her arm, and all but dragged her away from the patio, cutting between two bottle-brush bushes to a path that led to the pine grove.

'What do you think you're doing?' she sputtered as she tried to break free.

'That giggling redhead – Kitty something – was on a collision course with us. I've done my duty for tonight; any more of listening to Kitty would be cruel and unusual punishment of a guest, as any fair hostess would agree.'

Kitty Knowles. Carole was used to her giggling, but she acknowledged Kitty could be a trial. It occurred to her that Jerrold, as an actor, must often be forced to be polite to people he'd rather not meet in the first place. All the same, she had no intention of forgiving him. She dug her heels in, forcing him to stop.

'You deserve to spend the evening with her,' she snapped.

'No man deserves such a fate. I'd much rather be with you.' His hands rested lightly on her shoulders. Moonlight slanting through the branches of the pines silvered his face.

The fragrance of night-blooming jasmine sweetened the air. Music drifted from the house, one of Theda's slow and sentimental forties' ballads, a man singing about shadows and moonlight and love.

'You must know I can't keep away from you.' His husky voice blended with the singer's.

Nor she from him, no matter how hard she tried. His nearness stole her breath; she couldn't move, she could only continue to look at him in feverish anticipation. Where had her anger fled? Her indignation at his behavior? Her determination never to get into this kind of a situation with him again? With an intense effort, she managed to find her voice.

'Speaking of bad ideas – this is one.' Unfortunately her tone didn't match the words, being more of a whispered invitation than an angry denial.

His lips brushed hers softly. 'Righto,' he murmured against her mouth. 'Very bad.'

She hadn't forgotten his tantalizing taste and, as her lips parted in response to the delicate probing of his tongue, she feared she was already hopelessly addicted. She'd never be able to get enough.

He gathered her close and her hands rose to his shoulders to hold him to her. This time his kiss, rather than demanding, held a promise, one she longed to see fulfilled and, at the same time, a promise she feared to have fulfilled.

You're out of your mind, a voice in her head protested as she gave herself up to the wonder of his embrace. The rest of her paid no attention. The desire tingling along her nerves and the liquid warmth gathering inside her were far more persuasive than cool rationality.

Before she lost all sense of her surroundings,

Carole found enough strength to pull away from Jerrold. 'I must go back,' she gasped. The sound of her own voice, ragged with passion, frightened her. One touch from Jerrold and she'd be back in his arms, helpless to free herself a second time.

'This doesn't end here,' he warned her. 'We won't be shooting at all this weekend – I want to see you.'

His tone told her he meant to see her, never mind any protests. He didn't intend to take no for an answer.

She didn't want to refuse him, but she had to. Before it was too late to refuse him anything. 'I – I –' Carole struggled to find some excuse to take her away from Jerrold's dangerous proximity. 'I'm going to the mountains,' she finished. Thank God she'd remembered Rich's invitation. 'To enjoy the sequoias. With a friend.'

After a moment or two of silence, Jerrold laughed. 'Wrong,' he told her. 'It's plural. With friends. Rich Erskine invited me, too.'

'But . . .' She paused, unable to think of any way out. Unexpectedly, he took her hand and bowed over it. 'We're letting the music go to waste. I do believe that's a waltz. Shall we?' Without waiting for her to agree, he put an arm around her waist and swung her into the gliding steps of the waltz.

She could hardly refuse to dance with him, she told herself as she closed her eyes and settled dreamily into his embrace. Remembering a movie about Vienna, she visualized a lavishly decorated ballroom with glittering chandeliers, the floor crowded with richly gowned women partnered by splendidly uniformed officers. She and Jerrold were among the dancers.

While the orchestra played, one by one, the gentlemen whirled their partners through doors leading on to balconies, disappearing into the night until only she and Jerrold were left in the ballroom, dipping and swirling to the waltz. One by one the candles in the overhead chandeliers winked out, the music ended and they were left in darkness. Now that no one could see, soon he would bend his head, his lips seeking hers . . .

'A cloud's covered the moon,' Jerrold murmured into her ear, drawing her closer as he stopped dancing.

The moon? Carole's eyes popped open, her fantasy vanishing – all but the very end. Jerrold's mouth, warm and enticing, covered hers. She leaned into his kiss, parting her lips, bemused, aware they were no longer in Vienna but reluctant to return to reality. If only this moment could be frozen in time, she thought as she clung to him, desire fizzing inside her like champagne.

She wanted to be no place else in the universe other than in his arms, held close, feeling the warmth and strength of his body against hers.

His kiss deepened and she welcomed the sweet and sensual invasion as his tongue caressed hers.

When his lips left hers to trail down to her throat, she whispered his name, 'Jerrold . . .'

He heard the tremble in her voice as she said his name and a thrill shot through him. She was as enmeshed in this web of passion as he was. He could feel her longing in the way she pressed against him, her desire in the heat of her kisses. He wanted her more intensely than he could remember ever desiring any other woman and the depth of his need for her rather frightened him.

No commitments for him. He'd been down that rocky road and refused to travel it again. Ever. Still, he meant to take this affair to its conclusion – he meant to have her, had to have her.

His fingers brushed across her breasts, feeling, under the thin silk of her dress, the thrust of her nipples rising under his caress. She drove him wild. It was all he could do not to pull her down on to the grass, strip off her clothes and make love to her for the rest of the night.

'Carole,' he said hoarsely, breathing in her intoxicating scent – sweet and feminine, not a trace of that damn musky perfume he hated. 'Beautiful Carole. Do you know how much I want you?'

She wanted him, too. Now. Here. The moon slid free of the clouds, illuminating the naked passion in his eyes and setting her aflame. But the moonlight also revealed their surroundings, bringing her back to reality so that she heard the laughter and voices of party guests who were not all that far away, sounds she'd blocked out earlier.

'We can't,' she whispered, gathering all her willpower so she could force herself to leave his embrace.

He sighed and let her go. 'Not the best time or place,' he agreed. 'But it'll be right sooner or later, you can count on that.'

His words echoed in her ears: *It'll be right*. But would it? Once out of his arms, all her doubts returned. Right for him, maybe, but what about her?

CHAPTER 5

'Five thousand feet and still climbing,' Rich said, twisting the wheel to negotiate yet another curve on the mountain road.

Carole glanced at the live oak and the scant-needled digger pines on the hillsides below. Soon lodgepole pines and red firs would crowd close to the curving road they traveled. At this altitude the air was decidedly cooler than in the valley. When they reached the sequoias it would be downright chilly.

'I still can't get over you asking Jerrold to come along,' she said.

'Yeah, well, we got to talking about the mountains and all. He's nothing like I figured a movie actor would be – maybe because he grew up on a ranch. He was really interested in the big trees. I guess they don't have redwoods in Australia.'

'Apparently he wasn't as interested as he pretended to be. Otherwise he'd have come along.' As she spoke Carole tried to convince herself she really wasn't disappointed because Jerrold hadn't joined them.

Rich grinned at her. 'This way I get you all to myself.'

'You're sure you wouldn't prefer Marla?' Carole teased, remembering how Rich had followed Marla around at the party.

'Aw, come on, she's a star, she wouldn't give a guy like me the time of day.' Rich smiled dreamily as he maneuvered his four-wheel drive truck around a hairpin turn. 'Prettiest woman I ever set eyes on.'

'She's gorgeous.'

'Uh, not that you aren't a classy-looking chick when you dress up,' he added hastily.

It didn't bother Carole that Rich found Marla more attractive than he did her. She really didn't care how many other women he admired because, though he was her friend, she wasn't in love with him.

How did Jerrold feel about Marla? she wondered. He hadn't danced attendance on her at the party the way the other men did, but she knew there must be love scenes in *Bandido* between Murieta and Penelope White, the innocent American girl he rescued, Marla's role. A knife twisted in her heart when she pictured Marla in Jerrold's arms. Hadn't she heard somewhere that it wasn't unusual for the leading man and lady to continue the love scenes off camera, in private?

'Good thing we got an early start,' Rich said.

'I heard the edge of that northern storm'll hit us by this afternoon. That'll mean snow at this elevation. Not to worry, though –' he patted the wheel of the truck '– this baby'll get us through anything.' He glanced approvingly at Carole's jeans, heavy jacket and hiking boots. 'We're both dressed for snow anyway. Did I ever tell you about the time me and two buddies got stranded up here in the middle of a blizzard?'

Carole shook her head and Rich went on with the story. By the time he finished, they'd entered King's Canyon National Park. He pulled into a nearly empty parking lot and they got out.

'This is the way I like it,' he said. 'No tourists.'

Before they reached the trail to the big trees, a white Jaguar, the top up, turned into the lot. Carole's pulse rate jumped and she halted, waiting.

'Guess I spoke too soon,' Rich said, following her gaze. 'Hey, isn't that –?'

'Jerrold,' she finished, watching him get out, shut the door on the driver's side, walk around the car, and open the other door.

A woman in high-heeled boots, burgundy pants and a short pink suede jacket slid out. Rich drew in his breath audibly.

'Why that's her! That's Marla!' He hailed Jerrold, waving.

Now I know why Jerrold didn't come with Rich and me, Carole told herself. Because he wanted to be alone with Marla. Why did he pretend to be interested in me when it's obviously Marla he wants? Or is it automatic with him to come on to every woman he meets?

As Marla and Jerrold walked up to them, Marla thrust her hands into her pockets and shivered. 'Brr, it's polar-bear cold up here.'

Rich immediately peeled off his lined denim jacket and laid it carefully over her shoulders. Marla's smile of thanks rendered him speechless. Turning to Jerrold, he managed two words. 'Might snow.'

Jerrold glanced up at the sky, rapidly becoming overcast. 'How long do we have?'

'I'd say no more than an hour,' Rich answered. 'We better get a move on if you guys are going to see the trees and get out of here before the roads get too messy for the Jag.'

Annoyed as she was with Jerrold, Carole couldn't stop looking at him. His brown leather jacket and matching visored cap lent him a dashing European look that she wished she could find fault with. Unfortunately, it became him, as everything he wore seemed to.

Signs were posted reminding people to stay on the trails because of the fragility of sequoia roots, but Marla paid no attention, walking over to caress the fluted cinnamon trunk of the first big tree they approached.

'You're breaking the rules,' Jerrold pointed out.

'I just had to touch it to make sure it was real,' she said. 'I mean, don't you think all this –' she waved a hand to take in the grove of sequoias immediately ahead of them '– looks like some gigantic movie set?'

Rich smiled but Jerrold didn't appear amused. Carole had to admit that the huge trunks, with no branches for their first hundred or more feet and the sparse green-yellow needled foliage when the branches did begin, were unusual enough to seem unbelievable to a first-time viewer.

'I thought they'd look like the coast redwoods,' Marla complained as she picked her way back to the trail. 'I like those better, they're my kind of trees. These, I don't know why, aren't friendly.'

For the first time since she'd met Marla, Carole warmed to her. 'You're right,' she said. 'They're kings, lords of all they survey and they know it.'

Marla blinked, as if surprised Carole was supporting her view. 'Exactly. And I don't enjoy being made to feel like a peasant.'

'But the sequoias are beautiful in their own way,' Carole went on. 'Look how close those two are growing together – pairs like that are called loving couples.'

A loud chirring overhead made them all look up.

'A squirrel!' Marla cried. 'How cute. Isn't he just the darlingest thing you ever saw?'

'That's a Douglas squirrel,' Rich put in, the first words he'd said directly to Marla. 'They eat the seeds from the big trees.' He moved closer to her as he spoke. 'I'll show you how to tell a Douglas from the other kinds of mountain squirrels. First, there's his size —'

Carole stopped listening when Jerrold took hold of her hand and pulled her with him along the path, leaving the other two behind.

'While he's teaching her about squirrels, why don't you show me more about loving couples?' he murmured so close to her that his warm breath teased her ear.

She tugged against his grasp, but he didn't release her hand. Determined not to play his game, she took a deep breath and said in a pseudo park-ranger voice, 'Listen up, then. If you'll notice, some sequoias grow in threes rather than twos. They're called three graces.'

'Three's a crowd,' he said. 'That's why I didn't ride up with you and Rich. I figured if I brought Marla along with me, she'd distract him.'

Carole glanced at Jerrold. Could she believe a single word he said?

'Marla's distracting, all right.' Her tone was dry.

He shrugged. 'She's an actress.'

'And you're an actor.'

Jerrold shook his head. 'I admit I make a living acting but I'm damned if I'll let you file me into a slot as you keep trying to do.'

'Yet you filed Marla into one.'

'She'd agree she belongs there. Acting's her whole world. It's not mine.'

'It's snowing!' Marla cried from behind them. 'I just love snow, it's so beautiful.'

Carole had been so engrossed in her conversation with Jerrold she hadn't even noticed. He had his own share of ability to distract her.

'The trouble with my bright idea is that four's a crowd, too,' Jerrold muttered as Marla and Rich hurried to catch up up to them.

'I could walk in the snow forever,' Marla went on, throwing her head back and putting out her tongue to catch the snowflakes that were now falling thick and fast.

Rich watched her in admiration while Carole wondered if he wasn't feeling cold without his jacket. Maybe, like one of her grandmother's old songs said, love kept him warm. He certainly looked smitten.

'We ought to think about getting back,' he said.

'Good idea,' Jerrold echoed.

'I don't ever want to go back,' Marla said. 'Let's find a cabin and stay up here in the snow all winter.'

Carole pictured a cozy log cabin with a fire on the hearth while snow softly bombarded the windows. She imagined herself in front of the fireplace on a sheepskin rug with Jerrold's arms around her, just the two of them.

She was startled out of her reverie when Marla grabbed her hand, saying, 'Let's run away from these wimps. They're scaredy-cats, afraid of a little snow.' She began to run and Carole was forced to run with her.

Despite her protestations about damaging the tree roots, Marla pulled her off the trail and they darted between the giant trees until Marla, slipping and sliding in her high-heeled boots, halted.

'This is so beautiful with the snow and all,' she said, 'but neither of them appreciate it. Men just aren't romantic. Take Jerrold. All he thinks about is that damn palomino he rides. I swear he'd rather kiss the horse than me. Rich is sweet but . . .' she sighed '. . . squirrels! Maybe I'm losing my touch.'

Carole laughed. 'Rich is so stunned by you it's a wonder he can talk at all.'

'I suppose Jerrold's problem could be his ex-wife. I understand she was a real bitch.'

Startled, Carole stared at Marla. She hadn't known Jerrold was ever married.

'Marla! Carole!' Rich shouted.

'Come out or get left!' Jerrold added.

'I wouldn't put it past him,' Carole said. 'We'd better surrender peacefully.'

'Never!' Marla crouched and scooped together enough snow for a ball. 'Hey, this stuff is colder than a witch's hang-nail,' she muttered, juggling the snowball from one bare hand to another.

Carole blinked at the comparison – a witch's hang-nail? – but let it go, caught up in the pleasurable anticipation of smacking Jerrold with a snowball. She bent to make one for herself, peering around the sequoia trunk. The two men stood on the trail, no more than ten feet away.

'Enemy sighted,' she whispered to Marla as she stepped out from behind the trunk and let fly. Her snowball hit Jerrold square in the chest. Marla's glanced off Rich's shoulder.

'Just you wait!' Rich shouted as both men ran toward them.

Marla squealed and darted away. Carole fled in the opposite direction, angling back toward the trail. She didn't get far before Jerrold's hands grabbed her around the waist, halting her. He swung her around to face him.

'Now you pay,' he said, grinning at her. 'Want to know what the penalty is?'

'I suppose you intend to rub my face in the snow. Or put snow down my back.'

'Neither. Guess again. You've one left.' He drew her closer.

Marla's scream froze them both. Carole turned and saw Marla sprawled on the ground. Rich pounded up to kneel beside her. By the time Jerrold and Carole reached them, Rich had Marla's left boot off.

'She tripped and hurt her ankle,' he said. 'Might be broken.'

'Oh, no,' Marla gasped.

'The ranger station's not far,' Carole reminded Rich. 'You and Jerrold can carry her there for first aid.'

'The hell with first aid,' Rich snapped. 'Marla needs an X-ray, she needs a doctor. I'm driving her down the short cut to Porterville.'

'I'll help you carry her,' Jerrold offered.

'I'll handle it myself.' Rich's tone was clipped. 'I've been toting calves since I was fourteen. This little gal hardly weighs a thing compared to a calf.' He lifted Marla into his arms and she clung to him, moaning.

'I'll go with you,' Carole said.

'You'll just be in the way, there's not all that much room in the pickup.' Rich jerked his head toward Jerrold. 'You'd best ride with him.'

'Fine,' Jerrold said. 'You go ahead, Rich. We'll meet you at the hospital.'

Rich, carrying Marla toward the parking lot, called over his shoulder, 'Don't let him take the short cut, Carole. That Jag'll never make it in this snow.'

'He's right,' she told Jerrold. 'It's pretty hairy in the best of weather. We'll have to go back the way you came up.'

Jerrold shrugged. 'I hope Rich knows what he's doing.'

'Oh, he'll make it down all right, but I still think we should have gone to the ranger station. They'd have wrapped or splinted Marla's ankle until we could get her to a doctor.' She shook her head. 'There's no one more bullheaded than Rich once he makes up his mind.'

'You've known him a long time.'

It wasn't a question but Marla answered it anyway. 'Since we were kids.' She dusted the snow from her hair and pulled the hood of her jacket up over her head. 'It's really coming down. We'd better – '

Jerrold's look stopped her. 'Do you really think I'm going to let you get away without paying the penalty?' he demanded. 'No one attacks me without retaliation.'

She'd all but forgotten smacking him with the snowball. 'Okay, my third guess is it's going to be a snowball for a snowball but,' she taunted, 'I'll lay odds I'm better at ducking than you are.' As she spoke she readied herself to make a run for the parking lot, figuring she'd be out of range before he had a single snowball made.

He caught her arm before she got away. 'Wrong again,' he said, pulling her into his arms. 'Try ducking this.'

His face was as cold as hers, but his warm lips raised her internal temperature to feverish proportions. Despite the bulky layers of clothing between them, her desire blossomed, its seeking tendrils tingling along her nerve endings. Why was it Jerrold's kisses affected her so intensely? Before he came along she'd about decided a kiss was just a kiss. No longer! By the time he let her go she was weak-kneed.

'I call that cruel and unusual punishment for just one small snowball,' she said, striving for lightness.

'Lucky you didn't zap me with two.'

'Oh?'

He touched the tip of her nose with a cold forefinger. 'Bet your boots. Shall I show you what two snowballs would let you in for? I'll admit we may run into difficulties because of the weather, but you don't think I'd let a little snow stop me, do you?'

'I'm afraid nothing ever stops you,' she said. 'Thanks, but I'd rather remain ignorant. And we really must go or risk being stranded up here.'

'Is that so bad?'

'I don't know about you, but I don't care to spend the night in a ranger's quarters with him and his family. There isn't anything else available this time of the year.'

His dark gaze held her as surely as if he'd kept her there forcibly. 'And if there were, would you share a cabin with me, Carole?'

'That depends.'

'On what?'

'On whether I had any choice or not.'

'Do you really believe you have a choice?' His voice was as soft as the snowflakes and equally treacherous.

With Jerrold so close her willpower leaked away as quickly as water from a sieve. The warmth in his eyes left her with no choice but she was damned if she'd let him know that.

'Since I don't plan to be stranded anywhere in bad weather with you, the question is moot,' she said defiantly.

He grinned at her and, taking her hand, began walking toward the parking lot. 'You offer the most interesting challenge I've had in years,' he told her. 'I should warn you I never refuse a challenge. And I always win.'

Yes, and then what? she wondered. You go off looking for the next challenge, right? Well, *I* won't be one of your left-behind prizes.

'There's always a first time,' she said. 'To lose, I mean.'

'Watch it, you're talking to the king of the hill.'

'Like the sequoias? You're nowhere near as tall. Or as old. Or as . . .' She paused. Beautiful, she'd meant to say. But to her he *was* as beautiful as any sequoia.

Jerrold glanced at the giant trees. 'Righto. They do have a few hundred feet and a few thousand years on me. Since I'm on their hill, I'll abdicate gracefully in their favor.' He squeezed her hand. 'I'm glad I'm here with you; I'll never forget the sequoias in the snow. Not for as long as I live.'

His words brought a pang to Carole. He spoke

as though already looking back, anticipating leaving. Did he know she'd never forget him?

Just before they reached the car, he halted to put his hands on her shoulders. 'Like the sequoias, we could be a loving couple, Carole,' he said softly.

It wasn't fair the way he undermined all her defenses. She'd like nothing better than to be the other half of a loving couple with Jerrold, but he must be aware that, unlike the trees, their pairing wouldn't last.

To break the mesmerizing spell he cast, she blurted out the first thing that came to her mind. 'Marla said you were divorced. You never mentioned being married.'

Jerrold dropped his arms, turned toward the car and began brushing snow from the windshield. 'My marriage was over a long time ago. It has nothing to do with you and me.' He spoke without looking at her.

But it means you were part of a loving couple once before, she thought, helping to brush away the snow. What happened to end the marriage?

Neither of them spoke again until they were in the car, pulling out of the parking lot.

'The marriage was a mistake,' he said. 'Not mine, not Linda's. Ours. I'll never do it again.'

So now she knew where she stood. Though she'd certainly never expected Jerrold to marry her, in her heart of hearts she'd hoped for something more permanent than a month or two.

92

'Everyone believes it was Linda's fault I left the ranch,' Jerrold's voice was bitter. 'They're wrong. And, no, I don't carry a torch – the divorce was a relief to the both of us. Since the marriage wasn't the happiest time of my life, I don't often discuss it.'

'I've never been married,' Carole said, in a effort to lighten his mood. 'I've never even been engaged, though I almost was once. In college.'

'What happened?' He sounded relieved to change the subject.

'He wanted to live in San Francisco.'

Jerrold smiled. 'And you're a Harte. It's Harte's Way or nothing.'

'You've got it.'

'How about you and Rich?' Was his voice a shade too casual?

'Oh, we're good friends.' She strove to make it sound ambiguous, not wanting to reveal too much of herself to Jerrold.

'No marriage plans? After all, he's a rancher, too.'

'I don't happen to want to get married.' She spoke tartly. 'Wake up, it's no longer every woman's dream, you know.'

'Maybe not, but when marriage works, it's – pleasant.'

'Pleasant? What an anemic choice of words! Would you actually settle for pleasant?'

Jerrold laughed. 'What do you think?'

'Since you've told me in no uncertain terms

93

you'll never marry again, I refuse to answer what amounts to another moot question.'

'I'm beginning to think you studied law as well as agriculture at the university. But you're right – I'd never settle for just plain pleasant.' He glanced at her. 'For starters, I'd want what's between us.'

Carole caught her breath. Before she met Jerrold, she'd never dreamed a mere look from any man could make her weak with longing.

The Jag skidded on the slippery snow; Jerrold swore and returned his attention to the road. 'If you don't stop distracting me,' he muttered, 'we may never get off this damned mountain alive.'

'I'm not doing anything to distract you,' she protested.

'You're sitting next to me, close enough for me to touch you. If that's not distracting, what is?'

With a rush of pleasure, Carole let herself believe his words. It thrilled her to think he was as disturbed by her as she was by him and suddenly she didn't care if what was between them lasted a only a week or a month. For however long it turned out to be, she wanted to make love with Jerrold.

'Do I have a ghost of a chance with you?' he asked.

She didn't intend to touch that question with a ten-foot pole. Deciding she had to distract herself from how she felt about him, Carole searched for a change of subject, snatching at the first thought that came into her mind. 'Speaking of ghosts, why are all you film people so interested in Harte's Way ghost gold all of a sudden?'

He shot her a quick glance. 'Want me to back off, do you?'

'About the gold?' she said, deliberately misunderstanding.

'That, too? Righto. I can't speak for the others, but I enjoy solving puzzles. Unraveling mysteries. And hidden treasure is right up there with the best. I'm betting your bandit gold does exist. Wouldn't it be fun to find it?'

She sighed. 'José told you I searched all over the place without results when I was a kid. That was for fun. But today the ranch could use that hidden treasure – providing it's for real.'

'Then we ought to go treasure-hunting together. Who knows what we might find?'

'Nothing, is my guess.'

He smiled. 'You're wrong again. What we find depends on what treasure we're talking about. Gold's a precious metal, but some things are worth more than gold.'

Again he was venturing on to the same dangerous terrain. She refused to follow him. 'I hope Marla's all right,' she said.

'Don't worry, she's one tough lady. Marla will survive.'

'But if her ankle's broken, how can she finish the filming?'

'Herwin's innovative, he'll find a way. Besides, it's a period piece when long dresses were in vogue. A long gown hides much, including a cast, should one be necessary, and Marla's a trouper.'

They rode in silence until Jerrold said, 'I asked Sawa about the ghost gold, you know.'

'She told me.'

'I rather thought she might. I gathered she believes in it, but also believes in ghosts who guard the gold, and thinks the cache should be left alone.'

'Sawa doesn't know where the cache is,' Carole said firmly, in case he was toying with the idea that she might.

'Maybe not, though Herwin might disagree with you. He's convinced that most, if not all, old Native Americans possess spiritual powers that transcend those we poor, ignorant trespassers have.'

'Trespassers?'

'On their land, isn't that true? They didn't invite any of us here, did they?'

Carole smiled. 'My father told me that Sawa's husband once said it was too bad his people didn't have an immigration quota way back when the Europeans first sailed over here.'

'Too late now.'

She nodded. 'Much too late. I'd certainly have trouble giving up Harte's Way – it's been in the family for generations. Anyway, going back to

Sawa – she's a talented basket maker and she may believe in Miwok legends, but she'd be the first to tell you she doesn't possess any unusual powers.'

'Once Herwin gets hold of a conviction, he hangs on like a bulldog. He'll never believe Sawa isn't some kind of seeress or whatever. And, for him, the hidden bandit gold is a fact.'

Carole shook her head. 'He'll never find it and neither will I. Or you.'

'Is that another challenge?' Jerrold asked. 'If so, it's the second you've given me. Remember what I told you – I always win.'

'Winner implies a loser,' she said tartly.

He reached over and grasped her hand, bringing it to his lips. 'Going back to the first challenge – if I win, do you really think you'd lose?'

CHAPTER 6

As they drove down the mountain, the snow turned to rain at the lower elevations then, by the time the Jag approached the ranch, into a fine mist.

'We can call the Porterville hospital from the house,' Carole suggested.

'Good idea,' Jerrold said, turning into the winding drive to Harte's Way. He parked under the *porte-cochère*.

When they entered the house, Theda wasn't anywhere about. Leaving Jerrold in the living-room to make the hospital call, Carole went to the kitchen to ask Lollie where Theda was.

'Your grandmother and Mr Calvin, they packed up and drove off in his car.' Lollie shook her head. 'Holding hands and laughing and carrying on like teenagers, they was. Never said a word to me about where she was going or when she'd be back. Left you a note on the mantel, she did.' Lollie paused. 'Course I didn't read it, ain't none of my business.'

Frowning, Carole returned to the living-room and found the note tucked under a *cloisonné* vase.

'Dear,' her grandmother had written on her monogrammed blue paper, 'on the spur of the moment, Calvin and I decided to treat ourselves to a holiday in Las Vegas. I'll call to let you know where we're staying. Love, Theda.'

Carole read it twice, not quite believing her eyes. Theda had never done anything even remotely like this! When Grandpa Lyle was still alive, if he and Theda went anywhere, the trip was planned weeks ahead. He'd once said that the only impulsive thing he'd ever done in his life was to ask Theda to marry him.

'I talked to Rich,' Jerrold said. 'Marla's not seriously injured.'

Wrenching her thoughts back to what had happened at the Park, Carole turned to him.

'No broken bones,' he went on. 'Apparently she has a sprain. The doctor's sending her home with an elastic bandage on her ankle and orders to keep off it as much as possible for the next few days. Home being here on location.'

'That's good news.' Carole held out the note. 'I don't quite know what to make of this, though.'

Jerrold's eyebrows drew together as he scanned Theda's words. 'I'll tell you what it is,' he muttered, crumpling the paper in his hand. 'Bloody bad news. Damn the man!'

Carole bristled. She wasn't thrilled to find her

grandmother had gone off for a 'holiday' with Calvin Telford, but she didn't like Jerrold's attitude.

'They *are* adults,' she pointed out, unhappy to find herself defending what she regarded as her grandmother's impulsive decision.

'Exactly. And so at his age he should know better.'

Know better than what? Carole wondered. Know better than to choose someone like Theda for his companion on this Las Vegas trip? Theda might wear a bit too much makeup for over sixty and she might act a mite too girlish at times, but her grandmother was a wonderful, warm-hearted woman. She was amusing, attractive and interesting. A fit companion for a prince, let alone Calvin Telford.

'My grandmother –' she began.

'I don't blame Theda,' Jerrold cut in. 'This is my father's fault. He never should have asked Theda to go with him. He has no right to get involved with your grandmother. None at all.'

A horrible suspicion struck Carole. She knew Jerrold's mother was dead, but that didn't mean Calvin hadn't married a second time. 'Your father isn't married, is he?'

Jerrold shook his head impatiently. 'No. That's not the problem. When Theda calls you, let me know where they're staying.'

So he could call his father and berate him?

'Just what *is* the problem, then?' she demanded. 'Does he have some kind of serious illness?'

'Not exactly. My father . . .' He paused, frowning. 'It's not something I feel I can discuss with you until I talk to him.'

A disturbing thought struck her, distracting her from her annoyance with Jerrold. Could her grandmother actually be sharing a room with Calvin? A bed?

Carole struggled against her feeling that Theda had betrayed her in some way. Since Theda had been a widow for ten years, she had every right to involve herself romantically with anyone she chose, including Calvin Telford. But the possibility made Carole uneasy.

'I'm upset, too,' she told Jerrold. 'I never thought my grandmother would go off like this without letting me know ahead of time. But what's done is done. When they get back is time enough to –'

'You don't know a perishing thing about it. When they get back might be too bloody late!'

Jerrold's anger made him sound a good deal more like his father. Too bad he hadn't inherited Calvin's amiable disposition as well.

'There's no need to shout,' she snapped.

Lollie chose that moment to appear. 'Will Mr Jerrold be staying for dinner?' she asked.

'No, he won't!' Carole's tone was emphatic.

'In that case, I'll be getting along home,'

Lollie said. 'I left a crab casserole in the fridge.'
She retreated to the kitchen.

'I take it you want to get rid of me,' Jerrold
said.

'How perceptive.'

'Look, I didn't mean to yammer at you. I'm
sorry. How about if I agree there's no way to sort
out this mess until they return?' He smiled.
'Crab casserole happens to be a favorite of mine
– and we did miss lunch.'

Carole wasn't sure she was ready to forgive
him and she tried not to let his charm undo her.
After his intimation that he didn't find Theda fit
company for his father, she certainly wasn't in
the mood for a romantic dinner for two.

'I suppose you may as well stay.' Her tone was
grudging. 'Rich will probably stop by after he
drops Marla off and he can join us. Marla, too, if
she feels up to it.'

Jerrold grimaced, plainly disappointed but all
he said was, 'It's your casserole.'

Did he think she'd be willing to fall into his
arms after what he'd said? He might not be fond
of his father, but she and Theda were close, as
close as mother and daughter, especially since
her father had died. They were all each other had
and she didn't take kindly to any criticism of her
grandmother. And definitely not undeserved
criticism.

Only an hour ago she'd thought she wanted to
make love with Jerrold. She should have had

more sense. She'd never been one for casual affairs and that's all it would amount to with him. What if she did lose her head when he kissed her? That was no basis for trusting a man. And how could she make love with a man she didn't trust?

'Shall I light the fire?' he asked.

She turned to see him gesturing toward the hearth. 'If you like,' she agreed.

For a moment she imagined the evening as it could have been – a candlelit dinner for two, she and Jerrold alone by the fire afterwards, soft music, his arms around her, the magic that was between them casting its spell . . .

Carole shook herself free from her romantic reverie. That scene was definitely not in to-night's script. 'I'll see what else Lollie left for us,' she said and marched away from him into the kitchen.

Three hours later, the four of them lingered over coffee in the living-room. Marla lay on the couch, her head propped up by pillows, her left leg elevated, with Rich sitting on the floor beside her, alert to fulfill her slightest request. Jerrold lounged against the mantel, looking, Carole thought crossly, like an ad for some exotic virility potion. She sat in the rocker next to the hearth.

'That's the best food I've had since I came on location,' Marla said. 'I may kidnap your cook.'

She covered a yawn. 'I'd love to stay longer but I'm dead on my feet. Or at least one of them. I think I'd better say goodnight.'

Rich shot up, eager to please. Before he could open his mouth, Carole said, 'Mountain air and the altitude knocks everyone out – and you have a twisted ankle, besides. I'm sure Jerrold would be happy to drive you back to the trailers.'

'Any time.' Jerrold spoke so smoothly that Carole couldn't tell if he was annoyed with her or not. The smile he gave Marla suggested he'd been looking forward all evening to taking her home.

'I could just as easily drive Marla,' Rich protested.

'That's sweet of you,' Marla told him, 'but Jerrold and I are going the same way. I've been enough trouble to you for one day.'

'You'd never be any trouble.' Rich's tone was fervent. 'Never.'

'He's a dream, isn't he?' Marla spoke to Carole as though they were alone. 'I can't imagine why he's still single.'

'Ranchers tend to be cautious,' Jerrold put in, clapping Rich on the shoulder. 'I'll take you up on that tour of your spread as soon as I find a few free hours.'

'Just let me know.' Rich's gaze left Jerrold to fasten longingly on Marla. 'When your ankle's healed I'd sure like to show *you* around, too,' he told her.

'I'll remember that,' she assured him.

'No one's going to stop me from carrying you out to the car,' Rich asserted, bending to lift Marla into his arms.

It occurred to Carole that Jerrold would be the one to carry Marla into her room and she bit her lip. What would happen then? Would he be tempted to stay? And, if so, would Marla let him?

If I'd kept my mouth shut I wouldn't be wondering, she thought, because Rich would have driven Marla to the hacienda. But then I'd have been left alone with Jerrold and who knows what might have happened if he kissed me.

Carole shook her head. She knew very well what would have happened; part of her still wanted it to happen, wanted to nestle within his embrace and stay there until the time came for him to leave. Never mind how she'd feel when it was over.

Instead, she was sending him off with Marla. Sometimes she was too smart for her own good. She opened the door for Rich and he swept past her with Marla in his arms.

'Thanks again for the really great food,' Marla told her.

'Likewise,' Rich called over his shoulder.

Jerrold followed them out. Carole wasn't sure what to expect from him but his terse, 'Good food. Goodnight,' perversely disappointed her.

She stood in the doorway as the Jag pulled away. Rich watched from the *porte-cochère*. When the taillights disappeared from view, he turned to her. 'All right if I come in for a bit?'

She wasn't crazy about the idea but she nodded. At least if Rich decided to kiss her goodnight she wouldn't have to worry about his kiss making her lose her head.

After an hour of listening to him rave about how beautiful, charming, brave and unspoiled Marla was, Carole was sorry she hadn't said no. On further acquaintance she'd discovered she liked Marla well enough and didn't mind that Rich found her wonderful, but sixty minutes of just how wonderful was more than plenty.

'I'm getting quite sleepy,' she said when she could work a word in edgewise.

'Do you think Marla likes me at all?' he asked, paying no attention to her hint.

Carole saw she had to be blunt or he'd be there half the night. 'Rich, everyone likes you. But if you don't go home, I, for one, swear I'll start hating you.'

'Why didn't you say you were tired?' he asked, getting up.

After seeing him off and making certain all the doors were locked, Carole walked slowly toward her bedroom, wishing she had someone to talk to, to share her concerns with. When her mother died, Carole had been only seven and so Theda had become her confidante as she grew up. Some things, though, were impossible to discuss with one's grandmother, even if she had been on hand – like her feelings for Jerrold.

And now there was this problem of Theda and Calvin. With Jerrold's inexplicably hostile attitude toward his father, she couldn't expect him to be rational about the matter, so she had no one to share it with.

Passing Theda's memory room, Carole paused, remembering the youthful pictures of her grandmother in the albums. That was how Theda had looked when Grandpa Lyle first set eyes on her. Flicking on the light, she went in, sat down, took one of the albums on her lap and and opened it.

Theda had been a beautiful young woman. Her smile hinted at her vivacious and spirited personality and her eyes spoke of innocence and wonder. She was curvaceous enough to have been any man's dream of a pin-up girl.

'I was helping entertain servicemen at the Hollywood Canteen when I met your grandfather,' Theda always began the story.

Lyle Harte, twenty-eight to Theda's unadmitted sixteen – she'd passed as eighteen – had been deferred from military service because he was in a vital industry: food production. He desperately wanted to enlist when his younger brother Lowell did, but their father wasn't well and couldn't handle Harte's Way alone. Lowell had come home on leave before shipping out and persuaded Lyle to join him in LA for a night on the town.

'You have no idea what it was like in the forties during the war,' Theda often said.

Flipping through the album, Carole caught glimpses of the time from movie stills and photos Theda had saved: sidewalks were thronged with men in uniform – sailors, marines, airmen, soldiers – and quaint black cars drove along the roads. The women, young and old, wore bright red lipstick and many had long red finger-nails as well. Pageboy hairdos were in and skirts were at or just above the knee.

President Franklin D. Roosevelt waved from an open-topped car, his long cigarette holder at a jaunty angle, his dog, Fala, at his side; Joe DiMaggio swung at a pitch; couples jitter-bugged at the Hollywood Palladium while band leader Harry James raised his trumpet to the stars on the ballroom ceiling.

And Lyle Harte, in civvies, stood at the corner of Hollywood and Vine with Lowell who wore his full-dress Marine uniform . . .

'Come on,' Lowell urged. 'I'll tell 'em you're my brother and it's my last night here. They'll let you in.'

Lyle shook his head. 'I feel like a damn slacker.'

'Not you. Christ, you work hard enough for ten men. Dad's not well; if it wasn't for you the ranch would fold and you know it. So what if you're not in uniform? I don't care and you damn well shouldn't.'

Lyle smiled, trying not to show how much he did care. If Dad wasn't sick, he'd enlist tomorrow. 'You go ahead,' he urged.

'Nope. Together or not at all. Together we stand, divided we fall.' Lowell's voice slurred a little; he'd had more to drink than Lyle. 'Hey, I got a great idea to get you into the Canteen. What we'll do is tell 'em you're a visiting actor. A stage actor. From New York. What do they know about New York actors in Hollywood?'

'I'm no actor; I couldn't fool a two-year-old.'

'Sure you could. Pretend you've ridden up that favorite hill of yours back home. Squint your eyes and look off into the distance like you were gazing at the mountains. Don't say much. They won't know what to make of you and they'll believe anything I tell 'em.'

A combination of too much whisky and wanting to please Lowell on this, their last night together, finally pushed Lyle into half-hearted agreement. Once inside the Canteen, he concentrated so hard on looking enigmatic that he didn't notice the pretty blonde who came up to him. Not until she spoke and then he noticed nothing else.

'Are you really from New York?' she asked.

Lyle looked down into eyes as blue as a Valley sky in June and was lost. She was the prettiest

109

girl he'd ever seen in his life and she was smiling at him. He swallowed and tried to speak but couldn't. She must think he was a blooming idiot.

'If all New Yorkers are as quiet as you, the city must be a pleasant change from Hollywood,' she went on. 'I'm Theda Standish, what's your name?'

'Lyle,' he managed to say. 'Lyle Harte.'

'Real or stage?' she asked.

He didn't understand at first and by the time he did catch on, he decided it was too late. He was disgusted with playing this crazy role anyway.

'It's my real name, all right,' he admitted, 'but I'm no actor. Couldn't act if my life depended on it. I'm a rancher. Came in with my brother. He's a Marine. This is the last night of his leave and he wanted me with him. You ought to be talking to him, not me.'

She stared at him for a long moment from those trusting blue eyes and he knew he'd never get enough of looking at her. Now she'll walk away in disgust, he told himself, and who'd blame her?

Theda began to laugh, the sound as beautiful to him as crystal bells tinkling. The high notes of a clarinet blended with her laugh, the song about falling in love and not wanting to.

'A rancher,' she said. 'So that's why you reminded me of a cowboy.'

'I did?' Great, Harte, he told himself disgustedly. Just great. You're about as interesting as yesterday's newspaper.

What could he say, what could he do to keep her here with him? He might not be the world's greatest conversationalist but ordinarily he wasn't this tongue-tied. Theda Standish had knocked him for a loop.

'Are you in the movies?' he ventured.

Her smile was wry. 'I hoped you wouldn't have to ask.'

Damn! He'd said the wrong thing. How could be be so stupid? If she wasn't an actress she wouldn't be here.

'I haven't been to many movies lately.' His words sounded lame to him. 'I know if I'd ever seen you on the screen I never would have forgotten it. You're as beautiful as an orange tree in blossom.'

'That's the most original compliment I've ever gotten,' she said.

'It's more than a compliment, it's the truth.'

Someone called her name and she waved her hand to acknowledge she'd heard, but kept gazing at him. Fearing she'd disappear at any moment, he tried desperately to think of some way to keep her with him and could not.

'Where are you from?' she asked.

'The San Joaquin Valley. I live on a ranch we call Harte's Way. We raise beef and oranges. You'd like it there.'

111

'I'm supposed to be circulating,' she said after a pause. 'I have to go.'

He started to reach for her to try to stop her, but dropped his hand without touching her. He had no right to Theda, none at all.

She hesitated for a long moment. 'I've enjoyed meeting you, Lyle,' she said finally, her smile warmer than the Valley sun in June. 'I really have. Maybe I'd even like Harte's Way.'

He watched her walk away and, when she was swallowed up by the crowd of uniforms, for him the room darkened.

Theda must smile like that at all the men she talks to in the Canteen, he told himself. Isn't she an actress?

'I want you to love only me,' a woman crooned into a microphone.

He had no choice – he'd already fallen head over heels for Theda Standish. He knew it was hopeless. She was a young and pretty Hollywood actress, she'd have no interest in a staid, stay-at-home rancher. There was no use in him standing around mooning over her, she was as far out of his reach as a star in the sky. He spun on his heel, intending to wait for Lowell outside.

He reached the door and paused. Hopeless as it was, he couldn't leave. Not without telling her how he felt. If he could ever find her again in this crowd.

Theda gazed into the bright blue eyes of a sailor but saw instead the deep brown eyes of the tall man who'd looked at her as though he really saw *her*, not a Hollywood starlet. She'd come over to talk to him not because she'd overheard he was an actor from New York, but because he attracted her. Something about the way he moved spoke of open spaces and fresh air and honesty. She hadn't found a whole lot of honesty in Hollywood. In fact, she'd been downright dishonest herself – posing as eighteen when she wasn't even seventeen yet.

Her first impression had been right: Lyle was honest. He'd refused to go on passing as an actor when he wasn't.

'I really liked you in your last picture,' the sailor said. 'I sure never thought I'd get to meet you.'

Without even hearing her own words, Theda thanked him, smiled automatically and moved on. This was why she was here, to smile at and talk to the men going off to fight for their country and hers.

Lyle wasn't in the service, he was a rancher. Why couldn't she get him out of her mind? The San Joaquin Valley was only a few hours from Hollywood, but it might as well be on the moon. No one who was anyone lived in the San Joaquin Valley – or even visited there. And a ranch meant horses, didn't it? She was no friend of horses. Quite the contrary.

She was just beginning to be known . . . she was on her way up, she had no time for a rancher from the tules. Never mind how warm his eyes were, by tomorrow she'd have forgotten his name.

Theda put a hand to her heart, feeling a sudden pang at the thought of never looking into those brown eyes again. He'd made her feel strangely protected. And safe. Unlike those she'd met in this town, he was a man who'd never hurt her.

She shook her head. What was the matter with her? Noticing a red-haired soldier staring at her, she donned her camera smile and started to walk over to him.

'Lost love, where have you gone?' Helen O'Connell, at the microphone, wailed.

Theda stopped short. That's what was wrong with her – she'd felt lost since she'd left Lyle Harte. And now it was too late.

Or was it? Suddenly Theda smiled and pushed through the crowd to reach the stage.

Lyle's head throbbed from the smoke and the crowd and the beginnings of a hangover. He needed get out of here, he needed fresh air. He hadn't found Theda – for all he knew, she'd left by now.

'Lyle Harte!'

He blinked, staring around him, finally realizing the music had stopped and his name was coming from the loudspeakers. 'You've won this evening's door prize, please come to the stage,' a woman's voice continued. 'Lyle Harte. To the stage.'

Forget it. What the hell did he want with a door prize?

'Miss Theda Standish will award the prize,' the voice continued.

Lyle didn't remember how he got to the stage – all he saw was Theda. By some miracle he'd been given a second chance and he wasn't about to lose it.

Ignoring everyone else, he took her hand, holding it between both of his. 'You'll think I'm crazy or drunk but I'm not,' he said. 'I mean every word of what I say. You're the most wonderful girl in the world. If I searched all my life, I'd never find anyone else like you. I want you to marry me.'

Only when whistles, cheers and applause rocked the room did he realize the microphone had picked up his words and everyone there had heard his proposal.

Two months later Theda Standish became Mrs Lyle Harte.

'I never expected the greatest prize in the world,' he told his new wife. 'What more could a man ask for?'

Carole gazed at the wedding picture – her grandfather tall and handsome and young, Theda so beautiful in white it took her breath away.

'I gave up everything for your grandfather,' Theda had said more than once, 'and I've never really regretted it. Lyle is the only man I ever

115

loved – with the exception of our son, your father.'

Yet at this very moment Theda was in Las Vegas with another man. With Calvin Telford. Who wasn't, as far as Carole could see, anything like her grandfather. Or her father either.

She thought of herself as a modern woman, a liberated woman, but it made her uncomfortable to think of her grandmother being physically attracted to Calvin. Possibly she wasn't, possibly the feeling between them was one of companionship rather than passion. After all, they were both in their sixties.

'Holding hands and laughing and carrying on,' was the way Lollie had put it. Somehow that didn't sound like mere friendship. It sounded a lot like a couple of moonstruck teenagers.

Was Calvin a womanizer? Could that be why Jerrold was so upset about him taking Theda to Las Vegas? Carole clenched her fists. Calvin better not hurt her grandmother or he'd have her to deal with.

CHAPTER 7

Red roses flanked the bench Jerrold and Marla sat on. Carole could smell their enticing perfume as he stretched out his black-clad arm toward Marla until his fingers grazed her cheek in a featherlight caress. Her lips parted as she gazed at him with wondering blue eyes. He leaned closer and she raised her face to his.

'This is wrong, I know.' His voice, husky with pent-up passion, made Marla shiver.

Ever so slowly he bent his head until their lips were no more than a whisper apart. Carole closed her eyes, having seen more than enough, unable to bear watching the kiss that must inevitably follow.

The cameras are running, he's not Jerrold, he's Joaquin Murieta, she told herself for the fourth time since she'd begun watching the scene. And she's Penelope White, not Marla. If you were watching this on a movie screen, that's how you'd see it.

It was no use. As soon as she opened her eyes,

she could only view them as Jerrold and Marla.

Theda had called her this morning to give her the number of the Las Vegas casino – hotel where she and Calvin were staying and Carole, coming to tell Jerrold, had found the love scene being filmed in the hacienda courtyard. The fact that she knew it was an impossible love, a bittersweet, doomed love between a Californio don turned *bandido* and an innocent American girl betrothed to another, didn't make the scene any easier for Carole to watch.

She turned away. Behind her stood Sawa with a sack of basket reeds slung over her shoulder. Sawa motioned with her head and Carole followed her away from the cameras.

'He is *elsu*,' Sawa said when they were far enough away not to to be overheard. The old Indian woman settled herself comfortably on the ground under an old pepper tree with the tules beside her and began splitting the reeds into widths appropriate for beginning a basket.

Carole sat down, the spicy scent of the pepper berries surrounding her as she picked up a tule and copied Sawa. Miwok baskets, large and conical, with pointed bottoms, were used by the women in the old days to gather seeds and acorns. They carried the baskets on their backs.

As she worked, Carole pictured Jerrold as *elsu*, the Miwok word for hawk, almost able to see him soaring through the air, master of the heavens.

'He is a true man, he makes you feel like a

woman,' Sawa went on, thumping her chest with her fist. 'Even me, old as I am.'

God knows Jerrold made *her* feel like a woman, Carole thought. His touch roused passions she hadn't dreamed she possessed.

'And she is *woto*, bold and demanding,' Sawa said.

Woto was a coyote, never quite to be trusted. Carole admired Marla and liked her but, no, she wouldn't trust her. Not where Jerrold was concerned.

Sawa held up a finger for attention. 'If you keep hiding in the bushes like *petno*, you'll never get what you want.'

Carole blinked. Sawa saw her as a quail, that timid little bird?

'I hear them talk, those men who drive the trucks and move the cameras.' Sawa looked directly at Carole. 'They make bets about *woto* and *elsu* – will she or won't she? The odds, they say, are three to one. In her favor.'

'I'm not sure I understand,' Carole said, fearing she did.

Sawa shrugged. 'They say she takes all her leading men into her bed. I don't know if what they say is true, but this man she hasn't. Yet.'

'Everyone likes to gossip about movie people.' Carole heard the defensiveness in her voice.

'She is *woto*. When I was young my grandmother, she say when bad people die their ghosts go into coyotes. The bad ghosts make the coyote look human. Later, in school, they try to teach me there are no ghosts. Who knows the truth? But there is one truth I do know – if you want *elsu*, you can't be *petno*. Be yourself.'

Carole loved Sawa and would never dream of arguing with her about Miwok beliefs. Marla, though, was simply Marla. No ghost coyote, just a very beautiful woman. It was difficult to understand how Jerrold could kiss Marla and not feel *something*.

'It really makes no difference to me what Jerrold Telford does,' she told Sawa.

'Do you think I have no eyes to see?' Sawa spoke calmly as she began to weave the tule fibers together. 'It's bad you lie to me – worse, you lie to yourself. Always you watch him. And him, he tries to hide it, but he watches you. When I was young and saw the one man I wanted, I didn't hide, I took him.' She looked up and smiled. 'Many girls cried when he married me and not them.'

'You make me feel I should bring Jerrold down with a football tackle and drag him off by the heels.' Carole tried to keep her voice light.

Sawa chuckled. '*Elsu's* spirit belongs to the skies. You catch him by cleverness, not tackles.'

'But I'm not clever when it comes to men!'

'He's not men, he's one man. The one you want. Because he's the one for you, already you sense the secrets of his heart. Listen to your own heart, it will tell you what to do.'

Carole stared unhappily at Sawa. Her old friend's advice was well meant and probably was good advice . . . if she did want Jerrold. The problem was, her heart kept telling her she did while her head insisted that she'd be a fool to have anything more to do with him. How could she trust her foolish heart?

Dried pepper leaves crunched underfoot. Carole looked toward the sound and saw a man from the film crew approaching them. Carole remembered seeing him at her grand-mother's party — with his head shaved and boasting a ferocious black mustache he was hard to forget — but she didn't recall his name. Today he wore a red bandana tied around his neck.

He nodded to her, then turned his attention to Sawa, saying, 'They'll need you in about ten minutes. Bring the basket stuff with you.'

Carole rose, intending to go back to the set and wait until Jerrold was free so she could tell him where his father was. After that, she'd leave. Sawa began to gather the reeds and the begin-nings of the basket into her shoulder carrier.

'I'm Alex,' the man said to Carole. 'Mind if I ask you something?'

She smiled and shook her head. 'Ask away, Alex.'

'We've been hearing rumors about that hid-den contraband gold on your ranch,' he said. 'What's the real story?'

Carole glanced at Sawa, aware she'd paused in her loading of supplies. Looking at Alex again, she said, 'It's just ghost gold, I'm afraid.'

'Ghost gold? What's that mean?'

'That the gold has as much substance as a ghost, I suppose.'

Sawa stood up and faced Alex. 'Maybe the ghosts, they don't want the gold to be found,' she said. 'Wise men don't disturb a ghost.'

Alex grinned at the old woman. Nodding toward Carole, he said, 'If ghosts are insubstantial, as she claims, they're hardly a threat.'

Sawa eyed him searchingly. 'Ghosts are always evil.'

He threw up his hands in mock horror. 'Okay, okay, I consider myself warned.'

As he walked away, Sawa muttered, '*Lawati*,' before bending to retrieve her shoulder pack.

The word wasn't one of the Miwok words Carole was familiar with and she meant to ask Sawa what it meant but, as they began walking toward the hacienda, she caught sight of Jerrold and the thought skittered away.

Easy does it, she warned herself. You're here only to let him know where his father is. Tell him and take off.

'The White Knight?' Jerrold echoed, aware it was one of the new Las Vegas casinos. New and expensive. He'd expected as much. His father always went first class. 'Any word on when they'll be back?'

Carole shook her head. He noticed dark circles under her eyes, as though she hadn't slept well. *He* certainly hadn't.

'I watched you and Marla in that last scene.' The tone of Carole's voice alerted him to the fact she hadn't liked what she saw.

'I never claimed to be an Oscar winner,' he said.

'I thought your acting was excellent. Marla's, too.' She spoke stiffly, not looking at him.

He tipped up her chin so she was forced to meet his gaze. 'Then it must have been what happened in the scene that upset you.'

Her flush told him he was right. Did she have any idea how desirable she looked with her cheeks stained pink? It hinted at the passion simmering beneath her cool, standoffish beauty. He'd gotten enough of a taste of that wildfire to want more. If his father hadn't fouled things up with his ill-timed holiday, last night would have been a hell of lot different. A hell of a lot better.

'Does it really bother you to see me kissing Marla?' he asked.

She jerked her head away from his touch. 'Why should it?'

'I don't know. I've kissed more women than I can remember. In films, I mean.' Amusement tinged his tone. 'And got paid for doing it. We

123

actors do distinguish between business and pleasure, you know. Marla would tell you the same.'

'Would she?'

'Believe me.'

Her mouth tightened. 'I'm busy this morning; I have to be going.'

He laid his hand on her arm. 'Still peeved with me? Why? I'm the one who ought to be annoyed at the way you finessed me into escorting Marla home. I trust Rich didn't stay long?'

A smile tugged at the corners of her mouth. 'Long enough to have time to tell me ten times over how wonderful Marla was.'

He hadn't really thought Carole would let Rich make love to her, but it had bothered him all the same that she'd forced him to go while Rich stayed. He'd make damn sure it never happened again. She belonged in his arms, not Rich's – or any other man's.

'Rich invited me to tour his ranch,' he said.

'I heard him.'

'But I still haven't heard you invite me to tour Harte's Way with you. In spite of my hints.'

'I'm sure you're too busy with the filming.'

'Today, yes. And tomorrow. The next day the cast has the afternoon free, barring unforeseen acts of God.'

Some emotion flickered in her smoky yellow eyes and was gone before he could identify it. 'I'll try to find time,' she murmured.

'Marla hates horses.'

'So she said.'

'So we won't ask her along, right?'

Carole grinned. 'Righto.'

'I'll make an Aussie of you yet. As for Rich – we won't need him on the tour, either.'

'I'll do my best to remember.'

He watched her walk away from him to where Sombrita was tethered, unhitch the mare and swing on to her. Carole didn't have the studied grace of an actress: her movements were freer, more natural, reminding him of a bird in flight. She reminded him of a bird in another way. How often had she flown away from him just when he thought he'd captured her? As, sooner or later, he would.

When he did, he was determined nothing and no one would interfere. Not even his father, damn his hide. Although unfortunately his father's behavior often could be classed as an unforeseen act of God. Or the devil, if one believed in evil influences.

He fervently hoped he could finish the picture and get Calvin away from the ranch before the roof fell in, but he wasn't betting on it. He left that to dear old Dad.

Carole resolutely stayed away from the filming for the next two days. On the second night, Theda came home without Calvin.

'My first scene is being shot tomorrow morning,' Theda said, sinking down on to the couch with a sigh, 'so I flew back. Calvin's driving, he'll be here tomorrow. We had a perfectly lovely time – he's so much fun to be with.'

Carole sat in the rocker and eyed her grandmother appraisingly. Theda seemed to have an inner glow she'd never before noticed. 'I'm glad you enjoyed yourself,' she said, 'but I wish you'd mentioned the trip to me earlier. It was rather a shock to come back from the mountains and find you gone.'

'But, dear, I left a note.'

'Note or not, I was surprised. Jerrold was even more so.'

Theda frowned. 'I gather neither you nor Jerrold altogether approved.'

Carole couldn't think of the right words to try to tell her grandmother how it had made her feel. Logically, Theda wasn't being disloyal to Grandpa Lyle and yet somehow it troubled Carole that her grandmother had gone off with Calvin.

'Why didn't you talk it over with me ahead of time?' Carole asked finally.

'It was a spur-of-the-moment decision.' Theda's tone was unusually sharp. 'In any case, you have no right to question what I do. Or with whom.'

'I'm sorry, I didn't mean to imply I had the right. But you've never done anything like this before and it worried me.'

'I'm your grandmother, in case you'd forgotten. Certainly old enough to know what I'm doing. Or maybe you believe I'm growing senile, is that it?'

Carole, taken aback at Theda's anger, started another apology, then paused halfway through it. What had she said that was so awful? Just that she'd been surprised and a little worried. Her grandmother was being overly defensive. Why? Did Theda have self-doubts? Or had she been up to something Carole knew nothing about?

Come to think of it, this was the way her grandmother behaved after she'd loaned money to some acquaintance from the golden days, knowing Carole wouldn't approve.

'You didn't lend money to Calvin, did you?' she blurted out before she thought.

Her grandmother glared at her. 'Certainly not! And what business is it of yours if I had?'

'None, none at all,' Carole said hastily, aware she was now completely in the wrong. 'I've never once tried to stop you from doing whatever you wished with your own money. And I'm sorry I asked the question.'

'I should think you would be!'

Carole smiled sheepishly. 'Would groveling help? Or would you prefer me in sackcloth and ashes?'

Theda looked at her a long moment before she spoke. 'Your clothes are unfashionable enough already. I shudder to think how you'd look in sackcloth.' She rose from the couch. 'We won't discuss the matter again.'

Considerably subdued, Carole nodded and sprang to her feet. 'I haven't even asked you if you'd like something to eat. Lollie left –'

'Nothing to eat, thanks. I might make myself a cup of tea later. Right now I want to go over my lines again. After so many years away from the camera, I'm a bit nervous about tomorrow. I hope the makeup people know what they're doing. Have I shown you my costume?'

'No, but I'd like to see it.' Carole was ashamed that she hadn't taken more interest in her grandmother's role, but her fear that Theda might not be equal to playing the part had made her shy away.

She followed Theda into her bedroom where her grandmother opened the closet and took down a long black dress.

'What do you think?' she asked. Before Carole could respond, she went on, 'This gown is the height of dowdiness and respectability, of course. I've had to resist adding my own little touches because the dress represents the character to perfection, the dress *is Tia* Bella.'

The gown certainly wasn't Theda Harte, Carole thought as her grandmother held it up in front of her. 'It makes you look – well, older,' she said hesitantly.

To her surprise, Theda smiled. 'I hope so. Otherwise I won't be believable as Bella.' She turned this way and that in front of the long cheval mirror, appraising herself. 'I thought a white lace collar might be Bella's one touch of vanity, but then I decided if she did wear lace, it would be black. What's your opinion?'

'I really don't know the character,' Carole hedged, disturbed that her grandmother was taking the role so seriously. It would make it all the more difficult for her if she failed.

Theda returned the black dress to the closet and took out a pale blue satin robe. 'I'm glad Calvin won't be back tomorrow in time to watch my scene,' she said, surveying herself in the mirror again.

'Why?'

Theda glanced at her. 'Vanity. I don't want him to see me as a dowdy old woman.'

Carole hugged her grandmother. 'Even if you live to be a hundred and ten you'll never be a dowdy old woman.'

Theda smiled. 'That's sweet of you, dear, but I will be one tomorrow morning. If you don't believe me, come and watch the filming.'

Curiosity vied with fear of her grandmother's failure in Carole's mind. 'You're sure it won't bother you to have me there?'

'Not you, dear. Only Calvin. Maybe later on I won't care but right now . . .' Theda paused and smiled dreamily. 'I'd rather he thought me glamorous for at least a little longer.'

Carole took her grandmother's words and her

dreamy expression to bed with her, mulling over their meaning. She didn't care to speculate on what had happened between them in Las Vegas, but obviously her grandmother was infatuated with Calvin. The knowledge made her uneasy. It was as though the Theda she'd known all her life had suddenly turned into a stranger.

One thing was sure – though Calvin might consider Theda glamorous, his son couldn't possibly view Theda's granddaughter in the same way.

I'm just not the glamorous type, Carole told herself ruefully. I wonder if I ever could be? She smiled at the image of herself trying to do ranch work all duded up in fancy clothes. But her smile faded as she remembered her grandmother saying how unfashionable she was. What she wore had never really mattered to her before but, somehow, it did now.

What did Jerrold think about the way she dressed?

In the morning, having agreed to meet her grandmother at the hacienda later, Carole rode to one of the groves with José to inspect some orange trees that weren't thriving. He suspected citrus scab. She'd noticed José's eyes flicker when he noticed the bronze silk shirt she wore with her tan cords, but he'd said nothing.

The shirt might be a trifle dressy for looking at sick trees and she usually wore jeans for riding, but there was no reason she couldn't vary her pattern. Being completely predictable was boring.

'Your grandmother, she's acting today,' José said on the way back from the grove.

'I hope it turns out all right It's been so many years since she did anything like this.'

'After your father got big enough to go to school, she had offers, but your grandfather, he asked her not to take them.'

Carole glanced at him, astonished. 'I didn't know that. I didn't realize they ever discussed the possibility of her being in a film.'

'He was against it, he wanted her to be his wife and his son's mother, not a movie star.' José nodded in approval. 'I understand.'

How did Theda feel about it? Carole wondered. Her grandmother's generation believed that marriage was the be-all and end-all of a woman's existence, but that didn't mean Theda hadn't wanted more. Did she regret her lost opportunities or was her love for Grandpa Lyle so overwhelming it didn't matter?

Carole had loved her grandfather and never viewed him as a selfish man, but it seemed to her now that where Theda was concerned, he must have been.

'After your mother died, it was different,' José added. 'Then she had you to take care of.'

Did José mean her grandmother had been resentful of taking on the responsibility of raising a granddaughter? That she'd stood in the way of Theda pursuing her acting career? The thought had never before occurred to her.

'Your father, he expected your grandmother to raise you,' José said, his tone indicating, *what else?*

This new vision of her growing-up years disturbed her. She hadn't known either her father or Theda as well as she'd thought. How many times in her life had she been sure neither her grandmother nor her father understood her? For the first time it occurred to her that maybe the reverse was true – maybe no grandchild or daughter ever truly understood a grandparent or parent.

'Me, I'm going to watch your grandmother act,' José said.

Carole swallowed her apprehension. 'Me, too.'

José grinned at her. 'She'll steal the show away from everybody.'

Her return smile was half-hearted. A dingy black dress and makeup, no matter how cleverly applied, wasn't enough to transform Theda into an elderly Californio spinster – that would take a miracle.

She and José tethered their horses in the olive grove near the hacienda and walked to the set, obeying the instructions on where to stand so as to be out of the way. At least, she told herself, José would be sympathetic if the worst happened.

Members of the film crew darted about as Herwin Holden shouted orders. Neither Theda nor any of the other actors and actresses were anywhere to be seen. Carole's anxiety increased as the minutes passed. Finally everyone melted away, Herwin gave one last command to the cameramen and the hacienda door opened.

A dumpy black-garbed old woman shuffled into the courtyard, leaning on a cane. Though her gait was uncertain, her back was ramrod straight. The black lace *panuello* draped over her head concealed much of her hair but it appeared to be black, with scattered gray streaks. Her dark eyes gleamed with satisfaction as she snapped a blown rose from a bush.

'*Tia* Bella!' a woman's voice called from inside the hacienda. Then Marla, as Penelope White, ran out the open door, stopping short of the old woman.

Carole blinked in confusion. They must have realized her grandmother wasn't right for the part and found another actress to play *Tia* Bella. Theda would be crushed.

'The soldiers search for Joaquin,' Penelope cried in alarm. 'They'll be here in a few minutes. He must be warned!'

The old woman soothed her, explaining Joaquin was safely hidden and Penelope must be calm and give nothing away. 'You grow too fond of Joaquin,' *Tia* Bella scolded. 'He is not for you. You are forgetting your promise to another.'

José poked Carole's arm and, when she looked at him, he smiled broadly and pointed to the old woman, nodding his head.

Did he believe that was her grandmother? It couldn't be! The woman not only looked different, but moved and spoke differently. Carole watched the scene progress, growing tense with the uncertainty of whether Joaquin's hiding place would be discovered by the soldiers or whether *Tia* Bella would outsmart them.

She didn't find out before Herwin yelled, 'Cut!' and everything stopped.

As Herwin explained the changes he wanted before the scene was reshot, *Tia* Bella waved at Carole and José in a gesture that was unmistakably Theda's. Carole gaped at her. It *was* her grandmother!

A wig and contact lenses would account for the difference in hair and eye color, but only Theda's acting could account for the rest. A smile lighted Carole's face as she realized she'd been dead wrong about her grandmother's ability.

She watched the retake with heightened interest and grew more and more impressed with her grandmother. By the time the shooting was over, Carole was so proud of Theda she wanted to shout to everyone, 'That's my grandmother! Isn't she wonderful?'

Later, as she and José rode home, she realized

that since she'd been so wrong about about Theda's acting talent, wasn't it possible she was also wrong to worry that Theda might be going off the deep end over Calvin? Perhaps her grandmother knew exactly what she was doing there, too.

On the other hand, did a woman ever learn to use her head instead of her heart where a man was concerned?

CHAPTER 8

When Jerrold arrived at the house, Carole was still bubbling over about her grandmother's acting.

'I never dreamed Theda was so good,' she told him as they walked to the corral. 'I mean, I knew she'd been a Hollywood starlet way back when, and I've seen some of her old films, but I guess I thought she was in them because she was so pretty.'

'Theda gave a prize performance,' Jerrold agreed. 'Old Herwin's now convinced it was his idea and his alone to cast her as *Tia* Bella, that only he was astute enough to recognize Theda's talent ahead of time.'

'And did he?'

Jerrold shook his head, grinning. 'No flies on your grandmother. She wouldn't sign the agreement for Horizon to use the property until Herwin gave her a part in *Bandido*. He was convinced she'd be a disaster, but figured he could always cut her scene if he had to. Now he's had more lines written for her.'

Carole made a face. 'I'm ashamed to say I felt the same way. Only José believed in her.'

'You're wrong. Theda believed in herself enough to lay her ability on the line. I admire your grandmother.'

If he admired Theda so much, she wondered, why did it upset him when her grandmother went to Las Vegas with his father? Carole meant to find out.

'Theda and Calvin had a wonderful time in Las Vegas,' she said. 'I'm trying to come to terms with the fact that my grandmother is more than Grandpa Lyle's widow, she's a very attractive woman. Why shouldn't she enjoy a holiday with a handsome man?'

'I'm all for it – except when the man is my father.'

Carole stopped walking and turned to face him. 'Why? You're going to have to lay it on the line.'

Jerrold frowned. 'He's bad news.'

'Be specific. In what way?'

'Theda's no fool, she must know by now. I have a feeling that's why she came home without him.'

'But she behaved as though everything was perfect. She acted like a – a teenager with a crush on her first boyfriend.'

'Acted is the key word. Didn't you just see

another demonstration of Theda's acting ability?'

Carole stared at him. 'I'm not sure you're right. She seems genuinely happy.'

'For her sake, let's hope I am right. I'll find out when Calvin gets back. And so will you – then. Since there's nothing to be done until he arrives, let's shelve our elders for the afternoon.'

She decided Jerrold wasn't going to tell her anything more and she really didn't want to spoil their time together by prodding for information she wasn't likely to get.

Changing the subject, she said, 'Zaino hasn't been ridden for a couple of days so he'll be raring to go.'

Jerrold smiled. 'Think I can't handle that feisty chestnut?'

'Just a friendly warning.' Privately she thought he was as adept at handling horses as he was women. Too clever by half.

They led Sombrita and the chestnut gelding from the corral. Jerrold murmured to Zaino as he saddled him and slipped the horse something to eat.

'He's not supposed to have any sugar,' she warned.

'Do I look like a man who'd feed a horse sugar?' he demanded.

'You look like a man who might do anything.'

'You're confusing me with Joaquin Murieta.

138

Me, I'm merely a humble Aussie trying to make a few honest pounds – or bucks, in this case.'

'Humble! I'm willing to bet you don't have so much as one toenail that's humble.'

'I don't bare my feet for everyone – but for you I'd be glad to make an exception.' His smile made his words sound positively indecent. 'I'm all for stripping down to essentials. In the interest of research, of course.'

Before she could control her overactive imagination, a picture of Jerrold stripped to the essentials flashed before Carole's eyes. Excitement quivered through her as she imagined herself running her hands over his bare shoulders and then threading her fingers through the springy darkness of his chest hair. And then . . .

Belatedly noting his quizzical glance, she flushed, banished the all-too-vivid image, and busied herself packing Sombrita's saddlebags. When she finished, she swung into the saddle.

'Ready?' she asked after Jerrold mounted Zaino.

He inclined his head. 'I'll follow anywhere you lead, lovely lady.'

Even as she smiled, Carole wondered how often he'd charmed other women with those same lines. After all, as he'd reminded her about her grandmother, his profession was acting. But, acting or not, he beguiled her just the same. She wanted to believe him.

'What interests you most?' she asked. His assessing gaze swept over her and she added hastily, 'About the ranch, I mean. The orange groves? The Herefords?'

'I'm expecting the grand tour. I don't want to miss anything, from nematodes to wind machines.'

Carole couldn't believe he really was all that fascinated with Harte's Way. He'll be bored before we're half-finished, she told herself as she urged Sombrita toward the nearest grove.

'Are the wind machines automatic?' he asked as they walked the horses between orderly rows of navels. The fruit, still green at this time of the year, hung between the glossy leaves.

She glanced at the windmill-like machines rising high above the trees at measured intervals. 'They're temperature-controlled and will switch on if the thermometer drops below freezing, but they can also be controlled by hand. The wind they generate keeps the air moving so frost crystals can't form in the fruit. Citrus can stand temperatures down to twenty-eight without injury.' Carole grew enthusiastic as she described how efficient the machines were. 'Much better, easier and cleaner than when we used smudge-pots.

'I don't really remember those pots, but José says he can recall a pall of smelly, greasy smoke hanging over the entire Valley during every cold spell because all the growers had their smudge-pots lit. Talk about pollution!'

'When the wind machines are all going at once they must sound like a squadron of old-time planes warming up for take-off.'

Carole shook her head. 'It's a softer sound. When I was a child, their whirring used to lull me to sleep at night. I felt as though they protected me and all of Harte's Way – not just the oranges.'

'This ranch means a great deal to you, doesn't it?'

'I'm a Harte. It's my life.'

He nodded, but she doubted that he understood how the land and everything on it was a part of her, making her incomplete when she was anywhere else. At least he hadn't laughed at her dedication to the ranch as some of her classmates at Davis had done. Without planning to, she changed direction, guiding Sombrita toward her favorite spot, the tallest hill on the property. She'd never taken anyone there before, never stood on the top with anyone except her father. He'd told her that hill had also been Grandpa Lyle's favorite.

Though she didn't expect Jerrold to experience the same deep thrill that possessed her when she looked out over Harte's Way, somehow it was important to her that she bring him to that hill.

They climbed to the top of the rise and reined in the horses. Carole's gaze swept over the grazing Herefords and the green groves below, over the snow-crested Sierra peaks to the east and then, inevitably, to Jerrold. He seemed oblivious to her, his attention on the panorama spread out around him.

'I saw your car from here the day we met,' she said. 'Of course, I didn't know you were in the white Jag or that you were coming to Harte's Way.'

He half-smiled. 'And you wouldn't have liked it if you *had* known.'

She couldn't deny the truth of his words. And yet she'd been wrong in thinking Jerrold was trying to take advantage of her grandmother. 'Hartes aren't perfect,' she admitted with a smile. 'Occasionally we've been known to make a mistake.'

'So you've decided I'm a right enough bloke?'

She started to answer lightly, but his gaze caught hers and she was trapped, mesmerized by the warmth of his dark eyes. To break the spell, she slid off Sombrita and turned to face the east, her back to Jerrold. A cool breeze lifted strands of her hair across her face.

'I never get tired of the mountains,' she said.

'Meaning you do get tired of me?' His breath teased her ear as he spoke, telling her he'd dismounted and now stood all too close.

Before she decided what to do, he drew her back against him, wrapping his arms around her waist. The hard length of his body next to hers started the blood racing through her veins.

'Now, tired of me or not, you can't run away,' he murmured.

Running away was the last thing she wanted to do. 'I doubt if anyone tires of the famous Jerrold Telford,' she managed to say without giving away her breathlessness.

He whirled her around to face him, hands gripping her shoulders. 'I thought we came to an understanding up there in the sequoias, but since then you've been trying to renege. Why?'

Jerrold's nearness made her thoughts spin in her head as fast as the propellers of a wind machine, too fast for her to reach in and pull any one thought free. None of them mattered anyway when all she really wanted was to feel his lips on hers, to lose herself in his arms.

If he could believe the glow in Carole's amber eyes, she wanted exactly what he did, Jerrold thought. Why did she fight it?

God, she was *beautiful*, with the sun caressing her golden skin and the wind tousling her dark hair. Her jacket and riding pants emphasized her slimness and, at the same time, showed off her enticing curves. But, unlike many women he'd met, there was so much more to her than her looks. What she was intrigued him beyond reason. He wished he had time to spend with her, to find out all there was to know about her. If that was possible.

Unfortunately, they had so little time he'd be a fool to waste a moment. The shooting was going remarkably well; all too soon the film would be finished. And if Calvin took a prang before then, there'd be a prize dust-up and she'd probably never speak to him again. At the moment, though, she was close enough to kiss.

He lowered his head until his lips brushed hers and felt his blood surge.

'They can see us up here.' She breathed the words against his mouth, but made no move to pull away.

He cared not a perishing tick about 'they'. Still, she lived here; she'd be here after he left. Slowly, reluctantly, he lifted his head and dropped his hands from her shoulders.

Grasping Zaino's reins, he led the chestnut down the hill to where the orange trees began, circling to find the lee side, away from the wind. Without looking, he knew she followed him with the mare on the lead. He stopped and tethered Zaino to a branch.

'I brought sandwiches,' Carole said, tethering Sombrita and opening a saddle bag. She lifted out a striped blanket.

Food wasn't what he craved at the moment, but he took the blanket and spread it on the ground. When she knelt with paper plates in her hand, he dropped on to the blanket, swept the plates aside and pulled her into his arms.

'Nobody here but us and the nematodes,' he murmured as he kissed her. 'And they're underground.'

Her body fit against his as though she'd been made especially for him. Her taste was honey-sweet in his mouth and her scent surrounded him, heightening his desire. He'd never felt such a driving need for any other woman.

Her lips were warm and ardent, parting under his, allowing him entrance to the hot, delicious moistness of her mouth. He slid his hand along the curve of her hip and up to her breast, his thumb stroking the urgent thrust of her nipple. When she moaned in pleasure, the sound fueled his desire.

'You know I want you.' He spoke into the delicate shell of her ear, his voice passion-rough.

She shifted, raising up on one elbow to look down at him. 'You've kissed so many women.' Her voice was husky. 'How do you know when it's real and when it's not?'

He gazed into her eyes, gone a smoky gold with the same need that throbbed through him. 'Everything about you is real – your beliefs, your beauty, the very words you speak. How can I help but know the difference when I kiss a real woman?'

She sighed and lifted a finger to trace the curve of his lips. He caught her hand and brought it to his mouth. His tongue caressed her palm, feeling the ridge of callouses. Her hand was a working hand, a real hand, a hand to be trusted.

Deep within his mind a barrier fell.

Carole caught her breath at the glow in Jerrold's dark eyes. He offered a promise of passion unlike anything she'd ever dreamed of. He was a man outside her scope, a man from another world, a man living in the glitter and glamor of fame. Yet for the moment he was here, within her world. She didn't want his way of life for herself, but she did want Jerrold, here and now.

And forever?

What she felt wasn't simply dazzle and passion. Unlike Jerrold, she'd fallen in love. He'd go away soon – but no human relationship could last forever, anyway. Wasn't it better to take what he offered while he was here rather than have nothing to remember?

Still unsure, she eased back down into his arms. Jerrold kissed her quickly, then, to her surprise, set her aside and got to his feet.

'On second thought, we'd better have those sandwiches, after all,' he said.

Bewildered and hurt, Carole rose and walked over to Sombrita. As she lifted the food from the

146

saddlebags, she blinked back tears, determined not to let Jerrold see how upset his unexpected rejection had left her.

'What, no wine?' he asked from behind her, reaching around to pluck a container of orange juice from her arms. 'No wine and no thou, either. Ah, well, bread will have to do.'

Not quite trusting her voice, she said nothing. Retrieving the paper plates, she set out the chicken sandwiches and, sitting on the blanket, poured juice into plastic glasses.

Jerrold sat next to her and picked up a sandwich. 'I don't want you to regret making love with me.' His voice bore no trace of lightness.

'Regret it?' she echoed uncertainly.

'You told me once you were no actress.' He smiled wryly. 'It's true. Your expression gives away each and every one of your emotions. A few minutes ago I saw doubt written all over your face and I realized that for you this was the wrong time. Or place. And maybe even the wrong man.'

'But I –' she stopped, flushing. There was no way to explain to him just what had gone through her mind. Not unless she admitted she was in love with him – and she'd rather die than tell him that. Such a confession would certainly amuse him, at the very least. How many other women, she wondered, had said those words to him?

'Now I've embarrassed you.' Jerrold trailed a

finger along her hot cheek.

It was ridiculous to redden so easily, Carole thought, since she was twenty-five, not an inexperienced thirteen-year-old. Jerrold must think her incredibly naïve as well as gauche. She hoped he couldn't guess how his slightest touch unsettled her. The mere brush of his hand against her face sent her pulse mountain-high.

If only she'd inherited even a little of her grandmother's acting ability.

Jerrold bit into the sandwich with every evidence of enjoyment and she wondered how he could eat when she was sure she couldn't swallow a single mouthful.

'I like the touch of curry,' he said.

'Lollie made them. I'm afraid I'm not much of a cook.'

'Where would you find the time?'

She stared at him. Did he actually understand how hard she worked at keeping the ranch running or was he being sarcastic? He *sounded* sincere, but she couldn't be certain. Was he really interested in touring Harte's Way or had it been, as she suspected, a pretense to be alone with her? If only she could understand him.

Lifting a sandwich from the plate, he offered it to her. 'Eat up,' he urged, 'we've barely begun the tour.' Looking at her, he laughed. 'In answer to what I read on your face, I'll admit my

148

motives were mixed, but I did want to see the ranch, too. I still do. And I don't give up easily. On anything.'

Aided by sips of orange juice, Carole managed to coax down half the sandwich. When Jerrold insisted he'd had his fill, she gathered up the plates, glasses and leftover food while he folded the blanket. He helped her stow it all in Sombrita's saddlebags. She tried to think of the right words, light words to dismiss the abortive love-making as an amusing escapade but she couldn't. She'd never been good at smoothing over situations. Or lying.

And how could she tell him the truth?

Instead, she retreated to the safety of oranges. 'José said you didn't know much about oranges,' she said. 'They first grew near the South China Sea and from there were gradually spread by traders across Europe. There were no oranges in the western hemisphere before Columbus brought seeds here and planted them.'

'When I was a boy at school I used to have an orange for my morning tea – play tea, we called it,' Jerrold said. 'I remember my mother used to peel the orange spirally halfway down and replace the peel around it. I loved the taste of them so much I overused my orange crayon. The teacher got tired of pointing out to me that everything in the world wasn't orange.'

Carole tried to imagine Jerrold as a child. Had he been solemn? Happy? Full of the devil?

'Cold is what turns the fruit orange,' she told him. 'The ideal night-time temperature in a grove is forty degrees. If it stays too hot, like in the tropics, oranges ripen but remain green in color. But if you put bananas or McIntosh apples in storage with green oranges they'll turn orange because the ethylene gas the bananas and apples give off is absorbed by the orange peel.'

'Fascinating. I can see I've got a lot to learn about oranges. Among other things.'

She thought he was genuinely interested. Jerrold seemed equally interested in the Herefords, the irrigation system, the olives and the various vicissitudes of citrus growing, but Carole remained all too conscious of the unresolved awkwardness between them. She thought he felt it, too.

She was sure she was right when they parted with no definite plans to meet again. Jerrold might have been truly enthused about the ranch, but he'd lost interest in her.

When Carole met her grandmother at the hacienda the following afternoon, the sight of Jerrold walking off the set with his arm draped over Marla's shoulders drove a sliver of jealousy into her heart. The two of them were so engrossed in conversation he didn't even see her; he had no eyes for anyone except Marla.

What had Sawa said – odds of three to one?

No, Jerrold wasn't the right man for her, Carole thought morosely. Unfortunately, the fact didn't change the way she felt about him.

' – and what do you think he said?' Theda's words caught Carole's ear and, belatedly, she returned her attention to her grandmother, sitting next to her on a bench, dressed in *Tia* Bella's dowdy black gown but without the wig or makeup.

'Who said?' she asked.

'Why, I told you. Calvin. When he called me this morning.'

'I can't imagine.' Carole did her best to sound interested.

'He's all but closed some secret deal and, when he does, he has a proposition for me.' Theda's high, tinkling laugh sounded positively girlish. 'I wonder what it can be?'

Carole's attention sharpened and she gazed at her grandmother in some alarm.

Theda shook her head, smiling. 'You look like you mean to confront poor Calvin and ask if his intentions are honorable.'

Carole, who'd been thinking more in terms of Calvin possibly asking her grandmother for a loan, exclaimed, 'Theda! You can't be seriously considering marrying a man you barely know.'

'We haven't discussed marriage, but I know him well enough to consider his proposition –

whatever it may be.' Theda's tone warned Carole that her grandmother was annoyed.

'Jerrold informed me that his father . . .' Carole paused, then decided Theda had to be told – '. . . was bad news. I'm not sure what he meant, but shouldn't you talk to Jerrold before you make any decisions?'

Theda drew herself up. 'If I have any questions, I'll ask them of Calvin himself.' She eyed Carole. 'Children often complain their parents don't understand them, though they usually do. On the opposite side of the coin, I doubt that a son ever fully understands his father – or a granddaughter her grandmother, for that matter.'

'I'm trying,' Carole insisted. 'But I don't want to see you hurt.'

'The only way not to ever be hurt is to never take a chance. If you never take a chance, you might as well be dead and there's life in this old gal yet, dear.' She reached out and hugged Carole.

She returned her grandmother's embrace while Theda's words echoed in her mind: *Take a chance. Take a chance.*

Wasn't Sawa's warning the same? she asked herself. Why was she still acting like *petna*, hiding like a timid quail? On the other hand, quail were fair game for hawks and she knew full well that only the hawk survived the encounter.

But that was carrying the simile too far. She

152

really wasn't timid; no one had ever accused her of not having courage – in fact, she'd been called headstrong. Only where Jerrold was concerned was she hesitant about going after what she wanted.

He was what she wanted. True, she couldn't have him forever, but why settle for nothing when she could have a wonderful memory to cherish?

Yes, and a broken heart.

'Why so pensive, dear?' Theda asked. 'I do hope you're not brooding over Calvin and me.'

'I'm not, really.'

'Then what *is* bothering you? Maybe I can help.'

I wish you could, Carole thought. But no one can help.

It's my own fault for letting myself get in-volved. 'I'm fine,' she assured her grandmother.

Theda shook her head. 'It's Jerrold, isn't it? What's gone wrong between you?'

Carole jumped to her feet. 'Nothing!' Realizing she'd spoken too sharply, Carole took a deep breath and let it out slowly before trying to modify her abruptness. 'When there's nothing between two people, then nothing can go wrong.'

Theda frowned. 'While I'm fairly sure that's a true statement, I'm far from sure there's nothing between you and Jerrold. Even Calvin says Jerrold's taken with you and he ought to know his own son.'

'The truth is that Jerrold will be gone when the movie's finished and I'll never see him again.' Despite herself, Carole's voice quivered.

Theda reached up and took her hand. 'Do sit down, dear.' When Carole complied, she added, 'None of us can be sure of tomorrow, we only have today.'

Carole stared at her grandmother. Was Theda actually advising her to have an affair with Jerrold, come what may? Was that what she meant? 'I don't want to be hurt,' she muttered.

Holding Carole's hand in both of hers, Theda said, 'Who does? It's a risk we have to take if we want to be happy. Even when you do find happiness, it's not a constant, you know, there are ups and downs.' She glanced at her watch. Giving Carole's hand a final pat, she rose from the bench. 'Time to put on *Tia* Bella's face and persona. If you really want Jerrold, do take a chance, dear. Who can tell what the future may hold?'

Watching her grandmother disappear into the makeup trailer, Carole sighed. She was no seeress, true, but it didn't seem likely Jerrold planned to stick around once the filming was over. Hadn't he already warned her by making it clear he didn't plan to marry again?

I'll soon be reduced to flipping a coin, she thought, trying to find a touch of humor to lighten the situation. What will it be? Heads, I don't, tails —? She broke off the thought as the double meaning struck her and she began to chuckle. So much for coin tossing.

'Damn you, Jerrold,' she muttered. 'Why did you have to show up and complicate my life anyway?'

CHAPTER 9

After a restless night, Carole rose near dawn, dressed and rode into the hills on Sombrita. She told herself she'd get an early start on the day's work, but for the first time in her life she had no heart for ranch tasks. The unresolved attraction between her and Jerrold had ballooned out of proportion, out of reason until he was all she could think about.

She didn't really want a short-term affair with him, but she was beginning to believe anything would be better than riding the violent seesaw of her emotions as she had these past few weeks – the highs might be breathtaking, but the lows were cataclysmic.

'Why did I have to fall in love with him?' she muttered to the mare. Sombrita flicked an ear as though to say she had no idea.

'Wouldn't you think I'd know better?' The mare's head jerked down in a nod and, despite her depressed mood, Carole smiled. 'Okay, I freely admit that I don't have any horse sense whatsoever.'

The rising sun, still hidden behind the Sierra peaks, tinted cloud streamers apricot and gold, heralding another beautiful fall day, a good day for working – and for filming. How many more such bonanza days before the movie would be finished and Jerrold gone?

By then it would be time for the dense and dispiriting tule fogs to enshroud the Valley, turning the world chill and gray. Was that what her world would be like without Jerrold?

You'll get over him, you'll forget him, she tried to assure herself, knowing it was a lie. Life would go on, no doubt about it and so would she, but she'd never forget Jerrold, never completely get over him.

A flicker of motion to her left, near the ruins of an old shed caught her eye. What was it? Not an animal, for she was sure she'd seen something bright red. None of the workers should be in this part of the grounds. Curious, she turned Sombrito in that direction. Before she reached the dilapidated shed, she heard the roar of a dirt bike. By the time she had reached a vantage point the bike, and what looked like two men on it, was too far away for her to identify who the riders were.

Horizon people, she figured, since none of the ranch hands used a dirt bike. What were they doing poking around the ruined shed? Dismounting, she did a little poking around herself and, noting evidence of digging, decided what

157

had interested them was the remains of an ancient root cellar. It dawned on her that the digging must mean they had been looking for the bandit gold. Shaking her head – she'd searched the root cellar in vain years ago, they were out of luck – she remounted the mare and continued on her inspection ride.

She hadn't gone much farther when hoof-beats alerted her to a rider coming up behind her. As she reined in Sombrita and turned in the saddle, her pulse rate zoomed. Could it be Jerrold?

Carole's heart sank when she recognized José's ancient straw hat, but she rallied enough to wonder why he'd come after her. Another breakdown in the irrigation system? Or some other bad news?

'*Hola!*' she called as he pulled up his gray alongside her. 'Did you see who was on that dirt bike?'

José shook his head. 'Heard the bike, didn't see it.' He held out an envelope. 'Your grandmother, she give me this for you.'

What now? Carole thought apprehensively, taking the note.

'Dear,' Theda wrote, 'I'll be at the White Knight in Las Vegas again. Remember what I told you and don't ask for Mrs Harte.'

Carole stared at the pale blue monogrammed paper. What did her grandmother mean? Was she referring to Calvin's mysterious proposition?

By the time Carole reached her by phone, would Theda be Mrs Calvin Telford?

No! she thought. If Theda's bound and determined to marry Calvin, she mustn't tie the knot in some tinselly Las Vegas chapel – it wouldn't be right. I want to be with her for the ceremony. I won't let her get married this way.

'I suppose she's already up and gone,' Carole said to José.

He nodded. 'In one of those airport limos.'

She crumpled the note in her hand. Too late to catch Theda. 'Do *you* know what my grandmother intends to do?' she asked.

He shrugged. 'What she does – that's her business. Not my business.'

Carole frowned at him, certain he suspected Theda was flying to Las Vegas to marry Calvin, but had no intention of saying so. José didn't miss much. Was he also hinting that what Theda did was none of her business, either? Maybe not, but she couldn't help being concerned.

'She shouldn't go running off like this.' Indignation edged Carole's words. 'At her age she ought to know better, don't you think?'

'Me, I think she knows what she's doing. Maybe she writes notes because she don't want arguments.'

José was no help. The only person who'd share her concern was Jerrold. Carole thrust the crumpled note into her shirt pocket, told

José to take over the inspection tour and urged Sombrita toward the hacienda. With luck she'd find Jerrold before today's shooting began.

In the hacienda's courtyard, Marla sat in the sun. As Carole dismounted and greeted her, she was surprised to see Marla weaving an Miwok basket.

'This is fun,' Marla told her. 'Sawa's an excellent teacher. You know, I really believe I could get into baskets.'

Carole was too upset to make polite conversation. 'Where is everyone?'

Marla eyed her. 'If you mean Jerrold, he's galloping around on horses with the bad guys. They didn't need me for the scene, thank God. I much prefer basket making to horses.'

'Where are they shooting?'

Marla waved a vague hand to the east. 'Speaking of him, I've been wondering if he if he ever got around to telling you about his ex, Linda.'

Taken aback, Carole fought to keep her tone casual. 'Jerrold mentioned he was divorced. I didn't ask any questions.'

'Then you've never seen her picture. Guys are funny – no matter how many different kinds of women they run through, each man has a hang-up for a certain type and that type is the one he saves the serious moments for. Jerrold's weakness is tall slim brunettes with hazel eyes. Linda, as it happens, looks a lot like you.'

Somehow Carole managed to conceal her confusion enough to murmur, 'How interesting.'

Marla began weaving in another tule strand. 'Is our boy looking for another Linda? Think about it. You're not the average groupie, you're a real person – no use getting hurt if you don't have to. Be careful.'

Whether or not Marla meant to be kind or was warning her off for personal reasons didn't matter. Carole, stunned and unhappy, couldn't think what to say.

'There you are!' Rich's voice called.

Carole whirled to see him striding toward them, hat in hand. Though he smiled at her in greeting, he passed her by and crouched on his heels beside Marla. Carole couldn't recall Rich ever taking off his hat for her. And, by the looks of it, he'd bought a new Stetson. He must be seriously smitten.

'How's the ankle? he asked, making Carole ashamed she hadn't thought about Marla's injury.

'Practically cured,' Marla said. 'I guess I won't wind up with an interesting limp after all.'

'Then you're ready to go?'

Marla shook her head at Rich. 'Not unless you promise you won't take me anywhere near a horse.'

'Cross my heart.'

Marla looked up at Carole. 'Can you believe I've actually promised to visit his ranch?'

Carole summoned a smile. 'You'll enjoy the experience.'

'So he keeps telling me.' Marla rolled her eyes. 'Why do I go on believing what men say when you can't really trust a one?'

'Hey, don't include me,' Rich protested. 'With me, what you see is what you get.'

'I can't wait.' Marla's voice held amusement and a touch of anticipation as she leaned to kiss Rich on the cheek. 'Next you'll be telling me you're just a poor but honest farm boy.'

Rich shrugged as though to say that ought to be self-evident. He picked up a reed. 'Planning to sell baskets between movies?' he asked.

Engrossed in their byplay, they didn't notice when Carole turned away to Sombrita, mounted and rode from the hacienda in search of Jerrold. Firmly, she put Marla's words on hold. Her grandmother concerned her now, not Jerrold's taste in women.

Fifteen minutes later she crested a hill and saw camera trucks below. Saddled horses and their riders waited nearby. She identified Jerrold by his Californio garb. He was listening to a gesticulating, short man in jeans and a T-shirt – Herwin, she thought.

Since they weren't shooting at the moment, she decided it was safe enough to ride down the hill toward them.

'Let me see the note,' Jerrold demanded after she'd taken him aside and told him what had happened.

Smoothing the paper as best she could, Carole handed it to him. He read Theda's words and crumpled the paper all over again.

'Damn,' he muttered. 'Theda doesn't have a clue to what she's letting herself in for.'

'And just what is that?'

'My father can't be trusted.' He cast a scowling glance at the cameras, at the horses and at Herwin, now demanding to know where Alex was. 'And I'm stuck here, worse luck,' he muttered.

'Alex better show up pronto,' Herwin shouted, 'or I'll personally choke him to death by that damn red bandana he wears around his neck.'

Despite her preoccupation over what she feared was Theda's elopement, the word red caught Carole's attention and she remembered the flicker of red at the ruined shed. 'Does Alex ride a dirt bike?' she asked Herwin.

He turned to look at her and nodded. 'You see him?'

'I think he must have been heading here,' she equivocated, not wanting to get any more involved.

'If he values his neck, he better be,' Herwin growled and stalked off.

Carole returned her attention to Jerrold and

the matter at hand. 'Surely you can get away long enough to call your father at the White Knight,' she said.

Jerrold scowled. 'Not right now I can't. Come to that, whatever I might say to him on the phone wouldn't make any bloody difference. He's never listened to me.'

'Are you telling me you don't plan to do anything to stop them?' Carole's voice shook with indignation.

Jerrold spread his hands. 'What do you expect? You want me to tell Herwin to shove his scene? You saw for yourself he's already up the wall.'

'If you cared —'

He cut her off. 'Stick to ranching, you don't know a damn thing about film-making.'

'Telford!' Herwin called. 'Hurry it up.'

Jerrold laid a hand on her arm. 'I haven't got time now, wait until the scene's finished and we'll —'

'It's my grandmother we're talking about — I can't wait!' She pulled away from him, turned and hurried toward Sombrita.

He didn't follow her. By the time she reached the house, Carole's simmering anger was at full boil. Jerrold admitted his father couldn't be trusted. What could be more important than to warn Theda, to reach her before she married Calvin? Certainly not a mere movie scene!

It was clear Jerrold really didn't care what

happened to her grandmother. As for his father, he'd made no secret of his bitter feelings toward Calvin. Jerrold wasn't going to lift a finger to do anything. If Theda's and Calvin's marriage was to be stopped, it was up to her.

Jerrold was right about one thing – no phone call could prevent them from going ahead. To have any chance at success she'd have to catch, if possible, the next plane to Vegas.

Luck and a wild ride to the Bakersfield airport got Carole on the next plane to Los Angeles where she picked up a Vegas flight. After set-down she rented a car and sped to the White Knight, along the crowded Strip. Entrusting the car to a valet parker, she hurried past shrubbery cut into chess-piece shapes and into the lobby.

Inside, she paid little attention to the chess theme dominating the decor as she crossed to the desk. It gave her hope when she discovered her grandmother had registered under her own name after all. Her room number was not the same as Calvin's – though it was next door. But when neither of them answered their phones, or her repeated knocking at their doors, Carole feared she'd arrived too late.

Glancing at her watch, she saw it was almost three. They'd had plenty of time to find a justice of the peace and get married. Is that what they'd done? How could she ever locate them?

Back in the lobby, she made inquiries of the

sleek and ageless blonde at the information desk, describing her grandmother and Calvin.

The blonde started to shake her head, then paused. 'An Australian gentleman? I believe I do recall him – he bought two tickets for a tour to Hoover Dam.' She conferred briefly with a bellman and turned back to Carole. 'They left on the noon bus. I'm afraid they won't be back before six.'

Five minutes later, Carole was driving southeast in her rental car on her way to Hoover Dam.

Boulder Dam, her grandfather had persisted in calling it, even after Congress officially named the dam after the thirty-first President.

'I remember when they built the dam,' Grandpa Lyle had told her. 'They finished it on my birthday back in 1936 and it was Boulder Dam then, no one wanted any reminder of Hoover. Some day I'll take you and Theda to see it.'

But he never had. The ranch had always come first with Lyle Harte, as it had with her father, and neither of them had found the time for many trips away from it. At long last she was going to see Hoover Dam, but who'd ever have thought she'd be visiting the place under these circumstances? She couldn't help but wonder if her grandmother recalled Grandpa Lyle's unkept promise. If so, how would Theda feel being there with another man?

The pamphlet from the hotel told Carole the

dam was one of the highest in the world – 726 feet high and 1,244 feet long – but to her the most important information was that she had only twenty-five miles to drive. If Lady Luck was still smiling, she'd catch up with her grandmother and Calvin at the dam and they wouldn't yet be man and wife.

She'd planned her speech on the plane. After considering what José had said, that her grandmother's elopement was to avoid arguments, Carole had decided she'd offer no recriminations, no recital of why the marriage might not be a good idea, she'd just plead with Theda to wait until she and Calvin knew one another a bit longer.

As she drove past the western end of Lake Mead she saw boats scudding in the autumn breeze, their white, yellow and red sails bright against the sparkling blue of the water. Caught by the beauty of the scene, for a moment Carole forgot why she was there.

What fun it would be to tack across the lake, enjoying the cool wind and warm sun along with a friend. With a lover. With Jerrold. Then, at sundown, skin tingling pleasantly from the day outdoors, to anchor in a secret cove and sip wine between kisses. Later, they'd come together, she and Jerrold, and make love under the stars. In his arms she'd find the fulfillment she yearned for. In Jerrold's arms . . .

The sight of a vast, pale concrete wall connecting dark and rocky cliffs brought Carole back to reality. Hoover Dam. Theda. Calvin. She shook herself free of the dream of being with Jerrold and began looking for a parking place.

The noon tour group, she discovered, was presently underground visiting the power plant. After convincing a guide that she must reach her grandmother immediately, Carole was allowed to descend into the bowels of the earth on an elevator.

'We go down the equivalent of forty-four stories,' the guide, Ms Perkins, told her, 'until we're five hundred feet below the surface of Lake Mead.'

Following Ms Perkins along a dimly lit corridor where water dripped, she supposed, either from overhead pipes or from some invisible crack in the ceiling, Carole decided not to ask her what happened if the concrete barrier of the dam sprung a leak while they were underground.

She wished she didn't know how far below the surface she was. In the constriction of the shadowy corridor, she could almost feel the weight of earth and water pressing down above her.

'Claustrophobics must have trouble with this,' she said and was dismayed to hear a quaver in her voice.

Ms Perkins glanced over her shoulder. 'I hope you're not one.'

Carole shook her head. 'No, but I can't say I'd take to living or even working underground.'

As they approached a small chamber, Carole heard a man speaking. 'Lake Mead is one of the world's largest artificially created bodies of water,' he said and went on to quote statistics about the lake.

'This should be your grandmother's group,' Ms Perkins said in a low tone, leading Carole out of the corridor.

'I see her,' Carole said. 'Thank you so much for bringing me here.'

Theda's blonde hair shone even in the dim light of the chamber. Calvin Telford stood beside her, one arm protectively around her waist. Carol eased between people, making her way toward her grandmother.

'Why, Carole, whatever are you doing at Hoover Dam?' Theda exclaimed when she caught sight of her.

'Looking for you.' Carole nodded a greeting to Calvin as she took her grandmother's hand. 'Could we leave here? I came with a guide who'll show us the way back.'

Theda glanced at Calvin, who shrugged. Apparently interpreting this as agreement, Theda said, 'If you think we must.'

The silent trip back to the surface seemed to Carole to take forever. When she followed Ms Perkins off the elevator, she breathed a sigh of relief. Underground was definitely not her milieu.

'Look, love, what's the trouble?' Calvin asked Carole as soon as Ms. Perkins left them. He looked around as though expecting to see someone. Jerrold?

'No trouble, not exactly. Why don't we walk to my car? We can talk there.'

When they reached the car, Theda stopped and faced Carole. 'Well?'

Looking at the two of them huddling against one another like children expecting a scolding, Carole found it harder to begin than she'd expected. What right did she have to challenge her grandmother's actions? On the other hand, she hadn't come all this way merely to smile and say, 'Bless you,' to them.

Aside from whether it was right for her grandmother to marry Calvin at all, which wasn't for her to decide, she really did think it was wrong for Theda to marry in secret. Taking a deep breath, she plunged in.

'Your note upset me, Theda. Everything's too sudden, I can't take it in. I came here to ask you to wait.'

'How do you know it's not already too late?' Theda asked.

Carole blinked. Was it? She didn't think so. 'I can't believe you'd tour Hoover Dam if you'd just gotten married,' she countered.

Unexpectedly, Calvin laughed. 'She's got us pegged,' he told Theda. Sobering, he gazed at Carole. 'Wait how long?' he asked.

'Until after we've all gotten together and discussed the two of you getting married. Jerrold's as concerned as I am.'

'He would be.' Calvin's tone was wry. 'I was under the impression Theda and I were consenting adults, as you Yanks put it. Since we are, why do you insist our plans need discussion?'

Carole turned to her grandmother. 'You understand, don't you?' she asked.

Theda frowned. 'Not really.'

'Marriage is a serious step,' Carole pointed out. 'An important decision, an obligation, a contract not to be undertaken lightly.'

'Grandmotherly advice, if ever I heard any,' Theda observed. 'We seem to have our roles reversed.'

Carole realized she wasn't getting anywhere and changed tactics. 'Las Vegas is so unreal,' she said. 'Tinsel city. Do you really want to get married here?'

Theda glanced uncertainly at Calvin. He smiled reassuringly. Watching her grandmother, Carole saw the glow in her eyes when she looked at Calvin.

'Would you like to get married at home, love?' he asked Theda.

Theda's face brightened and she threw her arms around Calvin and hugged him. 'You're wonderful! You knew what I wanted before I did!'

Holding Theda close, Calvin gazed over her

171

shoulder at Carole. 'I'll see to it that Theda has her wedding at Harte's Way,' he said. 'But we won't wait long.'

'Calvin's right, dear. We don't care to wait much longer.' She slanted him such an adoring look that Carole felt she was trespassing.

On the ride to the hotel, Theda, in the back with Calvin, chattered nonstop about everything under the sun except her and Calvin's future plans.

'. . . so when Calvin said he'd like to compare Hoover to the Aswan Dam, I decided we *must* take this tour. He's been to Egypt and all sorts of other exciting places. When I was a child I used to dream of taking a trip around the world but I never had the chance.'

'I'd guess we've got a good lot of mileage in us yet,' Calvin assured her. 'Could be you'll have your chance at that trip.'

You can't trust my father, Jerrold had warned. *He's bad news.* Carole bit her lip. Theda hung on every word Calvin said, but could a single one of them be believed? Obviously Theda thought so. Her grandmother would surely be badly hurt and disillusioned when the truth surfaced. Yet it was better she discover the worst before marrying Calvin rather than after.

Carole wasn't sure just how bad that worst was, but the fact her grandmother had let slip that she'd paid for the first trip she and Calvin had taken to Vegas wasn't reassuring. Was Theda still footing the bills?

As soon as they got back to the ranch, she'd see to it Jerrold spelled out Calvin's problems. To her grandmother as well as to her.

'Don't you think those hot tubs in these Las Vegas hotel rooms are fun?' Theda asked.

Belatedly realizing her grandmother was talking to her, Carole shrugged. 'I didn't register so I haven't been in any of their rooms.'

'You don't need to see a room to have an opinion,' Theda persisted.

'I suppose it wouldn't be Vegas without jacuzzis,' Carole said grudgingly, not caring to imagine her grandmother and Calvin sharing one.

'I don't see why you're cross.' Theda spoke tartly. 'After all, you got what you came for. We're delaying our marriage.'

'I'm sorry,' Carole murmured, speaking no more than the truth. Her invasion of their idyll had made her feel like a heel. She was also tired. The lack of sleep plus the hectic rush and tension of the trip had caught up with her.

Theda said nothing more to her, contenting herself with talking softly to Calvin until they pulled up at the White Knight.

'What are your plans?' Calvin asked as they walked into the lobby. 'Are you taking a flight home tonight or staying over until morning?'

The sooner she left Vegas the happier she'd be. Carole opened her mouth to say so but, at the

173

sight of the man striding toward them, the words died in her throat.

'It's about time!' Jerrold's voice snapped like a whip.

She stared at him in disbelief. 'You didn't tell me you intended to come to Vegas!'

He scowled at her. 'You went haring off without waiting to find out what I meant to do. You're so bloody impatient I didn't get the chance.'

Her hands fisted and she glared back at him. 'You had plenty of time to tell me.'

'Wait a tick here, kids,' Calvin broke in. 'I was under the impression the two of you flew here for other reasons than to pick a spat with one another. Of course, I could be wrong. In which case, Theda and I will just tiptoe quietly away and leave you to it.'

CHAPTER 10

'Very funny,' Jerrold muttered to his father. But the remark had made him aware the hotel lobby was a very public place. Clamping down on his anger, he turned to Carole and asked in a low tone, 'Are they married yet?' As soon as she shook her head he sighed in relief and returned his attention to his father.

'Well, well, quite a reunion,' Calvin said, his gaze leaving Jerrold to sweep the crowded White Knight lobby. 'But the public rooms of a Vegas hotel are no place for a family natter, which I assume will come next. I suggest we go up to my suite.'

Jerrold's nod was curt.

Carole didn't realize until then that she'd been holding her breath, anticipating a renewed outburst from Jerrold. If his expression was any indication, he was seething with rage and she'd feared a scene.

The two couples started for the elevators, Calvin's arm protectively about Theda's shoulders. They'd almost reached their goal when a tall, tanned blonde stepped in front of Jerrold, stopping him.

'Excuse me, but could I have your autograph, Mr Telford?' she asked breathlessly, extending a crumpled 'The Castle' napkin, obviously from one of the hotel's restaurants.

To Carole's amazement, Jerrold managed a smile for the blonde as he said, 'I be happy to oblige, but I'm afraid I don't have a pen with me.'

'Use mine.' Calvin offered a monogrammed gold pen.

Carole noticed people drifting in their direction and she heard some of them mention Jerrold's name. He scribbled on the napkin and handed it to the blonde just as an elevator door opened. Grabbing Carole's arm, he pulled her inside, Calvin and Theda following on their heels.

Others crowded into the elevator, eyeing Jerrold. 'It is too him!' a purple-haired teenaged girl whispered to her friend. 'I know 'cause I've seen all those Australian movies he was in. Like, I could just die, you know?'

'This is our floor,' Calvin announced as the elevator stopped and the door opened.

For a moment it looked as though the purple-haired girl intended to trail Jerrold, but her friend pulled her back into the elevator. The door closed, leaving the four of them alone in the corridor.

Plush deep-red carpeting muffled sound as they followed Calvin. He stopped outside a door saying, 'Your key, love,' to Theda.

When she handed it to him, he opened the door and shooed Theda into the room. When Carole started to follow her, Calvin held up his hand.

'Your grandmother needs to be by herself for a few minutes.' He shut the door, closing Theda inside. 'Come along, my suite's the next.'

Moments later Calvin ushered her and Jerrold into his room – or suite, rather. They entered what she thought of as a sitting-room, carpeted in gold. She'd barely glanced around at the gilt and white pseudo-French furniture and the brass chandelier before Jerrold spoke, his words gritty with anger.

'You can't keep Theda from hearing what I have to say because I'm staying here until I tell her.' He scowled at his father.

'If your mind's made up I suppose I can't stop you. Give me a minute or two, I'll see if she's ready.' Calvin turned to Carole. 'Please do sit down, this may take a little time.'

To her amazement, Calvin seemed unperturbed by Jerrold's manner. Seating herself on the edge of a gilt chair upholstered in white velvet, she watched Calvin saunter to the connecting door between the rooms as though he hadn't a worry in the world. He tapped gently, said, 'It's me, love,' then opened it, stepped through and closed the door behind him.

Jerrold began to pace back and forth by the windows. 'I'm not looking forward to this,' he muttered. 'I wish I didn't have to do it. Why couldn't the old perisher stay in LA?'

'Maybe he wanted to be near you.'

Jerrold glanced at her. 'I find that hard to believe. More than likely he ran out of money.'

She frowned at him. 'You're his son, after all. He might miss you. Does he have any other relatives?'

'There's just the two of us left.' Jerrold shrugged. 'You may think we should be closer but the problem goes way back. I just can't trust him.'

'I can't understand what the problem is if you won't explain.'

Jerrold shook his head. 'Later.'

'Do you think he loves Theda?' The question surprised Carole almost as much as it did Jerrold since she had no idea she meant to ask it until the words were out.

'What the hell *is* love?' Jerrold countered, stopping his pacing to stare at her.

After a moment's thought, she said, 'One definition is being more concerned about the other than about one's self. Calvin certainly seems protective of Theda.'

Jerrold laughed, a short harsh sound that had nothing to do with humor. 'Concern can be faked as easily as any other emotion. Using your guidelines, I'd say my father hasn't the capacity for love.'

Maybe not, she thought. But do you? Is it a case of the pot calling the kettle black?

Jerrold ran his fingers through his hair. 'With him it's always been Calvin Telford first and to hell with the rest of the world. At sixty-two, I'd say he's too old to change.'

'My grandmother would disagree. She believes anyone can change their ways at any time in their life – if they truly want to.'

'A nice sentiment. But I'm afraid he doesn't want to change even if I'm wrong about how much he cares for your grandmother. Enough about him. You'll hear all you want to and more when your grandmother's ready to join us.'

'Why didn't you tell me you meant to come to Vegas?' she asked. 'You know you could have.'

'Did you really think I wouldn't do my damnedest to stop this marriage?'

She hated to admit that's exactly what she had thought. How wrong she'd been. Changing the subject, she said, 'I never realized how little privacy actors have when they appear in public. It must be bothersome.'

He shrugged. 'It goes with the territory.' Crossing to where she sat, he turned a quasi-Louis XIV chair around so it faced her and straddled it, crossing his arms over the back. 'What I do never impresses *you*. In fact, when we first met you'd never heard of me – right?'

She nodded ruefully. 'I'm afraid I'm not much of a movie-goer.'

'Or any other kind of fun-goer, it seems. All work and no play isn't the way to live.'

'I don't overwork.' She was dismayed by her defensive tone.

He smiled. 'That's not what I hear from José. Or Rich. Besides, I've watched you. Don't you know the ranch won't fall apart if you take a couple of days a week off?'

Carole bit her lip. 'How can I? The equipment is getting old and it *can* fall apart, in fact, it keeps doing so. Everything's mended – José is a genius at that. I need to be there in case of trouble, which seems a constant. If we don't break even this year –' She stopped abruptly. Why was she telling him this? Jerrold didn't want to hear her problems.

When she didn't go on, he said gently, 'Just how bad are things?'

She might have hinted to him before, but she'd never admitted to him or anyone else just how precarious their finances were. In fact, she hated to even think about it herself.

'We may not be able to meet the mortgage payment in January and it's touch and go for the next couple of months. If something large and expensive falls apart, we're in deep trouble.'

'Harte's Way is mortgaged?' Jerrold sounded shocked.

'Daddy couldn't help it,' she said, again defensive. 'We lost an entire orange crop a few years back because of bad weather; that same year, fifty head of cattle became infected and had to be destroyed and disposed of. We couldn't sell any of the others because of health regulations.

'I didn't know he'd had to borrow money to keep going until after I graduated from Davis and came home for good. He never did tell Theda. I had to break the news to her after he died.'

'Then the ranch isn't free and clear. How about your grandmother – does she have money of her own?'

Carole was taken aback by his question and her expression showed it.

'I don't mean to be obnoxiously nosy,' Jerrold assured her, 'but I do need to know.'

'Theda has a trust-fund income,' Carole said reluctantly. 'From when she was in Hollywood. That's why my father didn't tell her about taking out the mortgage. He kept her from realizing he needed money for the ranch because he didn't want to use hers and he knew she'd insist on giving it to him. When I told her what he'd done, she offered me her money to pay off the mortgage, but I couldn't take it – Daddy wouldn't have wanted me to.'

'And now? Does Theda know you're going to have trouble meeting the next mortgage payment?'

Carole shook her head. 'I may have to tell her,

though I hate to. I have to eventually, though. I run the ranch but it's in her name, not mine. Theda actually owns Harte's Way.'

'In *her* name? Damn!' Jerrold sprang up from the chair. 'I suppose she must have told him. He's bloody well not going to get his hands on Harte's Way and sell it – I'll see to that!'

He meant Calvin, she knew. At the mere mention of the ranch being sold, fear gripped her with bulldog teeth. Was it possible that was what Calvin intended to do? Talk Theda into selling Harte's Way? She shook her head. Even if he tried, Theda would never do it.

'What the hell's taking them so long?' Jerrold strode to the connecting door and knocked. When no one answered, he pounded on it. The door remained closed.

Carole rose, her gaze fixed on the door. Why didn't they answer? 'What's wrong?' she asked.

Jerrold tried the knob. 'Locked! I should have known I couldn't trust the devious old sod.' He rushed into the corridor and hurried to Theda's door. Carole, standing in the doorway, saw him turn the knob. Locked, of course. No one answered Jerrold's furious knocking.

He strode back into Calvin's suite, grabbed the phone and called the desk, explaining that they needed a key because they were inadvertently locked out of the other connecting room.

While they waited for someone to arrive, Jerrold pocketed the key to Calvin's suite and, in doing so, discovered his father's mono-grammed gold pen in his pocket. He flung it across the the room.

'We won't find them in her room,' he told the worried Carole. 'Ten to one he's convinced her to run off with him.'

Carole, who'd had unsettling visions of an accident or sudden illness or Calvin forcibly preventing her grandmother from opening her door, gasped. 'Are you sure?'

'I'd bet my last yellow Geordie. I know my father all too well.'

Whatever a Geordie was, she though distract-edly. 'But why would Theda go with him – willingly, that is?' she asked. 'You don't think he forced her?'

Jerrold shook his head. 'My father's not the type. If there'd been no such thing as sweet talk, Calvin would've invented it. He can talk almost anyone into almost anything. Theda included.'

'She's in love with him.'

Jerrold shot her a quick glance. 'Did she say so?'

'She didn't have to.' Carole's voice was wist-ful. 'I saw the way she looked at him. But what are they running from? You?'

'He knows I mean to stop their marriage and he's afraid I can. Once Theda hears the truth about him she'd be a fool to go on with the wedding. And she's no fool.'

'What *is* this terrible truth? You've kept me in

the dark long enough. I think I have a right to know.'

Jerrold seemed to debate with himself before finally answering. 'Calvin's a compulsive gambler. He's gambled away everything he ever had. He can't be trusted with money. That's why I don't want him to get his hands on your grandmother's trust fund. Or the ranch.'

A gambler. Carole didn't know what she'd expected to hear. Gambling could definitely make trouble for people, but somehow it didn't seem as bad as some of the other problems she'd worried that Calvin might have.

'Gambling's an addiction that can be cured,' she pointed out.

'Not unless the person admits he's ill and needs treatment. My father doesn't choose to admit to his addiction.'

Before Carole could comment on this, a housekeeper arrived with a master key and opened Theda's door for them, standing by while they entered the room. A quick look around confirmed the room was unoccupied. Pulled-out dresser drawers and hangers scattered on the closet floor made it obvious Theda had packed hastily.

'There's the key,' the housekeeper said, nodding at the night stand. 'I guess you don't need me any more.'

After they unbolted the connecting door and returned to the suite that had been Calvin's,

Carole turned to Jerrold. 'What do we do now?' she asked. 'Where do you suppose they might have gone?'

When he glanced at his watch, she looked at hers. It was after six.

'Who knows where they are?' he said. 'Las Vegas is a big city with far too many hotels to make searching for them practical. Anyway, they may have left town. I suggest we have dinner.'

'But what about finding my grandmother?'

'Do you know where to start looking?'

Carole didn't have the slightest idea. 'Your father told Theda he had a wonderful surprise for her,' she said. 'I wonder what it could have been.'

Jerrold's lip curled. 'He probably hit a lucky streak at the craps table.'

'I don't think that was it. If we knew, we might have a clue to where they've gone.'

Jerrold shrugged. 'One place they're not is the ranch. They could be any place else. We can't even be sure they're even still in Nevada.'

'On the way back to the hotel from Hoover Dam, my grandmother decided she wanted to be married at home. It won't be easy for Calvin to change her mind. She can be pretty stubborn when she has her mind set on something. She might have convinced him to take her home.'

'I don't think so. Calvin won't dare risk returning to the ranch. He knows I'll be returning there and he doesn't want me anywhere near

Theda. If she asks to go home, he'll find a way to sweet talk her out of the idea, at least for the time being.'

Jerrold's probably right, Carole thought. But how long would Theda and Calvin hide out?

'We can discuss this over dinner,' Jerrold said. 'I missed lunch and, despite the problem of our errant elders, I'm starving.'

Carole glanced at her gabardine pants, wrinkled from the flight and from driving. 'I'm hardly dressed for elegant dining. Maybe a casual café.'

'No problem, we'll call room service.'

'But these aren't our rooms.'

'I can't see that makes a difference, but if you'll feel better about it, I'll call the desk and straighten things out.' He smiled one-sidedly. 'Come to that, it'd be like Calvin to stick me with the bill, anyway.' He picked up the phone.

A wave of fatigue swept over Carole. Arguing over dinner wasn't worth the effort since she really didn't care where they ate. And, considering her clothes and how tired she was, she'd certainly be more comfortable in private. Why not eat here? Not waiting for Jerrold to finish talking to the desk, she crossed the sitting-room and sank on to the gold velvet settee.

To do the decor justice, she shouldn't be wearing practical and very wrinkled tan pants and jacket with a tobacco-brown shirt. She ought to be lounging in a wispy white negligee with feathered trim at the hem. Instead of sturdy ankle boots she'd need totally impractical slippers of some metallic gold fabric trimmed with faux fur.

As she leaned back on the settee, she imagined herself with her legs crossed, the negligee falling suggestively open while she dangled one of the slippers by her toes. Naturally she'd be wearing gold polish on her toenails.

She'd be holding a half-empty champagne glass in one languid hand. Her hair, instead of grazing her shoulders as it did now, would be arranged in an upsweep held by gold combs, with artfully casual strands escaping to frame her face. And she would have remembered to use makeup to enhance her eyes and add color to her lips.

When Jerrold turned to look at her he'd be struck dumb with admiration. She smiled and her eyes drooped shut as she imagined how he'd drop on to one knee beside her. No, what he'd do is sit beside her on the settee and pull her gently into his arms as he murmured how much he wanted her . . .

'Don't fall asleep before the food gets here.' Jerrold's voice jolted through her half-dream.

Carole's eyes popped open. He stood over her, smiling his devastating smile.

'I must not be at my best,' he said. 'Seldom is my company so soporific.'

Though she knew he could have no idea of

what she'd been imagining, she couldn't control her flush. He sat beside her and touched her cheek with the back of his hand. She felt the caress flame through her.

'Blushing becomes you,' he murmured.

Trying to overcome the effect of his touch, Carole moved her head slightly so that his hand fell away. He framed her face with both his hands. 'Don't turn away from me,' he said. 'I like to look at you.'

No more than she liked to look at him. But, if she did, she feared she'd regret it. Searching for a way out, she asked, 'What about the room?'

He hesitated momentarily. 'No problem. We have the use of this suite. I called room service and they suggested one of the specials – a veal in wine. I ordered two. With the trimmings. I hope you don't mind.'

She smiled. 'Veal's a favorite of mine.' Though she wouldn't like it to become a habit, she thought it was rather fun to let a man take over the ordering for once without consulting her.

Rising, she took off her jacket, laid it over a chair back and then explored the room. In an alcove between the sitting-room and the bedroom, the hot tub Theda had mentioned. Water swirled invitingly in the tiled tub that echoed the gold and white color scheme. Had Calvin filled it before he and Theda left for Hoover Dam, planning to use the tub later? With Theda?

Not caring to dwell on that, she erased the image, replacing it with Jerrold in the tub, naked to the waist, water beading his dark chest hair as he beckoned for her to join him. Before she did, she'd kick off the gold slippers and, with Jerrold's admiring gaze following her every move, ever so slowly untie the white negligee and let it drop to the floor. Underneath the frothy robe she'd be wearing a sleek, translucent white silk teddy . . .

A knock at the door startled her from her reverie. Surely not the food so soon. Leaving the alcove to look, she saw a waiter already in the sitting-room popping open a Mumms. He poured champagne into two flutes, returned the bottle to the ice bucket and left.

Jerrold picked up both the glasses and carried one to her. 'May we each get our wish,' he murmured, touching his glass to hers.

Before she could block it, a wish sprang into her mind, a wish that Jerrold would love her. Carole hastily sipped her champagne, wondering what he'd wished for. Probably that Theda would come to her senses and return to the ranch without marrying Calvin.

That should have been my wish, she admonished herself. I ought to be worrying about my grandmother instead of creating foolish fantasies about Jerrold.

But she found she was no longer so terribly anxious about Theda. Gambler or not, Calvin, she felt, wouldn't let any harm come to Theda. Unless he was a better actor than his son, Calvin's every gesture, his every word, led Carole to believe he truly cared for her grandmother. And, actually, Theda was no fool, not really. She'd seen through that phony count in record time and, if Calvin was really trying to dupe her, Carole thought Theda would sense it and set him adrift. Since she hadn't, chances were that Calvin truly loved her grandmother.

Jerrold fiddled with dials until a clarinet's high sweet notes floated in the air. He raised a questioning eyebrow and she nodded. Why not enjoy all the amenities for the short time they'd be here?

'You have beautiful eyes,' he told her.

'Like the sands of the Tanami Desert, I believe you once said.' She smiled coolly, determined to stay in control.

'The desert sands are beautiful, too, their golden hues always shifting, changing. I've never seen the color anywhere else. Until I met you.'

'I thought Linda had hazel eyes.' The words were out before she realized what she was saying.

He scowled.

Carole hurried on. 'At least Marla said so. Her exact description was "a tall brunette with hazel eyes". I think she meant like me.' Since she was digging the hole deeper with every sentence, she might as well jump down into it and bury herself. 'Marla thought perhaps you were attracted to me because I resemble Linda.'

'Marla's a bloody interfering twit.' Jerrold swallowed the rest of his champagne and retrieved the bottle. He topped her glass before refilling his. 'She trails trouble after her like a snail trails slime.'

'Marla means well,' Carole protested.

'Does she? Try telling your friend Rich that when she gets tired of her "poor but honest farm boy" and tells him, in no uncertain terms, to get lost. Marla's not one for tact.'

'Rich isn't stupid. I think he realizes the pitfalls of a relationship with Marla.'

Jerrold shrugged. 'We both know she'll hurt him.'

'Maybe the few weeks with her are more important to him than whatever comes later. Maybe the time they have together is worth any future pain.'

Was she thinking about Rich or about herself? Carole wondered. They were certainly both chasing delusions.

Jerrold gazed into Carole's amber eyes and wondered if he imagined he saw pain in their depths. For Rich? He didn't think so. He felt sorry for the poor bastard, but Carole didn't seem to since she obviously thought Rich could take care of himself. But then, she didn't really understand women like Marla.

How could she know how devious such women could be when she was so open and trusting herself? It was part of her charm.

'There's something I'd like to know,' she said. 'Do I remind you at all of Linda?'

He started to shake his head and paused. *Tell the truth and shame the devil*, as his grandma used to warn. 'Not any more. There's a superficial resemblance that unsettled me when we first met and once you wore the same French perfume she was fond of. But the similarity isn't even skin deep. You're nothing like Linda. Not your eyes nor your hair nor how you move and speak. You don't even think as she did. Thank God. If I'm to be completely honest, my first impression of you – that you resembled her – put me off rather than attracted me.'

He put down his glass, took hers and set it on a table and reached for her. She flowed sweetly into his arms.

'What changed my mind, what makes me want you is what *you* are,' he murmured before he kissed her.

As always, he lost himself when their lips met. His father's undoubtedly nefarious schemes didn't matter, it made no difference whether they ever got back to the ranch – who cared if *Bandido* didn't get finished? All that was important to him was here in his arms. Carole.

He relished her scent, her taste, the feel of her softness against him; he could never have enough of touching her, kissing her. She was what he'd searched for all his life and he meant to keep her here with him.

She might not be the first woman he'd ever wanted, but what he felt for her was different. Stronger. A marrow-deep demand he'd resisted far too long.

What had she said a few moments ago? Seize the moment and to hell with the future?

He bloody well intended to do just that.

CHAPTER 11

Holding Carole in his arms, Jerrold tried to ignore the persistent knocking at the door of the room until finally she pulled free of him.

'It must be room service,' she said breathlessly.

'He'll go away.'

'I thought you were starving to death.' As she spoke she rose and walked to the door.

Fervently wishing he hadn't called in the meal order, Jerrold watched her let in the man pushing a food cart. 'The table, ma'am?' the waiter asked. At Carol's nod he removed the basket of fruit from the table and covered its polished white surface with a gold cloth.

While the table was being set, Jerrold got up and wandered past the roiling hot tub and into the bedroom. Noticing an open closet door, he realized his father must have left his belongings behind and it would be up to him to pack and remove them.

When he glanced inside the closet, he was

surprised to find it almost empty. Was his father reduced to selling his clothes? He shook his head. Not Calvin's style. More than likely the old perisher had stashed some of his clothes in Theda's room – probably because he meant to share her bed and it was more convenient. Calvin couldn't have known he'd need to make a quick getaway. Or *had* he suspected? There was no denying his father was a wily old bird.

Various male toiletries were scattered on a bathroom counter. Jerrold scooped them into a cowhide kit and carried the lot into the bedroom, dumping it into an open suitcase in the closet. He yanked the few remaining clothes off hangers and crammed them in on top, then checked the dresser drawers and the bedside stand, noting in passing that the staff of the White Knight truly did think of everything. He put what he found of his father's into the case, snapped it closed, shut the closet door and returned to the sitting-room.

The waiter had just lit a white candle in a gilded holder and was shaking out the match. Jerrold handed him a tip and the man left with a smiling, 'Thank you.'

'Dinner by candlelight,' Carole said as Jerrold seated her. 'Room service is certainly efficient in this hotel.'

'Big gamblers are big tippers. At least when they're winning.'

'Do you ever gamble?'

'I won't say I've never made a bet, but I don't gamble in casinos. How about you?'

'I admit to pulling an occasional slot-machine handle at Tahoe when I was in college. Usually a nickel machine. Once in a while I ventured a quarter.'

'And you've been too busy to take a day off since you graduated.'

She frowned at him. 'That's the second time today you've disagreed with my life style and I don't appreciate hearing about it. Is it really any of your business?'

Jerrold held up an admonitory hand. 'No controversy at the dinner table.'

'You brought it up.'

'I sincerely apologize. From now on we'll stick to non-controversial subjects only. He lifted a second bottle of Mumms from the ice bucket and filled both their glasses. 'I didn't bother to check the wine list; I hope you don't mind champagne with veal.'

'To tell the truth, I'm not sure even at my best which wine goes with what dish. And, at the moment, I'm really too tired to appreciate gourmet dining. I didn't sleep at all well last night.'

For some reason this confession made her blush again and he wondered why until he remembered he'd also had trouble falling asleep following their abortive love-making among the oranges. Did he haunt her nights as she haunted his? He certainly hoped so.

He had every intention of spending all of this night with Carole instead laying awake, wishing she were in his bed.

'Champagne with the veal it is, then,' he said. 'And no controversy.'

'The problem with eliminating controversy is that then we've nothing left in common.' Her grin was impish.

'Half a tick, mate. You've forgotten horses. We both like horses. I hope to raise them one day. The question is, what breed?'

'Arabians would be my first choice.' Carole spoke with no hesitation. 'Though I've seen some lovely Appaloosas I wouldn't mind owning.'

'Convince me.'

As he listened to her totting up the many wonderful qualities of Arabians, he thought she was rather like one of those proud and spirited horses herself. Without doubt, if a man could choose a woman like a horse, she'd be his first pick.

But women weren't horses and, when it came to women, he'd already made one wrong choice. What made him think he'd do any better this time?

Carole halted her spate of statistics and narrowed her eyes. 'You've stopped listening,' she accused. 'I can tell you're thinking about something else entirely.'

'I'm thinking about you,' he answered honestly. 'About you and me.'

Carole caught her breath. When he looked at her with his eyes afire with the same need that burned inside her, all her defenses crumbled. She forced her gaze away from him and attacked the veal on her plate. The first few bites had been delicious, but now her appetite had fled and she might as well be chewing cardboard.

His words echoed in her mind. *You and me.* She wanted to ask exactly what he meant – what about us? – but was afraid his answer might not be what she wanted to hear.

Putting down her fork, she took a sip of champagne. 'I shouldn't drink any more,' she said, finding her own words inane. 'I'm already tired and the wine –'

'You can't ignore what's between us,' he interrupted. 'We've both tried and all it leads to is sleepless nights.'

She set her glass very carefully on the gold tablecloth. Since he refused to let her avoid the issue, she might as well be honest. What did she have to lose?

She squared her shoulders and met his gaze. 'You may be a man of the world, but I don't share your sophistication. Even though I'm not completely inexperienced, I've never had what you might call a casual affair. It's very difficult for me to discuss the possibility.'

He slammed down his napkin and rose, glaring at her. 'And just what the hell is casual about us?'

Carole pushed back her chair. 'Nothing. And that scares me.'

The anger left his eyes and he half-smiled. 'Me, too.'

She blinked in surprise. Handsome and famous Jerrold Telford, who could have any woman he wanted, afraid of the attraction between them? Could she believe him?

He stepped around the table and held out his hand to her. Carole hesitated only an instant before taking it. He pulled her to her feet and stood looking down at her.

'You're just a poor but honest farm girl, is that it?' His smile was tender.

Breathless from his nearness, she nodded. I'm no different from Rich, she thought. Never mind that I know very well what I'm letting myself in for, I can't make any other choice.

As though reading her mind, Jerrold said, 'All us movie people aren't alike, never think we are. Remember your grandmother was once in the business herself.'

Carole made one last try to extricate herself. 'You ought to be having an affair with Marla — the odds were three to one you would.'

He caught her by the shoulders. 'And you should have gotten engaged to good old Rich. Is that what you're suggesting?'

She started to nod, changed her mind and shook her head. She'd known before she ever met Jerrold that Rich wasn't the right man for her. As for Jerrold and Marla . . .

'Oh, I don't know what I mean!' she blurted out. How did he expect her to be able to think clearly when he was only inches away?

'I don't want an affair with Marla.' He spoke softly, his gaze holding hers. 'And you don't want Rich. Right, love?'

'Right.' She could hardly speak. He'd called her 'love', the same endearment his father called Theda. Maybe both of them used the word without its true meaning – it might be an Aussie-ism. Still, the word meant a great deal to her and she couldn't help but be thrilled to hear him say it to her.

His lips brushed across hers, his tongue delicately tasting her, making her shiver in anticipation.

'I don't know whether the odds are for or against us.' He breathed the words against her mouth. 'I don't care. You make me forget anything else exists except you and me.'

A current of pure pleasure flashed through her to know he was gripped by the same talons of need as she was, a need that shut out everything else.

'Hawk,' she whispered.

He couldn't know it, but with that word she admitted her vulnerability to him and surrendered to the demanding force that drove her into his arms.

Jerrold was the man she'd dreamed of as her

lover, that and more. Much more. He was the man she longed to spend her life with. She'd never tell him, of course. A woman's pride was her ultimate defense.

When he gazed deeply into her eyes, she realized he was searching for any hesitation. She knew he'd stop if she wanted him to.

She had no reservations. Not any longer. She loved him; she always would.

His hands slipped from her shoulders to gather her close, his lips claiming hers in a possessive kiss. She tasted champagne, a hint of spice and Jerrold's own seductive flavor. His tongue eased inside her mouth, triggering a rush of passion that whirled her into their own private world. This was their time, a time she wished would never end.

The hair at his nape was silken under her caressing hand, the hard strength of his body pressing against hers excited her and she longed to touch him everywhere.

Jerrold kindled fires within her no other man had ever before lit. Until he came into her life, she hadn't known what it was to be consumed by desire, hadn't even realized she could be.

He broke away and she gave an inarticulate cry of protest. With an arm around her waist, he led her from the sitting-room. Music still played softly and the low throb of a saxophone urged them past the whir of the swirling hot tub and on to the bedroom.

Beside the bed, he unbuttoned her shirt with agonizing slowness, finally sliding it off her shoulders. His hands slipped over the silk of her bra to cup her breasts, the brush of his thumbs over her swollen nipples giving her almost unbearable pleasure.

With a flick of his fingers he unhooked and disposed of the bra. 'You're so lovely,' he said hoarsely.

When he bent his head to her bared breasts, flame shot through her, making her cling to him, not certain her legs would hold her.

In the midst of a frenzy of kisses and caresses, she shed the rest of her clothes and he his. They tumbled on to the bed, the velvet of the spread soft and warm against her back. One last shred of sanity remained with her and she managed to gasp, 'I don't have – I didn't think – I mean I'm not –'

'It'll be right – I'll take care of things, love,' he whispered; his warm breath teasing her ear.

Love. Was she his love? Ah, but it didn't matter as long as he held her close. Nothing mattered but the wonder of his body against hers while his ardent caresses brought her higher and higher until they reached the peak together, clinging together in a ecstasy of fulfillment.

Afterwards she tumbled into a safe and warm haven of darkness and slept in his arms.

* * *

She woke to find sunlight filtering through a crack in the drawn drapes. Jerrold was propped on one elbow, regarding her, his expression bemused. She felt bemused herself, but seeing his gaze rove over her bare breasts unnerved her and she tried to pull up the tangled covers.

He reached for her hands, stopping her. 'You're far too gorgeous to hide under a satin sheet. I like to look at you.'

Since she also enjoyed looking at him, she played along, deliberately staring at his chest, liberally sprinkled with wiry black hair that arrowed down to disappear under the sheet. The satin failed to conceal his arousal.

He followed her gaze and grinned. 'You'd think last night would've taken the edge off,' he murmured, releasing her hands.

'Why would I?'

'Why, indeed? What it did was hone the need, making it sharper than ever.' He gathered her to him. 'Have you any notion of how much I want you?'

Despite the surge of warmth within her, Carole did her best to recover a few strands of sanity. 'We can't stay here,' she protested. 'I've got to get back to the ranch. We must find my grandmother and you have the movie to think about.'

He tightened his grip. 'Herwin's already mad at me, José's perfectly capable of taking care of the ranch and even if we left immediately we wouldn't be any closer to catching up with Calvin and Theda because we haven't any idea where they are.'

He kissed her deeply and thoroughly and one by one her concerns slipped away until nothing was left but the magic of Jerrold's embrace. She found he was right, that her desire was increased by her knowledge of how wonderfully and completely he'd satisfy her every need.

How meager her imaginings had been compared to the reality of making love with Jerrold!

When they'd floated down from the heights once again and were nestled together among the hopelessly disarranged bedcovers, Jerrold murmured, 'It's a shame to let a perfectly good hot tub go to waste – how about breakfast there?'

Enjoying their closeness too much to move, she said, 'I'm not going anywhere until you tell me what on earth a yellow Geordie is. You said something about betting your last one on something.'

He laughed. 'That was my grandfather speaking. Grandpa McLeod was a Scot through and through. My mother had a portrait of him in kilts and tartan, his skean-dhu, the black dagger, sheathed and thrust in his stocking, a white terrier at his feet.

'He treasured seven gold guineas handed down from his father's time. King George III's likeness was on the guineas – the reason the Scots called them Geordies.'

'And you have the yellow Geordies now?'

Carole felt Jerrold's muscles tense. 'I have one that my mother managed to hide and give to me before she died. My father sold the rest. For a gambling stake. He sold my grandfather's portrait, too.'

His words alarmed her. Calvin's gambling hadn't sounded so terribly serious before. But hearing that he'd been heartless enough to sell family treasures for money to satisfy his addiction made her fear he might well contrive to sell Harte's Way, too, if he married her grandmother. She fervently hoped Theda would hold out for what she wanted — a wedding at home. That would give her time to talk to her grandmother.

She sat up, ready to announce that maybe they'd better head back to the ranch.

'Last one in the hot tub's going to turn into a frog,' he announced, leaping up.

'No fair,' she cried, flinging herself after him. 'You have a head start. Besides, only males turn into frogs, not females — remember the frog prince?'

Jerrold paused. 'I'd forgotten. After you, love. But you have to promise that when I do turn into a frog you'll give me the magic kiss that turns me back.'

She grinned at him as she slid into the swirling water. 'You'll just have to wait and see.'

In the tub one thing led to another and

soon they were clasped in each other's arms, lost in a searing kiss. 'Now that I'm no longer a frog,' he whispered into her ear, 'it's every prince for himself. And this one wants the beautiful princess who freed him from the evil spell.'

Not any more than she wanted him. 'Here?' she murmured, having never before been naked with a man in a hot tub.

'Why not?'

Already breathless from his caresses. She couldn't summon up a single objection. Making love in a hot tub turned out to be a fantastically erotic experience, but she suspected any and all love-making with Jerrold would be equally spectacular.

Sometime later, she said, 'We'd better get back to the ranch, don't you think?'

'Calvin and Theda wouldn't have gone there,' Jerrold protested, reaching for her again.

'How can we be sure?' Evading his grasp, she climbed from the tub and, gathering her clothes, hurried into the bathroom.

Jerrold leaned against the side of the tub and sighed. So much for breakfast in the hot tub. He wasn't anywhere near ready to have this idyll end. Carole's initial shyness had dissipated; she'd proved to be even more passionate than he'd hoped. In fact, he couldn't imagine any woman being able to turn him on quicker and easier than she did. He'd been looking forward to more of the same . . .

Even absent, his father managed to make himself a bloody nuisance. He hoped against hope Theda had enough sense not to marry the man.

He'd never forgiven Calvin for selling Grandpa McLeod's portrait. Among other things. He meant to do all he could to prevent his father from getting his hands on Harte's Way. But the ranch wasn't in his name. Or in Carole's.

The more he thought about what Calvin had done in the past and might do in the future, the angrier he became. Finally he sprang out of bed and strode into the bathroom. Carole was in the shower and he pitched his voice to carry over the sound of the water.

'Why the hell didn't your father leave Harte's Way to you?' he demanded. 'You're the Harte, not your grandmother.'

The spray shut off, the glass door slid open a fraction and and Carole's hand reached out. He thrust a towel into it.

'Theda was his mother; he loved her,' she said, still hidden behind the door.

'More than he loved you?'

Silence from behind the door. He waited. A tiny, rational piece of his mind knew he was behaving badly, taking his anger out on Carole through her dead father, but he couldn't seem to stop himself. Reliving Calvin's past misdeeds had driven him too far along Fury Road to easily turn back.

Carole slid the door fully open and emerged with the towel wrapped around her. She looked at him, then away, as though his nakedness embarrassed her. After last night, why the hell should it?

'Daddy knew I could take care of myself.' She spoke higher than normal, in almost a child's voice. 'He wanted to be sure my grandmother had enough for the rest of her life. And, of course, he knew she'd eventually leave the ranch to me.'

'Didn't he ever consider that Theda might remarry?'

'I – I suppose not.' She burst into tears and fled into the bedroom.

Jerrold stared after her, his guilt at making her cry fueling his rage. Instead of going to her, he yanked open the shower door, stepped inside, slammed the door so hard the glass shivered and turned on the water full force.

When he was through showering and returned to the bedroom for his clothes, Carole was nowhere in sight. Since she wasn't in the sitting-room, either, he realized she'd split. He couldn't blame her, but her disappearance infuriated him just the same.

Muttering, he started back to the bedroom to get dressed. One of his feet slid out from under him and, arms flailing, he thumped down on his butt. Cursing, he looked to see what he'd stepped on. Something gold gleamed in the pile of the rug.

It was Calvin's monogrammed pen.

Carole's tears had dried by the time she reached the elevator. Damn Jerrold, he had no right to criticize her father. He was an insensitive, uncaring clod! He'd be lucky if she ever spoke to him again.

Once out of the hotel, she slammed herself into the rental car and roared off past the flashing, glittering neon lights of the casinos toward McCarran Airport. She wondered if Jerrold's lovemaking been any more real than the Las Vegas glitter. Would she ever know?

She was fortunate enough to get an immediate flight to LA and another, with only a hour's wait, to Bakersfield, where she'd left the pickup.

Driving to the ranch, she told herself it had been a bad day for her and her grandmother when Horizon Films came to Harte's Way. Horizon had brought Jerrold and, as a result, Calvin. The Telfords, son and father, were too damn charming for any woman's good. At the moment she couldn't decide whether she or Theda had behaved more stupidly. Perhaps it was a tie.

She was still upset when she turned into the drive, wondering what to do next. She didn't really believe her grandmother would be at the ranch and, of course, she wasn't. There were no messages from Theda the answering machine and Carole could think of no possible way to find her. She had no idea what to do next.

She'd just finished changing into fresh clothes when Lollie called to her. 'José's here.'

Carole sighed. Another ranch problem, no doubt. What else could go wrong? She ran a brush through her hair and hurried from her bedroom.

Instead of finding José at the kitchen table, having a cup of coffee with Lollie, she saw with some apprehension that he was standing in the middle of the living-room, waiting. His expression was far from reassuring.

'Really bad news?' she asked. 'What happened? Did the entire irrigation system break down?'

He shook his head. 'It works. The ranch, she's okay but Sawa, maybe she's not.'

'Sawa? Is she ill?'

'Who knows? No one can find her.'

'Do you mean Sawa has disappeared?' Carole asked in amazement.

'Me, I don't think she go off on her own.'

'José, you can't mean she was kidnapped! Who would do anything like that?'

He shrugged. 'Señor Holden come to me and say he need Sawa for the movie and she don't come. So I ride to her cabin. The door's not locked, she's not there. I know she don't always

210

lock her door so I don't get worried. But I don't like it that the crow's nowhere around so I send a man to see if she go off to visit on the reservation. Nobody there know where she is and, last night, she don't come home.'

Carole's anxiety rose. Sawa rarely left her cabin except for supplies or to visit the reservation. She usually walked everywhere she went and she wasn't a young woman – was it possible she'd been taken ill in some remote spot and had been unable to get to help?

'That old *curandero* on the reservation, he tell the man I send that he dream about Sawa,' José went on.

Curandero, in José's interpretation, meant, she knew, a combination of native healer and witch.

'Maybe you don't believe,' he went on, 'but *el curandero* tell the man he dream Sawa, she got bit by a snake.'

Carole gasped. Whether she believed in prophetic dreams or nor, the possibility Sawa had run afoul of a rattlesnake hadn't occurred to her. There were rattlers on the ranch, she'd seen them.

'What if a snake did bite her and she's out there somewhere, hurt and helpless?' she cried. 'We've got to search for her.'

'I sent some ranch hands out to look for her this morning,' José said. 'They don't find her. *El curandero*, he say Sawa's in the rocks.' He shook his head. 'Me, I look in many rocks. She's not there.'

211

'I'm going myself,' Carole said. 'Right now. Tell me where the hands searched and where you looked for her so I won't duplicate what's been done already.'

After listening to his explanation, she started for the back door, pausing to ask José, 'Did this medicine man happen to describe the rocks he saw in his dream?'

José looked uncomfortable. 'Ghost rocks,' he say.

'What does that mean?'

'Who knows? Maybe where the gold hides.'

Carole stared at him. 'I didn't think you really believed in the bandit gold story.'

'Some stories are true, some a lie. Who can tell which is which? You want me to go with you?'

'I'll go alone. One of us had better look after the ranch, okay?'

He nodded and walked out with her. His gray was tethered nearby and he mounted, riding off toward the north. Carole continued on to the stable where she saddled Sombrita.

She intended to check out Sawa's cabin first, just in case her old friend had returned from wherever she'd been, safe and sound. Thinking about it, she swung toward the hacienda first. Sawa had been teaching Marla how to make baskets. Was it possible she'd mentioned something to Marla that might lead to finding her?

Marla was seated on a bench under one of the pepper trees, working on her basket. She greeted

212

Carole with enthusiasm. 'At last, a friendly face,' she said. 'Herwin's tearing out what little hair he has left. When he's in one of his snits, no one dares to so much as smile. Without Jerrold or Sawa around he's stuck and he hates to let a day pass without shooting. "Time is money", that's Herwin's motto.'

'Jerrold ought to be back sometime today,' Carole said.

'He wasn't with you?'

Carole flushed. 'Not exactly. It's Sawa I'm concerned about. We can't find her. I wondered if she said anything to you that might help us.'

Marla started to shake her head, held and said, 'Wait. Sometimes she uses Miwok words and I don't understand a one. Maybe this might mean something to you – it didn't to me. We were sitting on the ground under that tree over there –' Marla gestured with her head '– and she put aside her basket and muttered something about ghosts in her dreams, in her head. It didn't make any kind of sense. Then she said a word that sounded like *lawati*, whatever that might mean. I asked her what she was talking about, but she didn't answer. Any help?'

Carole, puzzling over what Marla had told her, said, 'I'm not sure.' She recalled Sawa saying that same word to her. Why hadn't she asked its meaning then? Casting back, she remembered that one of the movie crew had been talking to them and it was when he walked away that Sawa had muttered, '*Lawati.*'

Alex, that was the man's name. He'd also been one of the men on the dirt bike who'd been digging in the old root cellar, searching for the elusive gold. Could he be involved in Sawa's disappearance? She certainly intended to question him!

CHAPTER 12

Though Carole searched through the the area where the film crew trailers were parked, Alex was nowhere to be found. And, apparently, no one had seen him for some hours. Giving up, she turned Sombrita toward Sawa's cabin, planning to check the cabin out just in case Sawa had returned.

She talked to the mare as she rode through the late afternoon, the lowering sun already casting long shadows. 'Sawa has to be all right,' she said. 'We'll find her, won't we, Sombrita?'

The mare's ears flicked, but she gave no indication one way or another.

She'd known the old woman all her life. One of her treasured photos was of herself as a baby bundled into one of the large Miwok baskets, peering out at Sawa who was smiling at her.

Think, Carole, she urged herself. Where could she possibly be? The Miwok medicine man had mentioned snakes and rocks. Ordinarily she wouldn't have put much faith in his dream but without any clues, if Sawa wasn't at the cabin, she'd try looking among the big boulders the glaciers had left scattered over the hills.

What could he have meant by ghost rocks?

What, if anything did Alex have to do with this?

And what on earth did *lawati* mean?

At the cabin she dismounted. As she was tethering the mare, Sawa's pet crow swooped down, cawing, and perched on the roof. She tapped on the door and called Sawa's name. Getting no response, she turned the knob. As usual, the door was unlocked, just as José had found it. Inside, nothing seemed disturbed and Sawa was definitely not there. She prowled through the three rooms, not sure what she was looking for.

Finally admitting defeat, she started to leave. At the door she hesitated, her attention caught by the basket on the left where Sawa stored a blue umbrella, her husband's two canes and the ancient narrow and twisty piece of wood she called her snake stick. The stick was missing. Sawa used it, she claimed, when she was going to walk through what she referred to as 'snake country'.

'Long time ago this old stick used to be a snake,' Sawa had confided to her. 'The dawn people lived then and they knew the right words to change things into something else. This stick got changed by them and none of us can change it back. We don't know the words, not any more. We lost the spirit power.'

'But why do you keep the stick?' Carole had asked. 'What do you use it for?'

'This snake stick tells me when snakes are near, so I don't go close to them and get bit. Got to have it along in snake country.' Sawa had never been too clear on how the stick 'told' her.

Carole frowned. Since the stick was missing, she must have taken it with her. Where *was* Sawa's snake country? In the ghost rocks? That didn't get her any further.

Leaving the cabin, she told herself she must take out all the pieces and try to put them together. There was the old story of hidden gold, the gold coin Sawa's husband gave her, the mysterious whirlwind, the medicine man's dream and the movie people's interest in the supposed gold. And now Sawa was missing.

'She wouldn't tell me where her husband was caught up in the whirlwind,' Carole complained to Sombrita. 'But I'll bet she knew.'

The mare eyed her, then snorted.

'You think that's self-evident, do you? If it *is* true, then Sawa may have a good idea – or maybe even knows – where her gold coin came from. But why would she go there? Well, we'll assume she had a reason. Now all we have to figure out is the probable site.'

217

Sombrita snorted again, louder.

'You think I'm forgetting something? Maybe that dream about the snake and the ghost rocks. Since I don't have any notion of what the rocks can be, all I can do is try to remember any rocky place where I've seen a rattler. Down by the creek's the most likely spot, wouldn't you say?'

The mare's response was to turn her head away from Carole.

'Yes, I know you don't like snakes, I'm none too crazy about them myself. Or maybe you don't think the creek's the right spot. You could be right – not too many rocks nearby. No convenient place to hide ghost gold. If there is any gold at all. I'm fairly sure there are no ghosts.'

Sombrita's head swung around so she faced Carole again. Her ears pricked.

'Is that a comment for me or do you hear something?' Carole asked. As if in answer, the crow, who'd vanished from the roof, flew over her head, cawing.

'Let's get going.' As she spoke, she swung on to the mare's back. 'It'll soon be too dark to search, but we have enough time to look at at least one spot. But which one?'

Deciding to let Sombrita choose the way back to the ranch, she slackened the reins. As they started off, the crow circled over them, keeping up its persistent squawking.

218

It occurred to Carole that she hadn't fit Alex anywhere into the puzzle but, actually, all she knew was that Sawa didn't like him and that he'd been digging in the old root cellar by the ruined shed.

Out of nowhere a memory sifted into her mind – Grandpa Lyle telling her how his father had a problem with squatters on the property. 'Digging for gold on the sly, Dad figured and ran 'em off.'

Her great-grandfather hadn't meant the ghost gold but gold nuggets or ore. The California hills and valleys were crawling with would-be gold miners at the time.

'He found a couple of 'em holding up in a shed once. Californios, they were. Didn't speak English. He understood some of their lingo, though, so as soon as he heard "*oro*" he knew they were after the same thing as the other squatters. He ousted them pronto.'

She couldn't help but wonder if her great-grandfather might have been referring to the ruined shed by the old root cellar. And wasn't it possible, she thought with rising excitement, if they were Californios, the *oro* they searched for might not have been native nuggets but already coined Spanish gold?

Like Sawa's.

So maybe the legend of Harte's gold was true, after all. After all, the hacienda was still in existence – Californios had once lived on the land. Even if it was true, though, that didn't get her any closer to finding Sawa.

The route Sombrita was taking would bring them near a rock formation she'd secretly named 'Alcatraz' when she was a child. Her father and Theda had taken her to San Francisco to the zoo and he'd pointed out the old island prison in San Francisco Bay. Alcatraz. The name had fascinated her. When she came home, she'd used the name for a rocky place that not so much resembled the prison as gave her the same feeling she'd had gazing over the water at that bleak structure in the bay.

'Alcatraz, it is,' she told the mare, tightening the slack so she could turn Sombrita to the right. She hadn't ridden near the spot in years. As they changed direction, to Carole's surprise, the crow stopped circling over them and flew off in the direction she'd chosen. For the first time it occurred to her that the crow might be trying to lead her to Sawa.

The rock formation she called Alcatraz was not made up of boulders but was a more rugged extrusion of rocks spewing forth from a hillside. The rocks thrust to either side so that when you came close to the formation, the view to both sides was cut off. Noticing the crow perched on a lone valley oak near the bottom of the hill, she decided they'd come to the right place. Tethering the mare to that oak, she stood looking up at 'Alcatraz', understanding all over again why she'd chosen the name.

Actually, though the place once held an eerie fascination for her as a child, she'd never liked to come here. She found she didn't like it much better now. Shaking her head at the uneasy sensation creeping over her, she began to climb. Why Sawa would come to this spot was beyond her. If it hadn't been for the crow, she'd doubted the old woman – or anyone else – would but, since she was here, she meant to give it a careful once-over.

The closer she came to the rocks, the more apprehensive she grew. It was almost as though a small voice somewhere inside seemed to be telling her to turn around and go back – but that was nonsense. The rocks rose above her, starting to crowd to either side until she could see nothing but them unless she turned entirely around. Many dark crevices, some tunnel-like, offered concealment – anything could be hiding within them. Including snakes. Ghosts?

I should have come here earlier, she told herself, before the sun sank low enough to be behind this hill. With more light it wouldn't be so spooky. Her glance darted from side to side, searching as much for something she could feel but not see as for any trace of Sawa. Though she'd intended to call Sawa's name, she hesitated. What might hear her?

Carole stopped dead, determined to eradicate the last trace of what she considered to be senseless fear. She was trying unsuccessfully to convince herself there was absolutely no reason to be afraid – after all, she stood on Harte land – when her gaze fell on a crooked stick lying to her left. Pouncing on it, she examined the stick and nodded. Sawa's snake stick.

'Sawa!' she called, throwing caution to the winds. 'Sawa, where are you?'

Without warning, a large rock plummeted from above, crashing down so close to her that she felt the wind of its passage. She flung herself to the left, pressing against the rocky outcropping as a shower of smaller rocks fell where she'd been standing. Heart pounding, she froze, afraid to move.

A natural rock fall? An accidental one caused by something – someone? – scrambling on the hill above her? Or a deliberate attempt to harm her?

Her impulse was to slip out of the semi-enclosure and rush down the hill, jump on Sombrita and hightail it for home. Instead, once the rocks ceased falling, she forced herself to edge the other way along the rocky side of the formation. She gasped when a whisper floated from the nearest crevice. 'Here.'

'S-Sawa?' she managed to stammer.

'Come in,' Sawa's muted voice urged. 'Come in where the ghosts can't find you.'

Snake stick grasped firmly in her hand, Carole ducked and inched a short way into the tunnel-like crevice. She jumped when a hand touched her. 'Sit,' Sawa ordered. 'We wait.'

Carole dropped down beside her. 'Are you hurt?' she asked the old woman.

Sawa replied with one of her typically ambiguous answers, 'I know better than to come near the ghosts.'

'But are you all right? Can you move? Walk?'

She felt Sawa grip the stick she held and released it. 'Ah,' the old woman said. 'This will help.'

The hair prickled on Carole's nape. 'Are there snakes in here?'

'A spirit one.'

Another unsatisfactory answer.

Keeping her voice low, Carole said, 'That rock fall out there wasn't caused by spirit snakes – or by ghosts either. We need to get out of here before something else nasty happens.' Recalling the medicine man's dream, she asked, 'Were you bitten by a rattler?'

'He took my stick from me.' Sawa's voice was so low Carole could scarcely hear her.

'Who?' Carole demanded.

'The snake grandfather. The ghosts called him.'

223

Though she'd always tried to respect Sawa's beliefs, so much different from hers, in this perilous situation Carole was hard pressed not to show her impatience.

'Ghosts or not, we're leaving,' she announced. 'Now. Come on.' Grasping Sawa's hand, she rose into a crouch and, tugging at Sawa, headed for the crevice entrance.

Sawa didn't resist. The two of them crept cautiously from the crevice, and keeping close to the rocks, made their way from the formation without further incident. At the bottom of the hill, Carole helped her mount Sombrita, then swung herself into the saddle with Sawa holding on behind her, the snake stick tucked under one arm. The crow deserted his perch atop the tree and flew ahead of them.

'I worked out where I thought you were,' Carole told Sawa, 'and your crow confirmed it. He knew where you were.'

Sawa nodded. 'He's my guardian.'

Dusk had cast its dark cloak over the land by the time they reached Sawa's cabin. Carole accompanied her inside, watching as her old friend thrust the stick into its basket, straightened her skirt and rearranged her braids before sinking onto a chair with a sigh.

'I'm growing old,' Sawa admitted, the first time she'd ever referred to her age. 'To make you come to rescue me.' She shook her head.

'Could you start at the beginning and tell me what happened?' Carole asked.

'We need coffee.' Sawa began to rise but Carole jumped up, motioning for her to stay seated.

'I know where you keep everything. Let me make the coffee. You can tell me while I get it ready. Was it Alex?'

'Alex?' Sawa's voice was puzzled.

'I know he's searching for the gold. And you don't like him.'

'True he is *lawati*, the snake, never to be trusted, but he hasn't harmed me.'

Now Carole knew what the word meant. Snake. Confused, she asked, 'So if Alex is *lawati* and you took your snake stick and then told me there was a snake up there on that miserable hill – didn't you mean him?'

Sawa shook her head. 'No human man was there.'

Carole took a deep breath, let it out slowly and busied herself with the coffee-making while she tried to sort out Sawa's answers. She waited until she finished and poured two mugs of coffee before resuming her questioning.

'Maybe I could understand better if you told me why you went to Alcatraz in the first place,' she told the old woman.

Sawa gripped her mug with both hands as though to gather warmth. 'Alcatraz?' she echoed.

'That's what I call the rock formation where I found you. It's not important.'

'We know it as the hill of snakes. We avoid it.'

'Yet you went there. Why?'

After taking a sip of coffee, Sawa said, 'My husband, he come to me in a dream. He say the gold coin is now tainted with evil. He say I must return it to the ghosts at the hill of snakes. That he was wrong to touch it.'

Carole started at her. 'I thought there was a whirlwind and all that.'

'He lied.'

After digesting this, Carole asked, 'Did you know he lied when he first told you?'

'In my heart.'

'Are you saying there really is a gold cache in those rocks and that your husband took one of the coins?'

Sawa shrugged. 'Who knows where the ghost gold lies hidden? My husband, he wouldn't trespass in those rocks. He find that one coin in the dirt at the bottom of the hill of snakes – his horse kick it up when he get spooked and throw my husband.'

'How do you know?'

'In the dream, I see him.'

'All these dreams,' Carole muttered. 'I found you because José went to the reservation looking for you and their medicine man had dreamed about you in ghost rocks. He thought you'd been bitten by a rattler.'

Sawa nodded. 'Grandfather Snake's warning to stay away from the hill of snakes.'

Carole looked at her in alarm. 'You did get a real snake bite then?'

'It's hard for you to understand.'

'You can say that again. Okay, it was a ghost bite, like the ghost gold. Except the gold really does exist, if that coin in any indication. I take it you did leave the coin in the rocks at the hill?'

'I hid it there, like the dream say, asking the ghosts to forgive me for wearing it. Maybe they will, maybe not.'

Feeling as though she had to pry each nugget of information from Sawa, Carole continued her questions. 'You haven't told me why you were hiding in the crevice – were you there all night?'

'A long time. First I hide the coin, then Grandfather Snake come up behind me, snatch my snake stick and shove me down hard. For a while, I don't know nothing. When I wake up my head hurt and I feel the ghosts seeking me and so I find a hiding place and I stay there.'

Carole fastened on the attack. 'Somebody pushed you down hard enough so you passed out? Does you head still hurt? Are you sure you weren't hit over the head and that's what caused you to fall?'

Sawa lifted a hand to her scalp. 'I feel a lump,

must have hit my head when I fell. Lots of rocks in that bad place.'

'Did you see anybody?'

'Nobody there. You don't always see a spirit.'

Eyeing her with resigned exasperation, Carole realized that, while she was all but certain a thoroughly human man or woman had attacked Sawa, she'd never shake Sawa's conviction she'd been downed by a spirit snake.

'I'm never going back there,' Sawa added.

Remembering her own uneasiness among the rocks, Carole said, 'I don't blame you.' At the same time, she wondered if Sawa's attacker, maybe scared off by fear he'd killed the old woman, could have later followed her back to 'Alcatraz' and tried to either scare her off – or worse – with the rock fall.

Whoever it was, he must believe the gold was hidden in those rocks. Had he originally followed Sawa, thinking she'd lead him to the cache? If so, why had he attacked Sawa? Was he afraid she'd see him?

Carole didn't have answers to any of those questions but she didn't like the idea that someone unknown might be planning to return to 'Alcatraz', search for the ghost gold and maybe even find it, with no one the wiser. The gold, if it existed, belonged to Harte's Way.

'You must be hungry after your long ordeal,' she said to Sawa, belatedly returning to her concern for her old friend. 'I'll fix you something to eat.'

Sawa shook her head. 'Me, I take no food as an offering to the spirits so they forgive me.'

'How's your head?'

'Hurt when I touch it, not otherwise. Don't worry, I'm old, like I say, but I'm still tough. You go home, I'm okay here in my own place.'

'You could come to the ranch with me.'

'Better here.'

'You're sure you don't want me to stay?'

'What, and worry your grandmother? No, you go home.'

Carole didn't think this was the time to burden Sawa with her worry over Theda. Sawa looked much as usual, with little indication that she'd been attacked and then spent the night and much of the day hiding in a rocky crevice. Would she be all right alone?

'I don't know,' she began dubiously. 'If you promise to lock your door, I might –'

She was startled into silence by a pounding on that door which she realized with some alarm that she hadn't locked after they'd entered. 'Who is it?' she asked as firmly as she could.

The door burst opened and Jerrold stood framed in the doorway. 'Where the hell have you been?' he demanded. 'I've searched over the entire bloody ranch for you.'

'I had to find Sawa,' she said, bristling.

'Come in, Mr Telford,' Sawa said.

Jerrold advanced into the room and closed the door behind him. 'Sorry to force my way in,' he told the old woman.

She smiled. 'You're welcome in my lodge.'

Carole recognized the old Miwok formula for assuring visitors of safe hospitality. A wry smile curled her lips as she interpreted. 'She means no one will attempt to kill you under her roof.'

'That's more than I can say for some places I've been in,' he said, abandoning his belligerent manner. 'Thanks, Sawa.'

Sawa asked, 'Coffee? My young friend has brewed it and served me, perhaps she'll serve you as well.'

Jerrold lowered himself into a kitchen chair. Glancing at Carole, he said, 'I'd like that.'

Somewhat grudgingly she handed him a mug of coffee.

'I could do with some explanations from the no-longer-missing,' he said.

Reminded of her grandmother and Calvin, she asked, 'Have they come back yet?'

He shook his head, obviously understanding who she meant. 'Not by the time I left the house to look for you. I finally found José and he told me you were searching for Sawa, who'd disappeared. I didn't think to ask where this cabin was so, later, when I couldn't find a trace of you anywhere, I had to backtrack and ask him. That's my story. What's yours?'

Carole glanced at Sawa, who shook her head, saying, 'You tell.'

Deciding to leave the could-have-been-natural rock fall, the dreams and the gold coin out of it, Carole launched into an terse explanation. 'Sawa was walking on this rocky hill when someone, she didn't see who, attacked her from the rear and knocked her out. When she came to, she was frightened and hid in a rocky crevice where she stayed all night and until I found her.'

'That's an abstract of the story,' he commented. 'I'm waiting for the details. For example, how did you know where to look for her? And, if she was hidden, how could find her?'

'If you must know,' Carole said, 'José went to the Miwok reservation in search of Sawa.' She went on to tell him about the medicine man's dream and how her interpretation of it led her to Sawa. 'I don't usually go by dreams,' she finished, 'but I had no other clue.'

'Why do I have the feeling you're still leaving some of the important details out?' he asked.

'Because my young friend don't believe in spirits, she don't believe in ghosts,' Sawa put in. 'She say attacker, but Grandfather Snake pushed me down, not a man.'

'That's a Miwok spirit, not a real snake,' Carole said, aware Sawa was grateful she hadn't told the entire story and was trying to help. She wondered if she'd erred in leaving Alex's name out of it, but Sawa didn't seem to think he was

231

involved and she didn't want to accuse him unfairly.

Jerrold looked from one of them to the other in silence, finally saying, 'Even the best of women are devious.'

Carole decided prudence forbade any comment.

'The question now is can Sawa be left alone?' Jerrold asked.

'The answer is yes,' Sawa said before Carole could open her mouth. 'I'll promise to lock my door after you leave, even though locks don't keep out spirits.'

'I'm not worried about spirits,' Carole told her. Sawa shrugged.

'I'll be back in the morning,' Carole added.

'Look for me first at the hacienda,' Sawa cautioned. 'Mr Holder wants me to make my baskets there.'

Jerrold had tied the movie palomino next to Sombrita. As he helped Carole mount, he said, 'You did give me a scare, you know.'

Taking that as an apology for bursting into the cabin and shouting at her, Carole said. 'Sawa is a dear old friend. I feared she'd been hurt.'

After letting the palomino fall in behind Sombrita as she picked her way home through the darkness, Jerrold said, 'I've had my fill of vanishing acts. First my father and Theda, then you taking off from the hotel in Vegas, leaving me behind. The last thing I expected was not to find you at home when I got here. Added to that was the discovery that Sawa had disappeared. I didn't know what to think.'

'Thank God I found her and she's safe and sound.'

'And thank God, so are you.' He sounded as though he really did care, that the time in Las Vegas had been more than a casual fling to him. Did she dare to believe it?

As she tried to decide, a wave of fatigue washed over her. 'All of a sudden I'm exhausted,' she said.

Although it was too dark to see his expression, he sounded amused when he said, 'Did some unfeeling bloke keep you awake last night?'

Carole smiled, a thrill shooting through her as she recalled the caresses – and more – that had kept her awake.

'I did sleep some,' she protested.

'Must be I'm losing my touch.'

'Oh?'

'Wait till next time.'

Was there to be a next time? She longed to feel his arms around her again, to experience the wonder of a complete embrace with him.

'Unfortunately, placating Herwin has to come first,' he said. 'He's waiting for me now, I'm in for what I hope amounts to no more than his standard chewing out – I'm used to those. Nothing's more important to Herwin than the film he happens to be shooting at the time. Not death nor taxes and certainly not wanting to hold the most beautiful woman in the world in your arms and make love with her all night.'

Though it pleased her to think he found her beautiful, she missed the words he might have said but didn't, missed any word of love. Not that she'd really expected any. She'd told herself from the beginning that anything between them had to be temporary. Hadn't she known their involvement couldn't last beyond the end of the filming?

'It's just as well,' she said. 'I'm really tired and anyway —' She broke off, unsure how to word what was bothering her. Somehow she didn't want Jerrold to make love to her in the ranch house, not did she care to go to his trailer, either. It might be irrational but that was how she felt.

He kissed her as they parted at her door, a long, intense kiss that melted her insides as well as thoroughly arousing him — she could feel he was.

'I hate to say goodnight,' he murmured. 'I'm tempted to stand Herwin up and to hell with it.'

Summoning her willpower, she pulled away. 'Your career's important,' she said.

He gripped her shoulders. 'So are you.'

José's voice floated out of the darkness. 'You find Sawa?' he asked.

Jerrold dropped his hands.

'Sawa's safe and sound,' Carole told José. 'I'll tell you all about it in the morning.'

As she shut the door behind her, leaving Jerrold and José outside, she sighed. Sawa was safe but she wasn't any too sure about her grandmother. Where was Theda? The house felt cold and empty without her.

Or maybe the emptiness was within her as she anticipated Jerrold's departure in a mere few weeks. How could she bear it?

CHAPTER 13

Carole woke early, uncertain what had roused her. Had she heard voices? She rose, slipped into her robe and padded from her room, only to stop short when she saw Calvin sitting at the dining-room table sipping coffee. He looked up, his expression guarded, and rose.

'Where's my grandmother?' she demanded when she recovered from her surprise.

'She just went to her room,' he said. 'I believe she intends to rest. I'm happy to see you arrived home safely.' He spoke as calmly as if there'd been no clandestine escape from the White Knight.

She stared at him, trying to decide how and where to begin.

'Do you mind if I sit down and finish my coffee?' he inquired.

'Please do,' she said, brought back to the fact he was, at the very least, Theda's guest.

'Won't you join me? There's more in the pot.'

She shook her head. The last thing she wanted

to do at the moment was sit with Calvin, sharing coffee.

'I hope that son of mine had the sense to keep the suite after I paid for the extra night,' he said.

His words left her speechless. Calvin had arranged for the room? Because he expected her and Jerrold to spend the night together? She felt herself flush and shook her head angrily. He was trying to confuse her, to throw he off balance.

'Why did you and Theda leave the hotel the way you did?' she demanded.

'I didn't want Jerrold upsetting her. Besides, we'd already decided to get married here – don't you remember?'

Yes, she remembered. It was one thing to listen to Jerrold tell of his father's profligate ways and another to confront Calvin's charm face to face. But she had to.

'Jerrold told me,' she said, 'about your gambling.'

Calvin waved a dismissive hand. 'A thing of the past. I haven't so much as played a slot machine since I met Theda. I'm cured. I'll never place a bet again.'

. . . *bet my last yellow Geordie* . . .

Jerrold's words echoed in her mind. Because of Calvin's gambling there was only one of those family heirlooms left. Knowing what his father had done in the past in order to keep gambling, how could she believe him now?

How could anyone believe him?

'Shall we go somewhere else to talk?' Calvin suggested. 'I don't want to disturb your grand-mother.'

He crossed to Carole and draped an arm over her shoulders, leading her from the dining-room into the music room. When he released her, she drew her robe closer about her, watching him as he gazed not at her but at the baby grand, a Harte heirloom.

'A shame no one plays this lovely old instru-ment,' he said. 'Theda said your grandfather's brother inherited all the Harte musical ability and that after he was killed in the Second World War the piano was never touched.'

'I found out early I was no musician,' she said.

Calvin sat on the round piano stool, lifted the lid, folded it back, put his hands on the keys and began a sprightly tune. ' "Country Gardens",' he murmured as he played. 'How well I recall Jerrold's attempts to learn this piece.'

Carole, though determined not to be dis-tracted from the main issue of Calvin's gam-bling, found herself asking, 'Jerrold is a pianist?'

Calvin continued to play as he talked. 'A better one than his old man. Surprising he got to be so good considering the ancient wreck he had to practice on. The McLeod ranch had been going to the dingos long before I ever set foot on the scene.' He glanced sideways at her without missing a note. 'I never pretended to be a rancher. What could I do but sell the old place after Doris – she was Jerrold's mother – died?'

Carole leaned on the piano, eager to learn everything she could about Jerrold's background.

'Jerrold never forgave me for selling the ranch and moving him into the city,' Calvin went on, his fingers dancing on the yellowing keys. 'But how in bloody hell would he ever have gotten into the movies otherwise?' He glanced at her again. 'Inherits the talent from me – I used to act when I was in school. That's where I met Doris, she painted stage sets.'

He finished 'Country Gardens' with a flourish and turned on the stool to face her. 'Doris's father hated me. True, I didn't have much but it wouldn't have mattered if I'd been King Midas himself as far as old McLeod – The McLeod, he called himself, implying he was clan head – was concerned because it was *me* he didn't like.'

'Is that why you sold his portrait?' The words tumbled out before Carole thought.

Calvin looked momentarily startled. 'Jerrold mentioned that to you? I'd have sworn he'd forgotten the bloody painting ever existed.'

'I got the impression he was fond of his grandfather and the portrait mattered to him.'

Calvin shook his head, his expression unhappy. 'When I take a prang, it's a beaut. Never would've sold the thing if I'd known. But that's Jerrold for you — close-mouthed as they come. Thinks it's a crime to admit he loves anyone or is attached to anything.'

Maybe because Jerrold learned early not to trust, she thought, but couldn't bring herself to say, dejected as Calvin looked at the moment.

'The boy should never have married Linda,' he went on. 'He hauled her off to the outback and tried to make a go as a ranch manager. I warned him the ranch was marginal and that Linda was a what's-in-it-for-me city gal, but what son ever listens to his old man? Both the marriage and the job crashed. Linda would've taken him on again when he went back into films, but by then he'd had more than enough of her ways. Curdled him on women, she did.'

Calvin eyed her appraisingly, making her wish she had on something more becoming that her terrycloth robe. 'You could change that. Soon as I met you I pegged you for a gal who could set him on the right path. Providing his hard-nosed McLeod stubbornness didn't get in the way.'

'Jerrold told me about Linda,' Carole said, deliberately ignoring what Calvin had said about the right path. 'But what I'm concerned with now is you and my grandmother. Does she know about your gambling?'

Calvin smiled wryly. 'I gave Theda a rundown on all my faults. Quite a list, it was. Would've discouraged most women, but she's one in a million.' He shut the piano lid and rested an elbow on it. 'Once she knew the worst she was still willing to marry me. Think you can put up with an old reprobate for a step-grandfather?'

Despite what Jerrold had told her about her father, Carole found it impossible to dislike Calvin. Accepting him into the family, though, was another matter. 'I don't know,' she replied honestly.

He grinned at her. 'Can't say a man doesn't know where he stands with you. You've got doubt written all over your face.'

'Jerrold told me the same thing,' Carole said, then flushed. Why couldn't she remember to think before she spoke?

The music room door opened. 'I couldn't sleep,' Theda said, gazing fondly at Calvin, 'and then I thought I heard someone playing the piano.' She looked charmingly fragile in one of her blue silk negligees. Catching sight of Carole, she added, 'I knew you were home, but I didn't realize you'd gotten up, dear.'

'You might have left a note for me at the hotel,' Carole couldn't help retorting. 'I wouldn't have worried so much if I'd known you were coming back to the ranch.'

Theda glanced conspiratorially at Calvin. 'But a note would have spoiled everything. You'd have come rushing after us. I was sure you'd eventually decide we were heading here. As you did. I assume Jerrold also returned?'

'Not with me, but he is here,' Carole said, hoping to discourage them from believing anything at happened between her and Jerrold at the White Knight. Had she and Calvin actually conspired to leave them together in that suite? She might believe it of him – but her grandmother?

'I really did want to be married here at home,' Theda said.

Carole sighed. 'Jerrold planned to talk to you about his father, but Calvin says you already know –'

'About his little problem? Yes, dear, I do. Calvin's been open with me from the first. There was no need for Jerrold to swoop down on us like some kind of avenging angel, no need at all. I'm really quite annoyed with him.'

Calvin's little problem? Carole chewed her lip. If what Jerrold said was true, and she had no reason to believe it wasn't, Calvin's gambling couldn't be dismissed so lightly. He claimed to have stopped cold turkey but that remained to be seen.

All things considered, she felt compelled to defend Jerrold. 'Jerrold was concerned, Theda. He still is. He doesn't want you hurt. And neither do I.' She flashed a stern look at Calvin.

He raised his eyebrows as he rose from the piano stool. Reaching for Theda, he drew her close to him. She nestled against his shoulder, her eyes glowing as she gazed up at him. They made a charming picture of a man and woman in love, Carole thought, wishing she could be sure he did love her grandmother.

She'd gotten over her initial objection to Theda's falling in love with another man – after all, Grandpa Lyle had been dead ten years – but her fear that her grandmother would be hurt by Calvin in one way or another kept her from accepting the pretty picture they made. And from accepting Calvin at face value.

'Calvin and I are quite capable of handling our own lives,' Theda said. 'Whether you and Jerrold can believe it or not, we have every intention of living happily ever after.'

Watching the two of them, Carole realized that nothing she or Jerrold could say would alter her grandmother's love-colored-glasses view of Calvin. Theda was determined to marry him, come what may.

'I hope you're right about being happy.' Carole was sure her expression showed her doubts. 'I hope everything flows smoothly for you and – '

'Oh, good heavens,' Theda said. 'That reminds me. While Calvin was getting the luggage earlier, José came to the door with a message for you. He said to be sure to tell you as soon as you got up. I forgot and I'm sorry.'

'What was it about?' Carole asked apprehensively.

'An irrigation line broke. Also someone's been digging in different places on the property.'

Carole groaned. Another problem to cope with when she already felt she had more than she could handle. She wasn't going to lose sleep over the digging, but the broken line was a disaster. Though it didn't involve people she loved or the turbulent emotions that unsettled her, she greatly feared it would involve an item she didn't have enough of. Money.

Later, when she rode with José to inspect the damaged line, Carole found the break every bit as bad as she'd anticipated. Because she couldn't afford it, she'd put off replacing the oldest section of the irrigation piping, just patching the leaks. The break was now beyond patching – a new line had to go in. Since José had shut off the valve above the break they weren't losing water, but everything growing below the valve wasn't getting any water, either.

The money for new piping just wasn't there. She'd have to wait and hope for rain as a temporary solution. She wanted to put off borrowing more money as long as possible. Always supposing the bank would lend it to her. She feared that was about as likely as her ever finding the damn hidden gold.

'We both better pray for a deluge,' she told José.

He shook his head. 'One time I light candles for rain, you know what happen? We get a flood. Your papa, he say, "*Basta*, José. Enough. No more candles."'

She summoned up a smile. 'Maybe just one very small candle this time.'

José shrugged and reached to help her back on to Sombrita.

'My grandmother said something about digging?' she asked as he climbed onto his gray.

'First by the old shed. Now by the tree that grow from the split rock. And down by the creek. Some of the movie crew looking for gold. Don't do much harm, but you should know. I tell that little boss man, he say he talk to them, tell me not to worry, maybe a week and they put it in the pot – no, the can – that's what he say.'

Carole's heart seemed to turn over in her chest. Maybe a week? José meant Herwin Holden, the director, and Herwin would know. With all she'd heard of movies in the making running behind schedule, she'd subconsciously expected *Bandido* to. She'd never once dreamed Horizon would finish shooting ahead of time. Jerrold would be gone sooner than she thought. How could she bear never seeing him again?

'Don't be sad,' José urged. 'My *madre*, she

have a saying. The words, they are better in Espanol but I give it to you in English. "Every time the eye shut don't mean sleep, every goodbye don't mean gone."'

As Carole tried to summon up a smile for José, she thought despondently that last night's kiss could be the last she might have from Jerrold. His goodbye kiss. Whether it was or not, he'd be going just the same. He probably was already committed to another film and, once he left Harte's Way, he'd forget her quickly enough. His life was in the thick of traffic while hers was winding slowly along a rutted country lane.

Ranch chores kept her occupied until late afternoon. When she returned to the house, Calvin wasn't there. Theda was as upset as Carole ever recalled seeing her.

'What's happened?' she asked in concern.

'Jerrold came by and insisted on talking to me about Calvin. I told him I already knew all I needed to about his father and refused to hear another word. I told him very plainly that his attitude toward his father was deplorable. I said if he didn't have anything good to say about the man who'd been responsible for his very existence, then he wasn't welcome in my home.'

'What did he say?'

'He muttered something about none of us being safe under my roof, which I didn't understand at all. Then he had the nerve to insist I should hear him out anyway.'

'Jerrold's only trying to make you understand the danger of –' Carole began to explain.

Her grandmother cut her off. 'I do understand Calvin. Far better than Jerrold ever could. Or you, for that matter.' Theda eyed Carole sternly. 'I refuse to hear one more negative word about Calvin. Is that clear?'

Carole remembered how her father had tried to protect Theda from anything unpleasant. Probably Grandpa Lyle had done the same. Now her grandmother was protecting herself from what she considering unpleasantness by not listening. If she persisted in trying to make Theda understand Calvin's gambling was no 'little problem', her grandmother would simply leave the room and refuse to talk to Carole until she apologized. Childish tactics, maybe, but effective just the same.

'Is Calvin having supper with us?' Carole asked, giving up temporarily.

'Who knows? Jerrold whisked him off somewhere, no doubt to browbeat the poor dear. I'd think twice before marrying *that* man.'

Carole blinked in confusion. 'Calvin?'

'I meant Jerrold and I meant if I were you. Considering the way he behaves toward his father, how can you be sure he wouldn't behave the same way toward a wife?'

In Carole's opinion, Jerrold had adequate

cause to mistrust his father but Theda had given her fair warning that she wouldn't listen to any explanation that wasn't favorable to Calvin. So she addressed another facet of her grandmother's statement.

'I've no intention of marrying Jerrold.' Carole fought to keep her tone disinterested, hoping the subject would be dropped.

'Then he *has* asked you,' Theda said triumphantly.

'No, he has not! Nor do I expect or want him to. And I wish you and Calvin had left well enough alone.' Despite her best efforts, Carole's voice broke of the last word.

'Oh, dear, you've quarreled with him, haven't you? I'm sorry you're upset.'

About to deny the quarrel, Carole decided it was useless to try to convince her grandmother of anything right now. She gestured sharply with one hand, saying, 'Can't we just forget about Jerrold?'

She might as well have saved her breath. Theda sailed blithely on. 'I know he was taken with you. And you with him. I do hope you're not trying to create obstacles to what may well turn out to be a perfectly wonderful marriage.'

'Theda! A second ago you were warning me he might turn into a wife-beater, now you're urging me to smooth the path to true love. Jerrold isn't in love with me and *Bandido* is all but wrapped up. Horizon, Jerrold and all will be leaving shortly and –'

Theda held up her hand. 'Yes, my part is in the can and Herwin informed me he's close to the end of shooting. Which reminds me. Did I tell you I'm planning a farewell party for the crew next week? I have the caterers booked, but I mustn't forget to send announcements to friends. Maybe you can help me with those. With all this dashing back and forth with Calvin to Las Vegas – what an interesting town – I've been too busy to think. Let me jot down what else must be done before the party or I'll forget. We'll talk more at supper.' Theda patted her arm and hurried off to her room.

Carole sighed as she sought her own room to change from her working clothes. Theda hated everything about horses, including their smell. She'd have to endure the party somehow. Smile at the guests. At Jerrold. Talk. Pretend her heart wasn't breaking.

Calvin didn't appear for supper. By nine he still hadn't returned to the house and Carole, too tired to stay awake any longer, went to bed and fell asleep immediately.

She woke at dawn to the welcome slash of rain against her window. She smiled in relief, wondering if José's candle had done the trick. If he was this successful, she thought as she dressed, she'd have to ask him to light one for her.

Not that a thousand burning candles could change the way she felt about Jerrold. Love, she was learning the hard way, couldn't be brought to heel like an obedient dog. It was more like a coyote, totally untamed.

Love was a creature of the wild – a hawk soaring in the air, wheeling, dipping, circling in unpredictable patterns. Difficult to manage.

Lollie didn't arrive until eight-thirty, but before she left at night she always set the timer so the coffee was ready earlier. In the kitchen, Carole poured herself a mug, drank it with a slice of Lollie's homemade orange-bran bread and then gathered her rain gear – poncho and hood. The best antidote for the blues was work.

As she saddled Sombrita, she wondered if Calvin had ever come back last night – she'd forgotten to look for his Cadillac when she left the house. Perhaps Jerrold had convinced him leave Harte's way . . . though she doubted it. From the warmth in his eyes when he looked at Theda, it would take more than Jerrold's dis-approval to pry Calvin loose from her grand-mother's side.

Jerrold seemed to believe it was only Theda's money and the possibility of acquiring the ranch that fascinated his father but she wasn't so sure he was right. While the money might interest Calvin, she thought his feelings for her grand-mother were genuine, as far as they went. The trouble was, she didn't know how far that was.

If only she could be certain he really loved Theda and that he really had quit gambling for good, she'd be the first to wish them every joy. Somebody in the family deserved to be happy.

Calvin didn't appear at lunch but his car was outside so he'd come back. Theda told her he was sleeping.

'I saw Sawa at the hacienda and she asked me to drive her into town,' Carole said, making innocuous conversation. 'Is there anything you'd like me to get?'

Theda shook her head. 'Is Sawa all right? Lollie told me she was missing for a while.'

'She seems fine.' Since Theda didn't appear interested in where Sawa had been or what might have happened to her, Carole kept mum. There was no point in getting Theda upset.

Later, driving into Hubbard's Corners with Sawa in the pickup beside her, Carole asked, 'Everything okay?'

Sawa grinned. 'I think I win my bet from those men,' she said.

'Bet?' Carole echoed. 'What men?'

'From the film crew. You know Alex, he's one. I got three-to-one odds. They know Marla but I know you so I'll win big.' She slanted a look at Carole who almost ran the pickup off the road as Sawa's meaning sank in.

'Maybe when the reservation builds the casino I'll be their first gambler,' she added.

Carole scarcely heard her. Three-to-one odds. On Marla getting Jerrold into her bed. But she'd gone after Rich instead, leaving Sawa the winner because the old woman figured he'd choose Carole instead. However she might resent such a bet, Sawa did have the right to make one.

'The movie's not quite finished,' she warned. 'You might lose yet.'

'I don't lose. Quail come out of hiding and hawk, he like what he see. He want you, no other woman. I know.'

'Then you know more than I do.' Carole couldn't help the sharpness in her voice.

'Much more,' Sawa agreed unperturbed. 'Not only about the hawk and the quail.'

Carole shot her a quizzical look. 'Like what?'

'Alex and his friend lose the bet. They won't get the gold either. That's what the ghosts told me while I hid in the rocks. No one gets the gold. It's theirs and they keep it.'

Carol stared at her in amazement. 'You know where the gold is, don't you?'

Sawa shrugged. 'The old ones, like me, we know the ghost gold lies somewhere in the rocks you call Alcatraz. We always knew. We know that gold is not for us so we leave it alone. We don't talk about it. We know better than to annoy ghosts. Look what happened to me.'

'You had a human attacker,' Carol insisted.

'It's true maybe Grandfather Snake got inside the man and made him push me.'

'What man? For heaven's sake, Sawa, why didn't you tell me before?'

'You don't understand, that's why.'

'Was it Alex?'

'Maybe. Maybe his friend. Don't matter. They won't bother me any more.'

'But how can you be sure? And what about the gold? We can't let them get it.'

'You don't listen. Nobody gets the gold. The ghosts, they keep it.'

Carole felt like shaking her. 'Men like Alex don't believe in ghosts.'

Sawa's smile chilled her. 'These ghosts don't care. Evil never cares who believes. I tell you not to worry. True, you can't have the gold – but then nobody can. Me, I win a bet so I don't care either.'

She got no more out of Sawa then or on the way back from shopping. After helping the old woman get her supplies to the cabin; Carole returned to the ranch, took off her rain gear and helped José mend tack in the barn.

'Sawa knows where the gold is,' she said after a time.

He nodded. 'They know many things, her people.'

'She says no one will ever find it, even though she admitted that two of the film crew know the gold is hidden in some rocks.'

José held up a hand. 'Don't tell me where. Bad luck to know.'

José, too? she wondered. 'What's to prevent these men from taking the gold once they find it?' she asked. 'I can't have them followed day and night.'

'No need,' he said. 'There are stories. Long ago men died for that gold. They guard it yet. Dead men's gold belongs to no living man.'

'You didn't try to stop me from searching when I was a little girl.'

'Because I know you don't ever find it so you won't come to harm.'

'We need money for the ranch,' she cried in frustration. 'We need new equipment. We could use that gold.'

José shook his head. 'Ghost gold is not yours to use. You will find another way to come up with the money.'

When Carole quit for the day, she shed her rain gear in the utility room before entering the kitchen where she greeting Lollie.

'Looks like you're eating alone,' Lollie informed her.

Carole looked at her in alarm. 'Has my grandmother gone somewhere?'

'Out to eat, she and Mr Calvin. And maybe a movie, they said. She told me she had enough of the house and that I should tell you not to wait up for her.'

Breathing a sigh of relief that Calvin and Theda hadn't taken off on another wild jaunt, Carole asked, 'Any other messages?' She hadn't meant to say it but the words slipped out. Why did she keep hoping that Jerrold would call?

'None for you,' Lollie said. 'Your grandmother had some. Nothing important.'

No messages for her. Jerrold hadn't tried to reach her. So much for his 'next time' . . .

CHAPTER 14

Lollie's cooking, as usual, was excellent, but Carole had little appetite. The empty evening stretched out ahead of her as long and unrewarding as a road to nowhere. She turned on the TV, turned it off, picked up a magazine, put it down, tried basket weaving and made so many mistakes she gave up. When the phone rang she ran to answer it.

Her 'Hello?' was breathless.

'Rich here, how's everything at *el rancho grande*?'

'Oh, Rich, how are you?'

'Hey, you sound funny. Something wrong?'

She couldn't very tell him that hearing his voice instead of Jerrold's was what was wrong.

'No, not really. We have a irrigation line break that's going to cost *muy mucho*, but otherwise . . .' Her voice trailed off. Otherwise she was miserable.

Atypically, Rich wasn't interested in the break. Usually he was fascinated by any mention of ranch problems. 'You're the only person I can trust,' he said. 'I want you to answer one question for me. Honestly, I mean.'

'I'll try.'

'Do you think I have a chance with Marla?'

'What kind of a chance?' she asked cautiously. 'Are we talking temporary or permanent?'

Rich groaned. 'Never mind, you've already answered. I had a gut feeling I wasn't much more than a diversion.'

'Well, obviously Marla likes you.' Carole tried to sound positive.

'Yeah. Likes.' His voice was despondent.

'Look, can you imagine Marla being permanently happy on a ranch? Think about it.'

'I have.' He sounded even gloomier.

'Can't you just enjoy whatever is between you right now?'

'Not without wishing for more. Hell, Carole, I don't want it to end.'

She sighed. 'I understand.' Rich could have no idea how well.

'Yeah. You've always been a good friend, a real buddy. Is your grandmother going to invite me to the farewell party?'

'She hasn't gotten around to sending invitations but consider yourself invited.'

'Thanks. It might be the last time I'll see Marla.'

And the last time I'll see Jerrold, she thought as she said goodbye to Rich.

If Theda and Calvin married, what would that make Jerrold? Her stepbrother? No, that wasn't right. If Calvin was his father and Theda was her grandmother, he'd be – what? She couldn't figure out how they'd be related, maybe an in-law of some kind. But it didn't matter what the relationship would be, she didn't expect he'd care to visit his father so she wouldn't be likely to run across Jerrold ever again, in-law or not, because of his father's marriage to her grandmother. And, on the odd chance that she did, he'd have lost interest in her, she was sure.

He'd never said a thing to make her believe his feeling for her was any deeper than Marla's interest in Rich, which was temporary. Jerrold's silence since Las Vegas told her in no uncertain terms just how temporary their relationship had been.

Why had she been such a fool as to fall in love with him?

After an uneasy night's sleep, Carole woke to an overcast day. Because her grandmother and Calvin hadn't come in by midnight, when she gone to bed, Carole looked to see if Calvin's Caddie was parked anywhere around the house. It wasn't.

Had he and Theda quarreled? Was he sleeping at the hacienda in the film-crew quarters? She doubted it. More probably he hadn't brought her grandmother home last night. Checking on her premise, though she hated to disturb Theda so early in the morning, she tapped at her bedroom door.

When there was no answer, Carole eased the door ajar and peeked inside. Her grandmother wasn't in the room and her bed hadn't been slept in.

There was no reason to worry. Or was there? No, Theda and Calvin were long past the teenage years. If they'd decided to stay in a motel overnight that was their business. Actually, they might have driven into LA or over to San Francisco or somewhere else too far to return without driving half the night. Yet her grandmother's failure to come home bothered Carole.

True, she and Calvin had taken off twice without consulting anyone but Theda had left a note each time. It wasn't like her grandmother not to let her know at all.

Carole took her anxiety to work with her; by ten, she decided she needed to find Jerrold and discuss it with him. He'd talked to Calvin yesterday and perhaps he knew something she didn't. It wasn't like she was using this as an excuse to see him, not this time – she was truly worried about her grandmother.

As she turned Sombrita toward the hacienda, the sun broke through the high clouds, brightening the day. She noticed some of the navels had started to turn, their green tinged with orange. It would soon be picking time. Money would come in from the sale of the oranges but first she'd have to pay the pickers with what should be the mortgage money.

The best she could hope for was to come out even. Which meant she'd still be short on the mortgage payment, with nothing at all for new irrigation pipe.

Carole sighed. If only Theda had charged Horizon more for their use of the ranch, the money could have covered the mortgage payment and the new pipe. But it was too late to look for money from Horizon. Too late to look for anything from Horizon.

That reminded her of Alex and his friend and their search for the gold. Harte gold. Gold she needed to save the ranch. And she thought she did know where it was – or at least approximately. If only she could find that gold.

After tethering the mare, she saw the cameras set up at the far end of the hacienda. She eased closer cautiously, keeping out of camera range while trying not to make any noise that might be picked up by the sound equipment.

Her heart leaped when she saw Jerrold, in Californio costume. standing beside the palomino. As she watched, Marla, all in white, rushed from a doorway toward him, her white gown trailing in the adobe dirt.

Joaquin and Penelope, she corrected herself.

With her gaze fixed on Jerrold/Joaquin, she entered into the story, suspending her disbelief.

She soon realized this must be the big farewell scene, Joaquin saying *adios* to the American girl he truly loved, preparing to ride away from her forever, leaving Penelope, though not realizing this was a final goodbye, distraught at his abrupt departure.

'You'll come back,' Penelope cried, her white fingers clutching his black sleeve, her beautiful face turned up to him with tears streaming down her cheeks. 'Promise me I'll see you again.'

Joaquin, his dark eyes sad with the knowledge he'd never return to her, smiled. 'If God wills.'

Penelope's arms encircled his neck as he bent his head until his lips brushed hers, then he gently freed himself. Swinging into the saddle, he waved to Penelope and rode away without looking back.

Carole, held by the momentary illusion that she was Penelope, suffered the pangs of being left behind by the man she loved but would never see again. Tears filled her eyes. Through them she caught a blurred glimpse of a red-tailed hawk soaring high above Jerrold and her tears flowed faster.

Not wanting anyone to see her crying, she retreated hastily, mounted Sombrita and urged the mare toward the ranch house. She was almost at the corral when she heard hoofbeats behind her. Hastily wiping her eyes, she turned and saw Jerrold, still in costume, on the palomino. She reined in Sombrita.

'You know you can't get away from me,' he said as he halted the palomino. 'Why do you keep trying?'

Hoping he couldn't see any evidence of her tears, she searched for the right words to defuse the tension crackling between them. 'Was that the last of the filming?' she asked finally.

'My last scene, at least. More or less, anyway. Herwin still needs a few atmosphere shots and the like and there'll probably be a retake or two. He's kept me so busy I haven't had a chance to see you.'

She shrugged. 'That's all right.'

'Is it? José told me about the irrigation line breaking. After the fuss over Calvin and your grandmother, that break must have been the last straw for you. I can't force my father to leave Theda alone, but I can help with the pipe. Get the line fixed and, whatever the cost, I'll pay for it.'

Carole stared at him, not believing her ears. 'As a loan?' she managed to ask.

'Hell, no. As a gift. God knows Horizon leased the ranch cheap enough. It's the least I can do.'

Pulling herself together, she said, 'I can't take your money.'

'Don't be a twit. Of course you can. It comes without strings.'

'I *won't* take it.'

He smiled one-sidedly. 'Won't you? Then I'll make the same offer to Theda while incidentally letting her know you're short of money for the ranch.'

'You wouldn't!'

His gaze was level. 'Try me.'

'Why can't you understand I don't want your money?'

'Or any other part of me?'

Carole flushed. 'If you're referring to the White Knight –'

'Hell, I'm trying to *be* one. But, since you brought it up, I recall that we spent a night there in rare and perfect harmony. Not to mention a number of other interesting –'

'Will you shut up!' she cried and kicked the mare into a lope with Jerrold in pursuit. How dared he offer her money and then, in the same breath, bring up the night they spent in each other's arms? How could he?

Sombrita and the palomino reached the corral neck and neck. He flung himself off his horse, dragged her from the saddle and held her by the shoulders.

'Just what the bloody hell is the matter with you?' he demanded.

'You make me feel like a – a call girl.' Her voice quivered.

His look was incredulous. 'You can't mean my offer to replace an irrigation line.' He rolled his eyes. 'Of all the convoluted reasoners in the world, you get the Oscar. Do you really see me as the kind of man who'd try to pay you off for a night of love by buying irrigation piping, of all things?'

Jerrold's outrage made it clear to Carole that she'd overreacted. She'd been insultingly wrong about what he'd meant. But she refused to apologize. 'Whatever the reason,' she said stiffly, 'I can't take money from you.'

'You're bloody well going to. One way or another.' He glanced toward the house.

'Theda's not home,' she said hastily.

'We'll see. Come along.' Taking her hand, he pulled her with him toward the house.

'The horses aren't tethered,' she protested.

He didn't miss a step. 'The palomino's trained to stay where he's left and Sombrita's at her home corral so I don't think she'll go far.'

Carole was torn between wishing Theda wouldn't be there and the hope that she'd returned. Because if she hadn't, where was she?

Wanting to avoid Lollie in the kitchen, Carole led Jerrold to the music-room entrance. Once inside, it became quickly clear that neither Calvin nor Theda were in the house. Lollie, when asked, said Theda hadn't called.

'When will your grandmother be back?' Jerrold asked as they stood facing one another in the living room.

'I don't know,' Carole confessed. 'She and Calvin supposedly went out to dinner and a movie last night, leaving me a message not to wait up. I didn't. Neither of them came home. Do you have any idea where they might have gone?'

Jerrold shook his head and groaned. 'They've taken off for parts unknown again?'

'Theda said you dragged – her very word – your father off someplace and talked to him yesterday,' she said. 'Did he tell you anything?'

'The usual promises. I don't believe a one. Not any more. He didn't mention planning any trips. But then the devious old sod wouldn't.' He leaned against the mantel. 'I don't like this.'

'They ought to be back soon because my grandmother's planning a party for the film crew next week and she hadn't finished all the details. It's not at all like her to go off leaving things undone. Theda's parties are always perfect.' Carole chewed her lip. 'Do you suppose they could have had an accident?'

'We would have heard. I'm sure they're all right. I blame Calvin. He's persuaded her again, that's his specialty, and who knows into what this time.'

'I don't think they've eloped, if that's what you mean. Theda hasn't given up the idea of getting married at home – she told me she really wanted to.'

'He's never before married any of them,' Jerrold said. 'I thought this time might be different but now I'm not so sure. I'll believe in the marriage when I see the certificate and not before.'

Carole was taken aback. 'What do you mean? Who are all these women Calvin never married? And why didn't you mention them to me before?'

'I told you I thought he might mean it this time. Besides, you were upset enough already.'

'You still haven't explained.'

Jerrold stepped away from the mantel. 'My parents weren't happy together, even though they remained married until my mother died. My father told me time and time again that once was enough, why let yourself in for hell twice. I understand what he means well enough. Marriage seems to bring out the worst in people.'

'I don't agree at all,' she said indignantly. 'My grandparents and my parents were happy together. And you still haven't answered my question about your father's other women.'

Jerrold grimaced. 'My father really enjoys the company of women so I can't prove he does it deliberately, but the ones he manages to ingratiate himself with always have money. Money they share with him. I've told you why money and

Calvin are a fatal combination. Anyway, there've been a series of wealthy widows interested in my father and he's never married any of them.'

'My grandmother isn't wealthy.'

'That's why I thought this time might be the charm. Remember, though, your grandmother does have her trust fund. And the ranch.'

Carole couldn't deny that. 'Does Calvin promise to marry each of his conquests?' How she hated to think of her grandmother as a 'conquest'!

Jerrold frowned. 'If he did, I never knew it. They may have assumed he would, but this is the first time the word "marry" has been mentioned by my father. Whether he means it or not is another matter.'

'You mean he's – well, seduced my grandmother with no intention of marrying her?'

'Come on, Carole, they're in their sixties and your grandmother isn't a virginal spinster, she's been married before. Seduce is hardly the right word.'

'But she's so trusting. She's fallen in love with Calvin and she'd believe anything he told her.'

'Unlike you.'

'Yes, unlike me.'

'The trouble with you is you don't believe anything I tell you. I think I've cleared things up between us only to find I'm back where I started.' Jerrold's dark gaze held hers. 'If I were Rich, you'd believe me. Why can't you trust me?'

'I grew up with Rich, that makes it different.' And I'm not in love with him, she could have added, but didn't. 'He called me last night, by the way, heartsick because he knows Marla will be dropping him.'

Jerrold waved Rich and Marla away. He took two steps toward Carole and put his hands on her shoulders. 'We're talking about you and me.'

Yes, she thought, but we sure as hell aren't talking permanence. Not once have you even hinted at that.

'You told me you weren't into overnight affairs,' he said. 'I don't want what's between us to be one.'

'What *do* you want?' She stared into his eyes, her pulses hammering because he was touching her.

'I want you to be happy.'

You make me happy, she thought, knowing full well he also made her miserable. 'Happy?' she echoed, hearing the edge to her voice. 'What's happy?'

He pulled her into his arms. 'For me it's holding you. Making love with you.'

How long will that make you happy? she wondered as her heartbeat tripled and her breathing increased in response to being in his arms. For however long it lasted – a week, a month, a year – she couldn't deny that she wanted Jerrold to hold her and to make love with her.

'I saw the farewell scene being filmed,' she confessed, looking into his eyes, 'and I felt you weren't Joaquin Murieta at all, you were Jerrold, saying goodbye to me.'

'I don't want to even think about saying goodbye to you, love,' he murmured before his lips came down on hers.

Lost in the magic Jerrold's kiss created, she didn't hear the door open, she didn't realize anyone had come in until her grandmother spoke.

'Oh, look, Calvin, they've made up. How nice.'

Carole and Jerrold sprang apart.

Theda and Calvin stood in the archway, smiling at them.

'Should we tell them now?' Calvin asked Theda. She gave him a melting look and nodded.

'I hope we didn't worry you by not coming home last night,' Calvin said, 'but we thought we deserved a short honeymoon. You see, after we left you at the White Knight the other day, we stopped and got married on our way back here.'

'It was my idea,' Theda put in.

'But you said you wanted to be married at home,' Carole protested when she'd recovered enough to speak. 'I was hoping to be a part of the ceremony.'

Theda smiled at her. 'I did. I still do. We'll

have a proper wedding here soon. But I didn't want to wait.' To Carole's surprise, her grandmother blushed.

Calvin chuckled and put an arm around her. 'Theda's an old-fashioned gal,' he said. 'When it came right down to the nitty-gritty, she couldn't bring herself to have an affair. So what could I do but make it legal?'

'I suppose it *is* legal,' Jerrold said.

'The sovereign state of Nevada says so,' Calvin assured him.

Tears pricked Carole's eyes and she wasn't certain certain if they were from happiness or sorrow. Whether she was for or against it, her grandmother was really married to Calvin. Making up her mind she'd do her best to be happy for them, she crossed to the newlyweds, first hugging her grandmother, then Calvin.

'This calls for a toast.' Jerrold's voice revealed nothing about how he felt, Though he smiled, his eyes remained guarded. He neither hugged Theda nor shook his father's hand.

'There's a bottle of Mumms in the fridge just waiting for this moment,' Calvin said.

The champagne was brought in by Lollie who was persuaded to stay and share the toast. Calvin popped open the bottle and poured the wine into flutes.

'Here's to love,' Jerrold said, raising his glass.

'Hope you find it, my boy,' Calvin said. 'It's a blooming glory, that's what.'

When everyone had taken a sip, Lollie blurted out, 'I knew you two came back married from Las Vegas that second time, it was writ as big as life over the both of you. Good luck, that's what I wish you.'

Calvin, his eyes twinkling, grinned at her. 'My son thinks I trust too much to luck as it is. But thank you, I'll take all the luck anyone offers. I want you all to know the luckiest thing that ever did happen to me was meeting my beautiful Theda.'

Lollie beamed at them and, glass in hand, retreated to the kitchen.

'May you live happily ever after,' Carole said.

Theda's eyes misted. 'How sweet of you, dear. I know we will.'

No one could look any happier than her grandmother did, Carole thought. Unless it was Calvin. But, as she sipped her champagne, doubts fizzed back into her mind.

Why shouldn't Calvin look happy? He not only had Theda as his wife, but might well be anticipating being allowed access to her trust fund. And, with his powers of persuasion, plus the fact Theda seemed bedazzled by love, it could possibly be only a matter of time before he'd be able to put the ranch up for sale. Hadn't he already warned everyone he was no rancher?

After all these years it would break her heart to have Harte's Way go to strangers. It hurt almost more than she could bear to even think about that possibility. Nothing in her life had ever meant more to her than Harte's Way.

Except Jerrold. But she'd soon be losing him as well.

'Cheer up, it's not the end of the world.' Jerrold's whisper tickled her ear.

'It may be the end of my world,' she murmured.

'Why don't we all go out and celebrate?' Jerrold asked, focusing on Theda and his father.

'How thoughtful,' Theda replied. 'I'm glad to see you've decided to change your attitude toward your father. But we'll have to say no for tonight, won't we, dear?' She turned to Calvin for confirmation.

He nodded. 'We'll take a raincheck, as they say over here. You young folks go out and celebrate for us. Tonight Theda and I plan a quiet supper by the fire and, afterward, early to bed.' His fond gaze sought Theda's.

Jerrold glanced at Carole, but she almost immediately looked away from him. Not wanting to discuss any plans for the evening in front of the newlyweds, he took her arm and gently urged her toward the room they'd entered through.

'I didn't have a chance to examine that lovely old piano when we passed by it,' he said. 'May I?'

After she accompanied him into the music room, he made a show of lifting the lid and fingering a key or two. The clear sweetness of the tone caught his interest and he began to genuinely explore the instrument, finding it in perfect tune.

'Who plays?' he asked.

'No one,' she said. 'We do keep it tuned, though, in memory of my grandfather's brother who was the real Harte musician. He was killed in World War Two.'

'A shame not to use such a beautiful instrument. The piano was made to be played.'

Her smile was impish. 'But not by those with no musical talent – like Theda and me. Maybe the piano's been waiting all these years for you Telfords to come along.'

He slanted her a mock frown. 'Calvin's been telling tales, hasn't he?'

She stroked the smooth rosewood of the piano's hinged top, relishing its cool, satiny feel. 'Will you play for me?' she asked softly.

He hesitated, then shook his head. 'The time's not right. Sorry.'

Will the time ever be right? she wondered.

Her expression must have showed more than she realized because he covered her hand with his. 'I want to play for you and I promise I will. But not now. I'm not sure I can explain.'

The truth was his reluctance to play lay in his roiled mood. Any attempt at an explanation would bog him down in his mixed, but mostly negative, feelings about his father's marriage. If only he could believe the old sod had reformed.

With regret and reverence, he closed the piano lid. 'I've got to get this –' he touched the silver ornaments of his black jacket – 'back to costumes before they come looking for me. I think they've fallen in love with my Californio outfit.'

Or maybe the man wearing it, she thought. Like me.

'I wouldn't want to interrupt Theda's quiet evening at home,' he said. 'I imagine you'll feel like a third wheel, too. Care to celebrate with me later?'

Carole bit her lip. 'To tell the truth, I don't feel much like celebrating. I don't mean I'm not happy for them but – oh, I don't know.'

He nodded. 'Don't try to explain. I understand. We both have some reservations. So, no celebration tonight. But how about sharing a pizza with me at Hubbard's Corners?'

'I'd like to get out of the house so they can be private,' she admitted. 'Thanks.'

'See you later, then.' He let himself out the side entrance and headed for the palomino, still standing exactly where he'd left him. José was unsaddling the mare.

'Theda and my father got married in Las Vegas,' he told José. 'They just told us.'

José nodded. 'Me, I see how they look at each other and I tell myself they marry quick.' He smiled slyly. 'Maybe you take after your father, *no es verdad?*'

It was definitely *not* true that he took after his

father in any way, shape or form, but Jerrold managed a smile for José and said lightly, 'You never can tell, can you?'

'Me, I can tell,' José assured him. 'Wait and you see.'

CHAPTER 15

Without thinking about it, Carol had expected Jerrold to come by in his Jag and pick her up for their excursion to Hubbard's Corners. She was in the kitchen talking to Lollie when someone tapped on the back door.

'I'll get it,' she said. To her surprise Jerrold was there.

He greeted Lollie, then smiled ruefully at Carole and said, 'I'll have to hitch a ride in your pickup. Shredded tires, two of them, after an unexpected confrontation with a jagged chunk of steel. I'll have to pick up two new tires before I can drive the Jag. So I rode the palomino over. José said he'd put him in the corral.'

After commiserating with him, she took in his wide-brimmed hat, jeans, shirt and boots and said, 'Genuine cowboy?' As usual, he looked drop-dead handsome.

'Smile when you say that, ma'am,' he told her. 'What you see is a genuine Aussie ringer.'

She grinned. 'You'll knock 'em dead in Hubbard's Corners. Since you came in this way, we'll scoot out the same door and leave our elders to their own devices.'

'If she asks, I'll tell your grandma you left, the both of you,' Lollie offered.

Since the pickup was hers, Carole assumed she'd drive, and did. Glancing at him as they sped along, she noticed that his clothes, though not excessively worn, were obviously not new. 'Working outfit?' she asked.

He nodded. 'Like I said – genuine Aussie. Haven't worn it in quite a few years. Brought the stuff along when I knew we were going to film on a working ranch – just in case.'

'Just in case what?'

'On the off chance I'd be escorting the farmer's beautiful daughter to Hubbard's Corners.'

'Yeah, sure. Really – why?'

He hesitated so long she began to wonder if he intended to answer. 'I miss ranching,' he said finally. And tersely.

'Why? Ranching's nowhere near as glamorous as being an actor.'

He shrugged. 'Glamorous is nowhere near as much of a high as people seem to think. I prefer ranching.'

Sure he did, she told herself dubiously.

Shortly before the last turn for the village, Carole noticed a sign by a graveled drive and pulled over on to the shoulder. 'Should we take a chance?' she asked, wondering if this was a good idea.

He read the crudely printed sign aloud: 'Benefit Barbecue. All welcome. Proceeds go to Hubbard's Corners High School marching band for trip to State contest.'

He smiled at her. 'Obviously a good cause. I'm game if you are.'

Carole swung the truck into the drive. 'These local barbecues are usually pretty good. The menu, besides the meat, will be beans, salad, rolls and an assortment of baked goodies for dessert – all homemade. The company's congenial with, I admit, a tendency to occasional rowdiness.'

'Sounds like my kind of do,' he said.

The cooking was going on under the sycamores down by a small creek with the rest of the food serve-yourself cafeteria-style. Picnic tables were set up under tiny lights strung from branch to branch.

'Almost like where I come from,' he said. 'Except down there it's not so often beef as it is mutton and lamb.'

Two other couples sat at their table and everybody introduced themselves by first names. Maybe because Jerrold told them he was 'Jerry', he wasn't recognized, which seemed to please him.

After they ate, a guy began playing a guitar and everybody started singing. Jerrold joined in

with enthusiasm, so obviously enjoying himself
that Carole couldn't help but have a good time.
Why had she worried that Jerrold would be
bored or that he might not fit in?

Hours later, they finally left in a chorus of
friendly goodbyes and, by the time they reached
the ranch, it was close to midnight. Carole
parked the pickup and they got out.

'Do I walk you to the door like a gentleman?'
he asked, 'Or do you, as a perfect hostess, see me
to my horse?'

How did he know she didn't want to invite
him into what had become, at least temporarily,
Theda's and Calvin's honeymoon house? Or
maybe he didn't want to linger.

'I'll choose the latter,' she said. 'It's better if I
get the palomino from the corral; the other
horses know me and you're a stranger.'

Once the horse was out, she helped him saddle
the gelding. 'All set,' she said as they finished.

'He is, but I'm not,' Jerrold told her. 'I'm not
ready to end this perfect evening.' He looked up
at the star-studded sky and the lopsided moon
half-hidden by a scudding cloud. 'Why don't we
saddle Sombrita and go for a moonlight ride?'

The idea struck Carole as incredibly romantic.

Once mounted, they let the horses set the
pace, drifting through the cool darkness silvered by the moon. Eventually they climbed
her favorite hill. At the top, Jerrold again

sought the lee side. Dismounting, he plucked a blanket from a saddle bag, spread it over the ground and waited, his arms held out, to catch Carole as she slid off Sombrita. When she was safely on the ground, he tethered the mare.

Pulling Carole down on to the blanket with him, he murmured, 'I like to finish what I start. Where were we when we interrupted our picnic the other day?'

She poked him playfully in the ribs. 'You planned this in advance – blanket and all. And you call women devious!'

'You wound me,' he said, laying a hand over his heart. 'I swear this was as spontaneous as the barbecue. You have to understand it's the palomino's duty to be prepared for anything and everything. Stunt horses always are.'

'So you're blaming this on the poor horse.'

He ran his fingers along her cheek and over her lips. 'Does it really matter what brought you into my arms?'

As always, his touch melted her. She was exactly where she wanted to be, where she'd longed to be ever since Las Vegas – no, since the first time he'd kissed her. With a sigh, she gave herself up to love.

Feeling her relax into his embrace, Jerrold drew a ragged breath, pulses pounding, as aroused as he could possibly be. For the time being, at least, she was his again, her incredible sweetness his to explore, her passion his to savor. He'd hungered for her from the beginning and after the night in Vegas; his need for her had become a permanent ache.

Now that he knew how memorable making love with her could be, anticipation heightened his desire. No other woman could ever satisfy him the way she did. He needed her so intensely, he had to have her. Now. Tomorrow. The next day and the next. How was he supposed to say goodbye to the best thing that had ever happened to him?

The depth of his feeling for her frightened him – but marriage was out. For him, the emphasis had been on the 'lock' in wedlock. He'd felt trapped and he could see now that Linda must have felt the same way. If marriage hadn't worked the first time and he was still the same man, how could he expect it to work the second time around?

As for love, the very idea of the word gave him the willies. When it came right down to it, wasn't love as make-believe as the movies?

But he was wasting precious minutes when the woman he wanted at this moment was in his arms. He covered her mouth with his, tasting the essence that was Carole, honey-sweet, compelling and enticing. She opened to him, her eager response driving his need into the upper register.

How soft she was, how smooth her skin. Her rounded breasts filled his hands and, when he'd bared them to his caresses, her engorged nipples and her little gasping moans told him she was as far gone as he was.

He wanted to prolong their pleasure, to touch her everywhere, wanted to feel her caress him and he did his best to go slow, enjoying every second as his need became more and more urgent.

When she whispered, 'Please, Jerrold, oh, please,' his control vanished. Unable to wait any longer, he slid inside her welcoming warmth and lost all track of time and place. He was where he belonged. Making love with Carole.

They reached the top together and spiralled down. Still he held her, reluctant to let her go. He never wanted to let her go.

Carole nestled in Jerrold's arms, content, feeling her entire world had compressed into this small space with him. She'd never known loving someone could be so wonderful. No, not someone. Because he was Jerrold, it was wonderful. If only they could hold each other forever.

The chill of the night breeze separated them at last. She dressed hurriedly, as he did, then snuggled close while he wrapped the edges of the blanket around them.

'Promise me you won't put yourself in danger again,' he said. 'I knew you hadn't told me the whole story of that escapade with Sawa so I checked out your "Alcatraz" in daylight. While I was there, a few big rocks slid down from above – luckily not anywhere near me. It's obvious what I saw wasn't the first rock slide in that formation, it's a dangerous spot.'

'Yes, you're right and I'm aware of the danger,' she said, her post-glow trance evaporating as she recalled how frightened she'd been.

He gave her a hug. 'Good.'

Whether he took her words for a promise, she wasn't sure. But actually she hadn't given him one, nor did she intend to. With the ranch in perilous financial seas and the lure of hidden treasure, how could she say she'd never go near the place again?

As if reading her mind, he said, 'You haven't got some goose-witted notion the bandit gold is in those rocks, have you?'

'It might be,' she said honestly. 'I think a couple of guys from Horizon have been searching there, among other places.'

'Herwin read the entire crew the riot act about that. Said there'd be no more searching for a gold cache, it was only a legend and digging up private property was illegal. You have any idea who the men were?'

'I'm pretty sure it's Alex, that guy with the bald head and the compensating mustache, along with a friend of his, age and looks unknown.'

'Maybe I'll have a little chat with Alex. Keep me posted. I won't have anyone bothering you.'

His tone was grim, giving her a tiny thrill because he wanted to protect her.

Not that she needed protection. As he'd pointed out, Alcatraz was a natural site for rock falls. She was probably totally wrong in believing the one she'd experienced had been man-made.

'I'd better get you home,' he said at last. 'Otherwise I'll have your clothes off again and we'll be here until sunrise and quite possibly wind up with pneumonia. I expect the wind machines to pop on any moment.'

It *was* getting cold, but how she wished they could stay together for what was left of the night. Knowing that was impractical, Carole rose reluctantly, helped Jerrold fold the blanket and watched him stow it in the palomino's saddle bag. Would she ever get enough of looking at him?

Back at the ranch, he waited while she unsaddled and took care of Sombrita, then walked her to her door despite her protest.

'Nothing will happen to me between the corral and the house,' she insisted.

'Maybe I want to be with you as long as possible – ever consider that?' he asked.

As long as possible. One of Carole's old songs spoke of the days growing short – and they were. All too soon he'd be gone.

His kiss at the door was tender and sweet and

lingering. Finally he broke it off and all but shoved her inside, saying, 'Never met anyone so difficult to part from, love. I don't want to leave you.'

She carried his kiss and his words to bed with her.

Wonder of wonders, in the morning Theda was up before she was. Not only that, but one of Carole's friends, Kitty Knowles, had arrived and was in the den addressing envelopes for Theda. Of course it *was* after nine. She hadn't slept this late in ages.

'Your grandmother said you were too busy with ranch work to help plan her party,' Kitty said. 'I know that's true, so I volunteered.'

Not until she was drinking her first cup of coffee in the kitchen did Carole realize that she hadn't heard Kitty giggle once. Usually a giggle punctuated every third word. Curious, she drifted back into the den.

'I'm glad Theda found someone to help her,' she told Kitty. 'I really hate doing stuff like this. But I thought you had a full-time job.'

'I do, but I'm on vacation at the moment and too broke to go anywhere, as usual.'

Not once did Kitty giggle. Nor did she rattle on, as she was inclined to do. She stamped another envelope, then paused and looked at Carole.

'I guess you noticed,' she said. 'I hoped you

would. It's all your grandmother's doing. At her last party she took me aside and explained what I was doing wrong. I guess she'd noticed how guys shied away from me. She told me jabbering and giggling were both nervous habits used to cover up shyness. She said she knew 'cause she had to overcome giggling herself when she first went to Hollywood. Just think, she was only sixteen! Anyway, she told me her secret way of changing a bad habit.' Kitty touched her silver concho belt.

'What you do is glue or tape a blunt pin of some kind to the inside of your belt or waistband, one long enough so you feel a prick when you press against the spot with your hand or arm but short enough not to jab you otherwise. When you feel extra-nervous, you press that spot and the pin-prick reminds you not to giggle. At that moment you have to turn to the nearest person and ask them a question so they'll talk and not you. It really works!'

Recovering from her amazement at her grandmother's thoughtfulness, Carole said, 'Good for you.'

Kitty grinned at her. 'So now all I have to do is meet some new guys who didn't know me when I giggled.'

'Maybe some of the ones you already know will notice you've stopped. I certainly did.'

'Girls always pick up on things quicker than guys,' Kitty said. 'Anyway, I'm not Marla Thurlow.'

Thinking that was an odd remark, Carole said, 'Neither am I. She's so drop-dead gorgeous she's out of our class, so why compare yourself to her?'

'Oh, no reason.' Kitty seemed about to giggle but nipped it in the bud. 'Don't you care that Rich trails after Marla like a lovesick calf?'

The penny dropped. Carole had never before guessed Kitty was interested in Rich.

'Rich and I are friends, nothing more,' she said.

'Yeah, I heard through the grapevine you were with Jerrold Telford at the benefit barbecue last night. Lucky girl.'

Talk about news traveling fast! She'd thought it was too good to be true that no one had recognized Jerrold at the barbecue. Obviously somebody had.

Seeing Kitty's avid look and aware she was waiting for details, Carol said, 'He's really not egotistical – I thought all actors would be.' She wasn't ready to share anything else about Jerrold with anyone, so she closed off the discussion. 'Well, I've got to run, I'm way behind this morning. See you later.'

Going in search of Theda to say good morning before she began her ranch duties, Carole found her in the memory room, beginning a new scrapbook.

'This one will be about *Bandido*, dear,' she said when Carole asked her about it.

'I'm glad you have Kitty helping you with the party,' Carole said. 'When I talked to her, though, she didn't mention your marriage. Does she know?'

Theda shook her head. 'Calvin and I have decided to keep it in the family until we have our wedding ceremony here at the ranch. But we are going to drive over to San Francisco for a three-day honeymoon – we'll be leaving by noon. Kitty has promised me she'll see to everything concerning the party so you won't have to lift a finger.'

'I could help, too,' Carole offered, feeling guilty.

'I doubt that's necessary. In fact, I don't think Kitty will have much to do once she finishes the invitations because I've already arranged everything. Lollie is in charge of any problems with the caterers, so that's taken care of as well.'

Theda rose from the longue and embraced Carole. 'I'm so very happy, dear. You have no idea.'

'You look radiant.'

'I am. Poor Calvin, though.' Theda smiled smugly. 'Apparently second marriages are harder on men than on women because he's still sleeping.'

As she walked toward the corral, Carole wondered if Jerrold was still sleeping, too. The mere thought of last night on the hill sent a thrill of memory through her. If only . . .

She quickly buried that thought before it was completed. There wouldn't be any 'if onlys'.

By the time she'd saddled and mounted Sombrita, clouds had covered the sun. Carole peered up at the overcast sky. Was a storm coming? Possibly, but it didn't feel to her like rain was on the way.

Though she told herself firmly she was not going to ride to the hacienda before making her ranch rounds, she found herself heading in that direction. When she got there, no one except Sawa was in sight. Dismounting, she walked over to the where the old woman sat weaving her basket.

'Where is everybody?' she asked.

'The little boss man herd the men off with their horses.' She waved toward the east. 'He say he needs some more shots. Your man, he go but the boss don't want Marla so she go with your rancher friend.' Sawa shook her head. 'He must like punishment.'

'Rich will survive.' At least Carole hoped so. At the moment she wasn't any too sure about herself.

Sawa shrugged. 'Why do they choose the wrong one to go after? It only causes pain.'

Because we can't help ourselves, Carole said silently. 'Have you had any more trouble with Alex?' she asked, changing the subject.

'Me, I don't see him. Maybe he go away from here.'

'I hope so.'

'Me, too. We don't want the ghosts to wake the sleeping giant. That's what they do sometimes when they get upset.'

Carole didn't know anything about this bit of Miwok lore. 'You mentioned that before. What sleeping giant?' she asked curiously.

Sawa looked around and lowered her voice. 'The snakes don't sleep yet.'

Carole knew what she meant because Sawa had told her the Miwok weren't supposed to tell the old stories until winter, when the snakes slept. 'But didn't you say the snakes only objected to creation stories told in the wrong season?' she asked.

Sawa put a cautionary finger to her lips and shot another quick look around. She leaned closer to Carole and whispered, 'You are right. But we have meddled in a bad place and maybe disturbed the snakes as well as the ghosts. I tell you this much, the giant sleeps under the mountains —' She gestured toward the Sierras' snow-capped peaks. 'When he wakes, the ground trembles. That's bad.'

Did Sawa mean an earthquake? About to ask, she held back, aware she'd upset her friend enough. 'I'd better get going,' she said instead. 'I'm already a couple of hours behind with the chores today.'

'Work can be good,' Sawa said in her normal tone of voice. 'Too much work is always bad.'

'So everyone keeps telling me. Maybe if I could afford a new irrigation system –' Carole broke off and sighed. 'Might as well ask for the moon.'

'Too much work means you don't get enough moon.' Sawa sounded amused.

Carole blinked, confused for a moment before she realized Sawa was teasing her and meant moonlight. Like last night. Love under the moon . . .

Freeing herself from her reminiscent trance, she mounted her mare, waved to Sawa and rode off. Determined not to relive last night's love-making, she forced her thoughts back to financial problems. No way would she touch a penny of Jerrold's! Maybe if he'd offered her a loan – but he hadn't. He'd wanted to give her the money and that was totally unacceptable. Especially after last night. She had to find another way.

Before she realized what she intended, she'd turned Sombrita in the direction of Alcatraz.

'I'll just take a quick look in a few likely places,' she told the mare. 'Very carefully. What harm can it do and I might be lucky, who knows?'

Sombrita snuffled.

'Okay, so you disapprove like all the rest. But I'm sure the gold is hidden somewhere in those rocks. Why shouldn't I have a go at finding it? The gold belongs to the Hartes, after all. Even the ghosts must know that.' Not that she really believed in ghosts.

With Sawa's sleeping-giant superstition pushed to the back of her mind – she was not Miwok, she had no belief in their legends – she continued on to Alcatraz.

When she reached the rugged formation, she left Sombrita tethered at the bottom of the hill and to the left where the mare would be safe from any falling rocks. Aware of this danger, she climbed carefully, keeping a sharp eye out for any movement that might signal a rock slide. But it hadn't rained for several days so she figured the likelihood of slides was reduced.

Once she reached the relatively level space where she'd found Sawa's snake stick, she eyed the crevices, trying to pick out the one she'd crawled into and found Sawa. Was it coincidence that Sawa had chosen that particular opening to hide in? Expedience, maybe, since it might have been the nearest to where she fell. Or was pushed. Or whatever had happened. Sawa had said that she sensed the ghosts all around them. Did that mean the gold was hidden farther along the tunnel-like crevice?

Carole shook her head. If ghosts didn't exist, why put any faith in Sawa's words? And yet, something had caused Sawa to pick that one opening.

Recalling Alex and his buddy, Carole scanned the areas above her, then checked all around. No

292

one was in sight; she heard nothing more than bird calls from the trees below and the distant hum of an invisible jet high above the overcast. Apparently Alex and friend had either been scared off by Herwin's orders or given up. Either way, she was alone. Good.

When she thought she'd located the crevice Sawa had crawled into, Carole hesitated, remembering how uncomfortable she'd felt being closed into that cramped space. Like being under Hoover Dam. Not exactly claustrophobic, but near enough to cause uneasiness.

She didn't have to go in there, she could turn around, remount Sombrita and get on with the day's business. Except she'd still be confronted with inadequate finances.

Don't be such a coward, she admonished herself. You've come this far, be brave enough to explore at least this one crevice.

After a last sweep of her surroundings, she crouched and edged her way into the dark opening, flicking on the small flashlight she always carried in her jacket pocket. No sign of snakes, at least. In cold weather they did crawl, sometimes *en masse*, into rocky holes to keep warm. It was, though, still a bit early for them to hole up and, besides, the weather had been quite warm for this time of year.

The thought of snakes, though, slowed her almost to a standstill and she had to forcing herself to keep crawling farther and farther inside. The hair on her nape began to prickle but the flashlight's meager glow showed nothing to alarm her. And no sign of anything but rock ahead. No glint of gold, no cloth bags or leather pouches that might contain gold.

Attracted by a streak of light a few feet in front of her, she soon realized that it was only a tiny opening in the rocks, allowing daylight to seep in. Beyond, though, what was that bulky mass? Not rock. Maybe she wasn't on a fool's errand, after all.

But, as she inched forward, her sense of wrongness increased. Just before she reached the light streak, it winked out, bringing her to an abrupt halt. What had happened? Though she didn't feel hot, perspiration coated her face and she began to shudder. It took her a few seconds to realize that she was not the one shaking – the rock all around her was. She heard an ominous rumble.

When the giant wakes, the ground trembles. Sawa's words echoed in Carole's ears as she began to back up on her hands and knees, not taking the time to turn around. Her mind focused on one thought – get out before it's too late!

CHAPTER 16

After the tremor – a small shake to anyone who lived in the LA area, Herwin had commented – he'd called a halt to the day's filming. 'No point in taking chances,' he'd said. 'They tend to come in pairs, that's been my experience, and the second one's sometimes worse.'

Jerrold, returning from the shoot, pulled the palomino up short when Sawa stepped into his path, her hand upraised.

'Find her,' she ordered.

Apprehension tensed him. 'What's wrong?' he demanded, knowing she meant Carole.

'The giant woke. Me, I think maybe she went to the bad place and that's why he woke.'

'Giant?' he repeated.

'The shaking,' she said impatiently.

'Oh, the earthquake. But why would you –?' He broke off and rephrased his question. 'Did Carole say she was headed for Alcatraz?'

'She say the ranch needs money she don't have.'

Money to fix that broken irrigation line? Money for the mortgage payment? To be paid for with bandit gold? He shook his head in disbelief. Carole couldn't have gone looking for the hidden gold, not after she'd promised him she wouldn't set foot on what she called Alcatraz again. Or had she promised? Thinking back, he wasn't sure.

'Damn the woman,' he muttered, wheeling the palomino and pounding off.

Sawa called something after him but all he heard of it was '. . . José . . .' Was José with Carole? Not likely. Dismissing whatever she'd said from his mind, he turned the horse toward Alcatraz.

The tremor had been a mild one, but that bloody place was nothing but unstable rocks. Was she out of her mind? She'd refused his offer to pay to have a new irrigation line put in; apparently she'd rather risk her neck than accept anything from him. Clenching his jaw, he urged the palomino on.

Call girl, she'd said. What in hell had he ever done to give her the impression he was treating her like a call girl? Of all the stubborn females he'd ever met, she got the prize.

He wouldn't allow himself to imagine anything had happened to her during the bloody quake. Hadn't lasted but a few seconds, not long enough nor intense enough to do any damage. A few rocks might have fallen, but she'd be all right. Unharmed. He needed to believe that and he hoped to hell the tremor had scared her enough to keep her from ever going there again.

Jerrold didn't think Herwin was necessarily an expert on earthquakes, but the director's words about one quake following another disturbed him. Sawa could be wrong, he told himself. Carole might not have gone near Alcatraz. But in his heart he feared she'd done exactly that.

The buzzing roar of a motor bike caught his attention. Looking to his right, he saw the bike, carrying two riders, heading toward him. He recognized Alex by the red bandana he always wore and he was almost positive the bike must be coming from Alcatraz. He slowed the horse, yanked the silver ornamented pistol from his holster and fired into a air. A blank, of course, which Alex would know, but the sound should attract Alex's attention and maybe he'd take it as a signal to stop.

The bike slowed, sputtering. 'What d'you want?' Alex called to him. Jerrold recognized the other man, but couldn't recall his name.

'I know you were on that damn pile of rocks,' he accused. 'Is she there?'

'Didn't see nobody,' Alex said.

'There's a horse tied up,' the second rider put in, earning a glare from Alex.

The bloody bastards. Anger mingling with his apprehension, Jerrold pounded on. He'd get to

Alex and his buddy later. Carole needed him now.

Inside the crevice, Carole, still on her hands and knees, backed as rapidly as she could toward the entrance, choking on the dust filtering into the tunnel. Though the dreadful roar and crash of rocks over her head had diminished to a rattle of stones, she continued to fight against increasing panic.

Once I get out of here, she vowed, I'll never crawl into anything like this again. Ever.

Her foot struck an obstruction. She kicked at it but it didn't move. Something blocked her way, she couldn't get out. At the same time, the light from her tiny flash dimmed perceptibly. The batteries were going, she'd soon be in darkness. Trapped in darkness. Panic clogged her throat, preventing her involuntary scream from escaping.

If you don't control yourself you'll die in here, a tiny rational part of her brain told her. Forcing herself to take several deep breaths, she let them out slowly. What could she do to help herself?

First of all she had to get turned around. Gathering herself into a crouch, with difficulty she turned in the tight space until she was facing the obstruction. The fading beam showed what she already knew must be clogging the way out. Rocks. The quake had caused a rock fall, a bad one this time, and the top of the tunnel had been smashed in. She was doomed.

* * *

298

When he saw Sombrita tethered at the foot of the hill, Jerrold flung himself off the palomino and climbed rapidly up toward the jumble of rocks. He tried to keep himself from admitting that the contours of Alcatraz looked different than they had when he'd visited the place before, telling himself he might be wrong.

Finding no sign of Carole, he began shouting her name. When she didn't answer, his chest grew heavy with dread. Where was she? If anything had happened to her . . .

Falling apart wouldn't help. He must find her! Warning himself against his impulse to rush around shouting, he began to wind methodically among the tumbled rocks, pausing every few seconds to call her name, hoping against hope to hear her respond.

The flashlight winked out, the batteries shot. Trapped in the dark, Carol's control all but disintegrated completely. She'd begun to whimper when she thought she heard someone shouting very far away. Was it her name? Or was she only imagining she heard something?

She tried to call out but choked on the dust instead. Frantically clearing her throat and swallowing, she managed a tiny, hoarse, 'Here.' Her next attempt emerged louder and stronger. 'Here. Here I am!'

The voice outside came closer, now calling, 'Where? Keep talking.'

She shouted until she began to cough. When the spasm passed, the voice had moved to overhead and she recognized it. 'Jerrold!' she cried. 'Help me. I can't get out. Rocks are in my way.'

The clatter over her head told her that he'd started to roll the rocks away. Time passed, the clatter continued but her path was still blocked. 'Hurry,' she begged. The word seemed incredibly hard to get out as breathing itself became more difficult.

Jerrold stared at the huge pile of rocks with dismay. No matter how fast he worked, no matter how many he moved, the heap didn't diminish perceptibly. He had to get Carole out, he would get her out, but would he be in time? Every time she spoke, she sounded weaker.

A shout from the bottom of the hill made him pause momentarily to glance in that direction. To his surprise, Alex and his buddy were climbing toward him. He couldn't believe they'd come back to help until he saw José behind them with a shotgun, herding them upward.

'Me, I track them,' José said. 'Where is she?'

'We have to move this rock pile to get her out,' Jerrold said. 'Pronto. She's stopped talking.'

José nodded at the two men. 'Begin,' he ordered. 'If she lives, you live.' Cradling the gun under one arm, he stood back watchfully.

Jerrold approved. José was getting on and two young men could work more than twice as fast as

300

one old guy, especially under pressure. With three of them tossing rocks aside, the pile went down rapidly until at last they had to reach inside an opening to pick up the rocks.

Jerrold paused. 'Carole!' he called. 'Are you okay?' His heart sank when she didn't answer.

It seemed to take forever for the three of them to lift out enough rocks so that he could let himself down into the opening. Crouching, he peered into the tunnel. She lay huddled no more than a foot away but the space was too confined to let him reach for her.

'Carole,' he said urgently. 'Wake up! We've moved the rocks, now you have to help me. You have to help yourself. Carole! Hear me!'

Jerrold's voice came from a great distance. She knew he was urging her to help him, but it was too great an effort to move. If he'd stop calling her, she could slip back into the drifting nothingness. But he persisted until she decided she had to open her eyes.

Terror rushed in as she gaped at rock walls. Where was she? In the light that filtered in dimly from above and ahead of her, she saw a man's legs. He was standing on a small heap of rocks. 'Jerrold?' she quavered.

'Thank God!' he cried. 'Carole, can you move?'

She moved an arm experimentally. Her legs also worked, as best she could tell in the cramped space. If only she didn't feel so weak. 'I think so,' she told him.

'Good. I'm going to climb out. You follow me.'

She watched his legs disappear from view, then inched her way toward where he'd been standing. Supporting herself by bracing her hands against the rock walls, she slowly man-euvered herself on to her trembling legs, her head poking through the roof opening.

Jerrold's strong arms reached down and hauled her free of the tunnel, then held her against him. Hardly able to stand, she leaned her entire weight on him. Looking dazedly around, she blinked. Alex and his friend stood in front of her.

Confused, all she could think of was that she'd grown tired of not knowing the guy's name. Pointing a finger at him, she blurted, 'I know Alex, but who are you?'

'Brad,' he muttered.

Then she saw José with the shotgun and grew more confused than ever. 'What's going on?' she asked Jerrold.

'Never mind, we'll sort it out later,' he told her. 'Do you think you can ride Sombrita home?'

'Yes,' she said, not at all certain she could, but determined to try because she desperately needed to be away from this horrible place. To be home.

Jerrold helped her down the hill and lifted her

on to the mare. She swayed in the saddle momentarily, but regained her balance. 'I'll be okay,' she said.

Looking dubious, he mounted the palomino, never taking his eyes off her.

'What about –?' she began to ask.

'José can handle the other two. Don't worry about anything except getting home.'

So she didn't. Actually, it took all the strength she had left to stay in the saddle. At the corral, Jerrold dismounted and held his arms out. She slid into them and he lifted her, carrying her to the house. She closed her eyes and nestled against him, knowing she was safe.

He carried her directly to her room and laid her gently on to the bed. 'She needs rest,' he told Lollie who had followed them into the room.

Leaning over Carole, he ran his fingers gently along her cheek. 'And a bath – later,' he added.

'I'm thirsty,' she said drowsily. Lollie brought her a glass of water. The last she remembered was Lollie helping her undress and get into her sleep-T.

She woke from a terrible dream of suffocation, sitting up abruptly in bed, her heart pounding. The dim glow of her nightlight showed her where she was, but shreds of the dream clung unpleasantly to her, making her unsure she could believe her eyes. Was she really in her own bed, in her own room?

As she sat on the edge of the bed, she grew aware of various aches and also realized her arms and legs were filthy. Hadn't she been told she needed a bath? Or was that in the dream? She was vaguely aware of holding some unpleasantness at bay as she rose and headed for her shower. With hot water sluicing over her, she discovered that even her hair was dirty and, somehow, that opened the barrier and everything rushed back.

By concentrating on shampooing her hair, she managed to adjust to the knowledge that, through her own foolishness, she'd come very close to killing herself.

Toweling herself dry, she donned a clean nightgown and padded into the living-room, belatedly recalling that Theda and Calvin were gone and so, of course, was Lollie. She was alone. Being in the house by herself at night had never frightened her before, but it did now. She didn't fear an intruder as much as she needed someone to be with her.

As if her thought of an intruder had conjured one up, a dark form rose from the couch to loom over her. She bit back a strangled scream and started a quick retreat.

'It's me,' Jerrold said, turning on a lamp. 'I didn't mean to give you a scare.'

'I'm edgy,' she admitted, considerably relieved.

'I didn't like to think of you being alone after

what happened so I rode over to my trailer for a shower, changed into these sweats and returned before Lollie left.'

He looked as good to her in the gray sweat-suit as he had in the fancy Californio getup. She longed to bury her head against his chest and feel the safety of his arms around her, but pride kept her from moving. She'd already been enough of an idiot for one day.

'You look like you need a spot of comfort,' he said. 'Pretend I'm the elderly uncle you never had and come sit with me on the couch.'

When would she learn to conceal her feelings instead of plastering them all over her face? She let him lead her to the couch where he pulled her down next to him, one arm holding her close. With a sigh, she snuggled against him and closed her eyes. Safe. Protected. She'd never thought she'd ever need to be protected, but now she acknowledged her mistake. There were times . . .

When he felt Carole relax against him, a strange emotion gripped Jerrold, one he wasn't entirely sure he cared to decipher. The sensation had nothing to do with desire, it was more akin to – what? Nurturing was a pop word with the Yanks just now; maybe he'd call it that. Probably only a case of taking care of someone who needed his protection, that might account for his pleasurable glow.

He certainly couldn't call himself a hero. All

he'd done was initiate the search, thanks to Sawa, and he'd found her. José's brilliant idea of forcing Alex and Brad to help free Carole had saved her life – by himself he wouldn't have been able to move the rocks fast enough to get her out in time. At the moment, though, he was here when she needed him.

Carole stirred, distracting him. 'You said you'd tell me what was going on,' she murmured.

'José got his dander up about Alex and Bard searching for the bandit gold,' Jerrold said. 'When he found out Herwin had forbidden any more of it, he collected his shotgun and began watching for them, waiting to catch them in the act. He heard the dirt bike, climbed a hill and spotted them on their way to Alcatraz. He let them stash the bike and grab a pick-axe and shovel they'd cached in the rocks, then made a beeline for Alcatraz.'

'But no one was there when I arrived,' she said.

'Something must have given José away. Anyway, they took off before he got to Alcatraz. On his way there, he heard the dirt bike, changed his course and eventually nabbed them. Before then, he encountered Sawa and told her what he was doing while she shared her worry over you. She told me you'd woken the giant by going to Alcatraz. Whatever that means.'

'Earthquake.' She didn't elaborate.

'Some giant. Anyway, after José corralled those two, he decided he might need their help if you were in trouble because of the quake. A shotgun is a great persuader.'

'Sawa told you I was there?' she asked. 'I wasn't intending to go to Alcatraz when I left her. How did she know?'

Jerrold decided this wasn't the time to go into ranch finances. Nor was it a good time to scold her. She'd been through too much.

As if reading his thoughts, she said, 'I'm lucky to be alive.'

'Very lucky.' His arm tightened around her as he realized how much it mattered to him. He wanted to crush her to him, to kiss her, to make her so irrevocably his that she'd always be with him. Instead, he deliberately loosened his hold and said, 'I think we missed a meal. I'm hungry. How about you?'

'Now that you mention it, yes.' She sat up, away from him.

'Lollie told me she'd left cold chicken for salad or sandwiches.'

'Sounds good to me.'

After she retrieved her robe, they ate in the kitchen. 'It's a good thing Theda wasn't here,' she said when she was halfway though her sandwich. 'She'd be beside herself. She'll be upset anyway, but at least everything is over before she comes home.'

'My offer still stands,' he said.

She blinked at him a moment before nodding in comprehension. 'About the irrigation line, you mean. No gifts, but maybe we could discuss a loan. With interest, of course. I won't hear of anything else.'

'I have a better idea. I'll put a new line in as my wedding present to Theda. You can hardly object to that.'

She frowned, remaining silent. 'I suppose I can't begrudge my grandmother a wedding gift,' she said finally, her tone indicating she didn't think he played fair.

He grinned at her. 'Mark one up for me.'

Carole opened her mouth to respond but was interrupted by someone banging on the back door. 'José?' she muttered as she rose.

Jerrold sprang to his feet. 'Let me answer it.' He didn't think it would be José because he'd talked to him on his return after changing clothes and José had said everything was taken care of.

He was right. It wasn't José. Rich stood at the back door. He didn't seem especially surprised to find Jerrold opening it.

'What on earth are you doing here?' Carole said as Rich accompanied him into the kitchen.

'She's dumped me,' Rich said lugubriously, taking off the new stetson and turning the hat in his hands.

Poor Rich. 'Have a cup of coffee with us,' she invited, gesturing to a chair.

Jerrold raised his eyebrows, but brought another mug and the pot to the table.

Sinking on to a chair, Rich slumped dejectedly. 'I knew it couldn't last but, you know, I hoped it would just the same. She's so beautiful, so wonderful . . .' He sighed.

'Marla's not known for long-term relationships,' Jerrold commented.

'Yeah, well, like Carole said, she's not cut out to be a rancher's wife.'

'Any more than you're cut out to be a groupie,' Jerrold agreed.

'Groupie?' Rich stared at him. 'You mean like those noodle-heads that hang around the rock groups?' He scowled. 'No, not even for her. Hell, no!'

'That's the spirit,' Carole said, forcing brightness into her voice. Jerrold's words had hit her hard. Did he think of *her* as a groupie? The idea made her sick to her stomach.

Still frowning, Rich downed his coffee. 'I feel like a damn fool,' he muttered.

'At least you've stopped bawling like a motherless calf,' Jerrold said drily. 'That's an improvement. Look at it this way – you got picked over the competition, had a fling most guys would die for and now it's over.'

'Over and then some. In a week she'll be off to Hawaii for her next film.'

'Good,' Carole said briskly, putting aside her own heartache in her attempt to prevent Rich

309

from sliding back into the morass of self-pity. 'Marla will be far away from California. As Theda used to tell me, "Out of sight, out of mind."'

Rich shrugged, but she thought he looked a lot less unhappy than when he'd walked into the kitchen. He was her friend and she hated to see him hurting.

He set down his empty mug and rose, for the first time seeming to take in the fact she wore a robe. He glanced from her to Jerrold and back. 'Uh, hope I didn't interrupt anything,' he muttered. 'Sorry. See you around.' He bolted through the kitchen door and vanished.

Carole and Jerrold looked at each other. Neither spoke and the silence grew into a tangible force. Is he wondering if I'll act like Rich when it's time for him to go? she asked herself. Does he think I'll go around weeping on everyone's shoulder?

'I wonder if Marla ever gives the guys she leaves behind a second thought,' Jerrold said at last.

How about you? she was tempted to ask. I can't be your first left-over.

'Why should she?' Carole said tartly. 'According to you, they should be grateful for whatever attention she gave them before she took off.'

He gave her a puzzled glance. 'I thought you liked Marla.'

'I do. I even believe she's honest enough in her own way.'

'So it's my remark you're reacting to. You don't think Rich is grateful?'

'Let's drop it,' she suggested, unwilling to explain her feelings.

He ignored her. 'It must be the word. Grateful does sound a bit smug, although, come to think of it, you used that word first.'

'Much more of this and I'll become ungrateful,' she snapped. Calming herself, she added, 'I never did thank you for rescuing me.'

'José had as much to do with it as I did. Sawa, too. And, to stretch a point, Alex and Brad.'

Thankful to find a legitimate change of subject, she asked, 'What happened to Alex and Brad?'

'José said he turned them over to Herwin and told him what had been going on. I imagine Herwin kicked them off the ranch and will be reporting them to whatever union they belong to.'

'I'm glad no one called the sheriff. They were just a couple of treasure hunters, after all. And they did help move those rocks.'

'Motivated by a loaded shotgun. Don't forget that they saw your horse, but didn't bother to look for you until José caught up with them.'

'They weren't around when I crawled into that – that –' She shuddered and didn't finish.

311

'How do you know they didn't hide and watch you until the quake scared them off?'

Carole blinked. That hadn't occurred to her. Had Alex and Brad been hidden when she got there? Did they know the quake had entombed her and deliberately left her to die? She bit her lip, unwilling to think anyone could be so cold-blooded.

'I dreamed about being suffocated,' she whispered. 'That's what woke me up.'

Jerrold rose, pulled her to her feet and put his arms around her. 'It was a real nightmare,' he agreed grimly, not adding, *for me, too*. Because it had been. The endless time it had taken to move the rocks so he could get to her still haunted him. What if José hadn't come along? He dismissed that thought immediately.

But her ordeal had been far worse than his. Cradling her protectively, he said, 'Do you think you could sleep if I came with you?'

She didn't answer immediately.

Not wanting to be misunderstood, he added, 'Not to make love, just to hold you.' That was an offer he'd never made to any woman before.

'I don't want to be alone tonight.' She spoke so softly he had trouble hearing her.

Taking her words as agreement, he led her toward her bedroom. She slipped off her robe and he caught his breath when the night-light's glow revealed a nightgown of material so thin he could see her curves through it. He'd left his shoes by the couch. Considering his arousal, he didn't dare take off anything else so he crawled under the covers with his sweats still on.

Holding her close, he struggled with two warring impulses. He longed to kiss her, to experience the delicious sense of her warming to his caresses and then feel her passion rouse. Their lovemaking, he knew, would banish the ghosts haunting them both. On the other hand, what she needed from him right now was comfort and the security of being held by someone she trusted.

Wouldn't it be a violation of that trust to seduce her into making love?

CHAPTER 17

In the morning, Carole awoke to the smell of coffee. She stretched, unable for a moment to account for the aches she felt. When she remembered, she realized Jerrold was gone. He must have gotten up sometime earlier without her hearing him because he was no longer in bed with her. She smiled, thinking of how safe she'd felt in his arms, how she'd fallen asleep almost immediately and no bad dreams had troubled her.

A quick check of the clock told her he wasn't responsible for the coffee – Lollie had arrived. She was almost certain he'd taken care to be gone from the house before Lollie got here. It was like him to consider how she might feel about Lollie finding him in her bed.

When she entered the kitchen, she could hear the washer running in the utility room and Lollie called to her from there, coming into the kitchen with something in her hand.

'Them clothes you wore yesterday got kind of

tore up,' Lollie said. 'Specially your jacket. I found this caught under the lining.' She opened her hand and Carole stared at the glow of gold.

A gold coin. Old, with a hole pierced near one edge. She was surprised by the dagger thrust of revulsion that shot through her. She didn't want to touch the thing, she didn't want it anywhere near her.

'So here it is,' Lollie said, obviously wondering why she didn't take it.

Reluctantly, Carole plucked the coin from Lollie's palm and examined it closely. To get inside her jacket lining, it could only have come from that horrible tunnel she'd been trapped in. Had she actually found the ghost gold? After a moment's thought, she shook her head. The holed coin must be the one Sawa had returned to that same tunnel.

'This belongs to Sawa,' she said aloud.

Once she'd recognized the coin for what it was, her feeling of unease abated. But she still didn't want to be responsible for the gold coin. She'd take it to Sawa as soon as she finished breakfast.

'Hope you feel better this morning,' Lollie said. 'When Mr Jerrold brought you in yesterday you looked like death warmed over.'

'I'm totally back to normal.' Which was more or less true, barring a few bruises.

'Guess you had company after I left,' Lollie said. 'Three dirty cups.'

Lollie was a jewel, a treasure and she'd hate to do without her, but she tended to be a tad nosy. 'Rich dropped by,' she said, aware Lollie knew Jerrold had been at the house when she left for the day.

'Singing the blues, like as not,' Lollie commented.

Carole nodded; there was no point in denying it. Lollie didn't miss much.

José was waiting for Carole at the corral. 'You feel okay?' he asked.

'I guess I got off easy, thanks to you.'

'You don't go there no more.'

'You can count on that! I was never so scared in my life. Jerrold said he needed all the help he could get with those rocks – your arrival was a godsend.'

José smiled. 'I make those two work hard, serve 'em right.' His smile faded. 'The one they call Brad, he don't seem too bad but that Alex – *muy mal.*'

Was José right, was Alex very bad? Carole bit her lip. He'd left her to die, hadn't he?

Not wanting to dwell on it, she said, 'Well, they're gone for good anyway.'

'The little boss, he tell them to go, but I keep my eye out,' José said. 'You do, too. Can't trust that kind of *hombre.*'

Eager to get rid of the coin, Carole nodded without really heeding José's warning. Herwin had ordered both Alex and Brad off the property and she doubted they'd dare to come back.

Once mounted on Sombrita, she decided to look for Sawa at the hacienda first but, when she got there, no one was around, neither Sawa nor anyone else. Denying to herself that she was disappointed in not seeing Jerrold, Carole headed for Sawa's cabin.

On the way, for some reason, Sombrita began to act spooked. She didn't actually shy at things, but kept tossing her head as though she might at any moment. Carole halted the mare, murmuring soothingly to her as she stroked her neck, meanwhile listening for any sound Sombrita might have picked up with her keener-than-human hearing.

She heard nothing out of the ordinary. When she urged the mare on, Sombrita seemed calmer, but her behavior had affected Carole, who kept glancing behind her. No one followed. Why would they? She was on her own property; she was perfectly safe.

Sawa was sitting on a bench in front of her cabin in a patch of sunlight, weaving willow strands into a basket. The crow who usually perched on the cabin roof was nowhere in sight. Carole pulled up Sombrita some yards away, near a tree, dismounted and tethered her. She called a greeting to the old woman as she approached. Without answering, Sawa gestured to the bench.

When Carole sat beside her, she said, 'Are your ears open today?'

Not understanding, Carole touched her right ear uncertainly. 'I guess so.'

'You closed them yesterday. No words reached you.'

Grasping Sawa's meaning, Carole said, 'I'm sorry. If I'd listened to you I'd have saved everyone a lot of trouble, including myself.'

Sawa laid the basket aside and put her right hand over her heart. 'The bad feeling don't go away. It stays here.' Before Carole could speak, she added, 'Don't talk to me about heart attacks, my feeling is of the spirit. My friend, the crow, knows. He stays away.'

'I noticed he wasn't around. But I'm okay, I survived, safe and sound.'

Sawa's dark gaze assessed her. 'Did you?'

'Barring an ache or two and a few bruises.'

'Something troubles you, I can tell.'

Carole shook her head. 'Not really. Except maybe this.' She extracted the coin from her jacket pocket and offered it to Sawa. 'I didn't know it at the time, but this got caught in my torn clothes yesterday. I'm sure it's yours.'

Sawa recoiled from the coin so violently she almost fell off the bench. She couldn't have reacted more negatively if she'd been offered a rattler. 'No! That's not mine. I take no ghost gold.'

Carole stared at her. 'But, see, here's the hole.

318

I'm sure this is the same coin you –'

Shaking her head, Sawa sprang up and, leaving her basketry behind, hurried to her cabin, entered and shut herself in. In surprised dismay, Carole heard the click as she locked the door.

I've been locked out! Carole told herself in disbelief, looking from the door to the coin she still held on her palm. Sawa locked me out. As she started to rise from the bench, realizing there'd be no point is staying, the hair on her nape rose in warning. What was wrong?

Sombrita snorted and pawed the ground, distracting her. She slid the coin into her pocket and got up to check the mare, tethered to a nearby tree. As she reached her horse, something hard jabbed her in the middle of the back.

' "The gun's loaded," a male voice told her. 'Do what I say and you won't get hurt.'

Recognizing the voice as Alex's, apprehension tensed her. José's word's – *muy mal* – echoed in her head, reminding her Alex was dangerous.

'Untie and lead the horse,' he ordered. 'Disobey and I'll shoot her first.'

Shoot Sombrita? Carole bit back a furious objection, tamping down her anger. Best to stay as calm as she could. She needed to keep her wits about her.

'What do you want?' she demanded as she untied her mare.

'You'll find out. Head for that clump of willows ahead and to the right.'

Leading Sombrita, she did as he directed. He ordered her to stop near the thickly growing willows and, keeping her covered with a long-barreled revolver, hauled his dirt bike free of the concealment of the trees.

'Hide the horse in here,' he said, 'and tie her up. Keep in mind if you try anything foolish, she gets shot first.'

Carole obeyed.

'So far, so good,' he said. 'Now get on the bike. You're going to sit ahead of me and I'll tell you what to do.' He mounted the bike the same time she did, sitting close behind her. He grabbed her around the waist, the gun jabbing into her stomach.

She listened to his instructions about starting and working the various pedals of the bike. 'We're heading for those rocks we dug you out of yesterday,' he told her. 'Keep the bike upright. If we go over, the gun goes off.'

Carole swallowed and, carefully following everything he'd said, started the bike and pointed it toward Alcatraz. They jounced off.

'Been trailing you,' he said into her ear. Unable to shrink from the enforced intimacy, she forced herself to ignore her revulsion. 'Figured you found the gold cache. Knew you had when I heard what you told Sawa. You can hand over that coin you showed her when we get there. Then you're going back into that hole and bring me out the rest of it.'

Terror gripped her, making the bike wobble.

'Careful,' he warned. 'Keep her steady. Don't want to hurt you. I won't if you do what I say.'

'The gold's not there,' she shouted over the bike's roar. 'I don't know where it is.'

He laughed. 'You're lying. I heard every word you said. Sawa put her coin back with the others in the cache and when we dug you out, you had that coin. Don't waste your breath on denial.'

He didn't believe her. In despair, she tried to think of words that might convince him she was telling the truth. She found none. I can't crawl into that awful tunnel again, she thought. I just can't.

But she'd have to if the alternative was to die. Carole shuddered. He'd probably kill her anyway when she couldn't produce the gold because it wasn't there. To survive, she had to get away from him. How could she possibly do that without having him shoot her? The gun – she'd have to get the gun first. But how?

Did Sawa see what went on after she locked herself in the cabin? Does she know I'm Alex's captive? Hope flared for a moment before Carole realized that even if Sawa did know, with no phone and no transportation she hadn't any way of summoning help quickly. There'd be no one coming to the rescue.

They were at the bottom of Alcatraz Hill when the handlebars twisted from Carole's grasp. Before she could understand why, she found herself flying through the air as the bike tumbled away from her. She managed to curl herself up before hitting the ground. Even so, the impact stunned her. Moments passed before she regained her wits enough to realize the ground beneath her was shaking.

Earthquake!

Staggering to her feet, she glanced quickly around. Alex was pinned beneath the bike. She couldn't see if he still had the gun or not but she couldn't wait to find out. Luckily she didn't seem to be hurt. Unfortunately she'd fallen part way up the hill and he was below her. Her best chance not to get shot was to run farther up the hill where, concealed by the rocks, she could make her way around to the opposite side.

As soon as the ground quit moving, she poised herself to sprint uphill only to hear the ominous roar of a rockslide. To go uphill in the face of a slide was crazy. Whirling around, she flung herself downhill, swerving in an arc to avoid Alex who, she saw, had squirmed from under the bike and was getting to his feet, apparently unhurt.

He yelled at her and grabbed at the bike. Her heart sank. Even if he'd lost the gun, if he got on the bike she'd have no chance to outrun him. A massive boulder crashed down to her left, startling her. Was the entire rock formation coming down? Refusing to give up, she ran as fast as she could, heading back toward Sawa's.

The sputtering roar of the bike starting blended with the crashing rocks, shutting out all other noise. Not until she looked up did she see the palomino pounding toward her. Jerrold! Glancing over her shoulder, she saw Alex, mounted on the dirt bike, racing at her.

Realizing Jerrold wouldn't have time to dismount and pull her on to the horse with him before Alex reached her, a vision sprang into her mind – Jerrold leaning over from the horse and pulling the stunt woman up and on to the palomino. Halting abruptly, she did her best to assume the stance that woman had used. Would he understand?

As the palomino swept past her, she felt Jerrold grasp her and pull her upward. She scrambled to sit in front of him as he swung the horse to one side to avoid the rush of the bike.

The palomino pounded past Alcatraz Hill, heading away from Sawa's. Craning her neck to peer around Jerrold, Carole drew in her breath, watching in horror as Alex twisted the bike, fighting to avoid a tumbling boulder. He almost made it, but not quite. The bike glanced off the boulder. Its impetus flung the bike violently aside, throwing Alex into the air. He came down, hit the ground and lay still.

'Jerrold!' she cried. 'Turn the horse. Alex had an accident.'

He was unconscious when they reached him. Because he lay in the path of possible rockslides, Jerrold plucked a blanket from the palomino's saddle bag, rolled Alex on to it and pulled him aside to a safer spot. He left the smashed bike where it was.

'We'll send someone back for him,' Jerrold said. 'Looks like his left leg is broken, can't risk trying to put him on the horse.'

He reached to help Carole remount, but she slipped from his grasp and ran part way uphill to where gravel and small rocks were still slipping down. Digging into her jacket pocket, she pulled out the holed gold coin and flung it into the slide before hurrying back to the horse.'

Both mounted on the palomino, she directed him to the willows where she'd been forced to tie Sombrita. On the way, they met Sawa, trotting toward them.

'You're safe,' she said. 'I give thanks.'

'I threw your coin into the rocks on the hill,' Carole told her.

Sawa nodded. 'You did right. It was never my coin. The ghosts have it back, now maybe they stay quiet and let the giant sleep.'

Whether she believed in Sawa's ghosts or not, Carole was glad the coin had been returned to where Sawa's husband found it. Where she, like Sawa, felt it belonged. 'Alex is hurt,' she added. 'We'll send help for him.'

Sawa shrugged. 'So the ghosts let him live.

Too bad. I thought they'd kill him.' She turned and began walking back toward her cabin.

After retrieving Sombrita from the willows, Jerrold rode along with her as they headed for the ranch house. They were almost there when Carole began to shiver. By the time they reached the corral, she could hardly hold on to the reins. Jerrold pulled her from the saddle, holding her close and she leaned on his strength.

'I d-don't know w-what's wrong with m-me,' she quavered.

'Delayed shock,' he said.

José rode up on his gray. 'I see you riding home and I get a bad feel in my head. So I come here, too. What happened?'

Jerrold sketched what had occurred, finishing by asking José to send help to Alex.

'So he got hurt,' José said. 'Serve him right. You don't mess with ghosts. But he don't belong there, we got to get people to take him away.'

Jerrold led Carole to the back door. Once inside, she refused to be taken to her bedroom so he persuaded her to lie on the couch in the living-room and pulled an afghan over her. Lollie bustled off to make her some hot tea, which was her universal remedy for any and all upsets.

'He had a gun,' she told Jerrold. 'He threatened me.'

'Sshh, you don't have to tell me now,' he said.

'I do have to,' she insisted, squirming up until

325

she was braced against the pillows leaning against the couch arm, feeling too agitated to lay flat.

He eased down next to her, sitting sideways. 'All right, let's hear it.'

'First, how did you know I was in trouble?'

'Sawa interrupted the shoot. Her cabin is just over the hill from where we were filming. That's why I had the palomino.'

Carole stroked the black sleeve of his Californio costume and managed a weak smile. 'At least you didn't have to ruin this one rescuing me like you did the one you wore yesterday.'

He brushed a strand of hair from her forehead. 'My heart was in my mouth when I realized you were poised to have me sweep you off your feet and that I had to do it to save you. I was afraid I'd fail.'

She wanted to tell him he'd swept her off her feet the first time he kissed her. Instead she said, 'I can't imagine you failing at anything you do. Thanks again. I'm doubly in your debt.'

'Sawa said Alex captured you at her cabin.'

Carole nodded. 'He saw that I had the gold coin – Lollie found it in the lining of my torn jacket – and he misinterpreted the reason. He thought the gold cache was in the tunnel you rescued me from yesterday. He was going to make me crawl in there and get it for him.' She hugged herself. 'He wouldn't believe me when I told him Sawa had put the coin inside

326

that crevice and that there wasn't any other gold.'

Jerrold shook his head. 'You were wrong; he was right. Sawa told me the gold was hidden in that miserable hole. She said it didn't matter if I knew because the crevice would be gone after the giant shook the hill. Then the ghost gold would be hidden forever.'

'As far as I'm concerned, it can stay there throughout eternity,' she said fervently.

'Your Alcatraz is pretty well destroyed. This last quake and the slides completely rearranged the rocks. I'd say Sawa's right about the disappearance of the crevice.'

'Sawa's right about more than I realized.' A stray thought occurred to her, making her smile wryly. 'Did you know she won quite a bit of money betting on you?'

He frowned. 'Betting on me?'

'Didn't I tell you it was three to one that Marla would seduce you before the filming ended? Apparently you're her first failure as far as leading men go.'

He slanted her a look. 'Good for Sawa. At least somebody believed in my virtue.'

'Virtue?' Carole was mortified when a giggle escaped her. She wasn't given to giggling. Must be the delayed shock.

Lollie bustled in with a pot of tea and a plate of Saltines. She was an staunch advocate of hot tea for settling nerves and crackers for settling stomachs. Noting there was an extra cup for Jerrold, Carole said to him, 'Would you pour, please?'

He did the honors with grace and dispatch but then, she reflected, Aussies were more or less English. Actually the tea did taste good and she'd always liked Saltines.

When she finished, she felt so much better that she flung off the afghan and sat up. As it turned out, she was barely in time. Moments later, Theda swept into the living-room, Calvin trailing her.

Jerrold rose. 'Back so soon?' he asked.

Theda shook her finger at him before sitting next to Carole and taking her hand. 'Are you all right, dear? José called me. He told me he was concerned about you and thought I should come home. He wouldn't tell me why, so I'm waiting for you to.'

'He shouldn't have bothered you,' Carole insisted. 'It's all over with and I'm fine.'

'Had a spot of trouble, did you?' Calvin asked, looking at his son.

Jerrold shrugged. 'Some.'

Since he didn't elaborate, Carole launched into an somewhat edited version of what had happened over the last two days. 'But it's all over and done with. Everything's back to normal and the bad guy's out of the picture,' she finished.

'Good heavens, dear, what a trial this has been

for you.' Theda patted her hand. 'And to think I wasn't here to help.'

'Jerrold filled in,' Carole said drily.

Calvin glanced from her to Jerrold and back, and smiled. 'Admirably, I'm sure.'

Theda looked at Jerrold. 'How brave you've been.'

Carole thought she'd never seen him look so discomfited. For once words seemed to have failed him.

'Shall we take the youngsters out for dinner to celebrate their survival under odds?' Calvin asked Theda, thus letting Jerrold off the hook.

'Actually Carole and I were planning to have dinner out tonight,' Jerrold said quickly. 'Alone. After she rests, of course.'

She stared at him in amazement. Why had he said that? Couldn't he stand the thought of spending a few hours with his father?

'How nice,' Theda said. 'To tell the truth, I do believe I'm too tired to enjoy an evening out so it's just as well you'd already made plans. We'll do as Calvin suggested at a later date.'

Great, Carole thought. Now Jerrold and I are committed to going out to dinner. She wouldn't have minded if he'd asked her because he wanted to, but he hadn't. She was only part of a ploy to avoid being with his father.

'I'd best get back to Herwin,' Jerrold said, 'before he self-destructs. This is the second time I've ridden off on him in the middle of a shoot.'

329

He glanced at Carole. 'I've got new tires on the Jag. See you later. Say about six?'

Carole realized there was no way she could gracefully excuse herself from the evening out, so she nodded.

Hours later, staring into her closet, she despaired of finding anything decent enough to wear. Why hadn't she bought a few really chic dresses? Even just one would have done. As she stood there dithering, someone tapped on her door.

'May I come in?' Theda asked, pushing the door open.

'I don't have a thing to wear,' Carole wailed.

Theda came up beside her to poke in the closet. 'I've waited years to hear you say those words. You know why you're saying them, don't you?'

'I suppose because I failed to listen to you for umpteen years. If I had, there'd be something in my closet I could wear.'

Theda smiled, 'That, too. But the real reason is because you've finally found the right man and you want to look your best for him. So somehow we must devise the right clothes for tonight.'

'Right man?' Carole asked. 'I thought you didn't approve of Jerrold.

'Dear, I've always approved of him. The more so since he's proved himself as a knight errant. He has flaws, of course, but what man doesn't?'

Calvin certainly has, Carole thought but

didn't say. Why should she upset her grandmother? It was too late for any warning about Calvin to be of any use. Besides, despite herself, she liked him.

'I've decided Jerrold would make an acceptable husband,' Theda added.

Carole frowned. 'If you're thinking that Jerrold has it in mind to ask me to marry him,' she warned, 'you're way off base. He's not going to do that. Ever.'

'He may think he won't, but he's wrong.' Theda spoke with complete assurance as she shifted hangers back and forth in the closet.

Carole shook her head. Her grandmother always expected things to go the way she wanted them to. This time she was in for a disappointment. 'And even if he did, how do you know I'd accept?' she challenged.

Theda raised her eyebrows, not bothering to comment. obviously believing Carole's words were too ridiculous to take seriously.

He'll never ask so I don't have to wonder if I really would refuse, Carole told herself.

Theda lifted out a hanger holding a black faille suit, removed the skirt and put the jacket back, saying, 'This skirt might do. I have a white silk blouse that I've never worn because it's a trifle large for me. It'll be stunning on you. You can't possibly wear that jacket – it's totally *passé* – but we'll find you something appropriate.'

Although Carole wouldn't have picked black

and white for herself, when she looked in the mirror after dressing, she had to admit her grandmother had chosen well.

'Sophisticated without being blatant about it,' Theda said, handing her an oversized mohair cardigan, black with flecks of red. 'This is so far out of fashion it's chic again. And do put on that old garnet pendant of your great-grandmother's.'

Feeling closer to her grandmother than she had in weeks, Carole smiled at her. 'You know more about clothes than I'll ever learn. I should have listened to your advice years ago. I promise to pay more attention in the future.'

Although when Jerrold's gone, it won't make any difference what I wear, she thought.

Theda kissed her cheek, obviously pleased at Carole's words. 'Goodnight, dear. We'll be turning in early so I won't be waiting up for you. Nevertheless, don't overdo – you know what I mean. You've had a terrible experience and that does take its toll.'

Don't overdo? She was afraid to ask what her grandmother meant by that – could it be what she thought? Surely her grandmother wouldn't bring up . . . well . . . *sex*. Or would she?

After Theda left, Carole fastened the garnet pendant around her throat, nothing how the deep red of the stone glowed in the light. Great-grandmother Harte, she knew, had worn the heirloom necklace on her wedding day. She grimaced, reached up to remove the pendant, then paused.

Stop this nonsense, she admonished herself. So he's not going to ask you to marry him. Forget there may be no tomorrow and enjoy tonight.

CHAPTER 18

'Let's hope your girlfriend stays out of trouble for the next few hours,' Herwin said sarcastically when Jerrold returned to the shoot site. 'I'd like to wrap it up today. If you think you can spare the time.'

'Alex caused this problem,' Jerrold said. 'He came back after you threw him off the property and had a collision with a boulder for his sins.'

'Kill him?' Herwin asked.

Jerrold shook his head. 'Possibly a broken bone or two.'

'Bad cess to all troublemakers, that's my world-view.' He turned from Jerrold to call out, 'Okay, everybody in position, let's get this show on the road.'

Later, after Herwin, finally satisfied with what he'd captured on film, dismissed them all, Jerrold rode slowly toward the hacienda. After seeing the palomino to the temporary corral, he dismounted and stroked the gelding's neck. Thanks to the horse's specialized training, Carole was alive and safe. 'Going to miss you, mate,' he told him. 'You're a real pro.'

As he walked toward his trailer to change, he caught sight of Marla sitting on a blanket under a tree surrounded by basketry supplies. She beckoned to him and he sauntered over to her.

'A new hobby?' he asked.

'I'll have you know that I find basket-making intensively creative.'

'For the time being, anyway.' He hadn't intended to mark any such remark but Rich's woebegone face still haunted him.

Marla bristled. 'My baskets are going to be as much in demand as Liz's perfume,' she said. 'This is a lifetime commitment.'

'Baskets not being as expendable as men, then.'

She put down the willow strips and glared up at him. 'Just what in hell is eating you, Telford?'

Jerrold got himself under control and started to apologize, but he was too late.

'If you're referring to Richie, as I expect you are, that's none of your business,' she snapped. 'What I —' She stopped abruptly to eye him narrowly. 'Can those snide remarks be a case of guilty conscience, Telford? You're leaving this place unencumbered just like me, right?'

He didn't reply and she read his silence as agreement. 'The shoe pinches when it's on the other foot, doesn't it?' she crowed. 'Join the short-shrift club, Telford. Sooner or later, it's what all of us in this business are forced to do to people we like. Can't be helped, I suppose, but it hurts us in the long run. We can't be trusted in any relationship and people get to know that. But what can we do? I can't be a rancher's wife any more than Carole could fit comfortably into the glamor crowd.'

He stared at her unhappily, unable to refute a single word.

'Hey, don't look so down in the mouth,' she said. 'If we hadn't come along, they probably would have married each other. With luck and a little time, the two of them will still make a match and forget us.' Her expression turned bleak. 'While we go on our heartless way. On and on and on . . .'

Jerrold shook his head but her words stayed with him as he entered his trailer. *Heartless.* He wasn't that kind of man, no way. Damn it, he didn't want to leave Carole, but what other choice was there?

Isn't it possible Marla doesn't really want to leave Rich, either? he asked himself. But she's a realist and understands there's no permanent solution for the two of them so she'd cut the ties and got out. While that might be true, he didn't believe he and Marla were much alike.

He thought Rich had distracted and amused her, much as the baskets were doing. But baskets were easy to set aside when you grew bored and then pick up and work on later, if you wanted to. People weren't baskets.

Would Carole turn to Rich after he was gone? The possibility couldn't be dismissed. The idea of her in Rich's arms made him clench his fists. Carole was his! He didn't want her to belong to any other man.

Yeah, great dog-in-the-manger act, he told himself in disgust. He had no right to Carole, none at all. Right implied some kind of long-term commitment, marriage being the most binding. He'd failed at one marriage, he couldn't risk another.

He and Linda had married too young, each had unrealistic expectations about the other. He'd envisioned her being happy as a ranch manager's wife, whereas in truth she was a born-and-bred city girl who was out of her element anywhere else.

She'd expected him to remain in the city and continue with what looked to be a promising acting career. She didn't understand how he hated the artificiality of the business and she was stunned when he threw it over and hauled her off to an outback ranch. They'd been fated to part.

He smiled wryly when he considered the present situation. Talk about role reversal. Here was Carole, a born-and-bred rancher while he was now, thanks to his dear father's debts, a full-fledged actor, neck-deep in the business of artificiality. Never the twain shall meet? Given Carole's stubbornness, probably not.

Whatever else happened, though, he couldn't let her lose Harte's Way because of either financial difficulties or Calvin. The ranch was her life. It'd be easier to come up with a solution to that than to find a way not to lose Carole completely.

He hadn't realized how much she'd come to matter to him until he'd found her trapped by those rocks and was forced to face the fact she might die before he could rescue her.

What would his life be like without Carole? He pushed the thought away, not wanting to deal with the coming actuality.

Instead he concentrated on where to take her tonight. He'd didn't know the area, she did; he'd let her make the choice. It had to be a decent restaurant, one with ambience. He'd enjoyed the rural barbecue, but tonight was for the two of them, he didn't intend to share her with a crowd.

Dancing? A good excuse to hold her in his arms if she could come up with somewhere to go. There'd be no problem in finding an appropriate place to dine and dance if they drove to San Francisco, but that would mean an overnight stay. Much as he'd enjoy that, somehow he doubted she'd agree.

He'd never forget holding her in his arms last night while she slept. He'd savored the knowledge that her trust in him made her feel safe enough to go to sleep. Then again this morning, while trying to escape from that bastard Alex, she'd waited with utter confidence for him to sweep her up on to the palomino, certain he wouldn't fail her. Thank God, he hadn't.

He didn't want to harm her in any way. At the same time, he couldn't seem to break it off cleanly as Marla had with Rich. He wasn't ready to give up making love with her – no other woman had ever made him feel the way she did. Her sweet passion beguiled him to the point of enchantment.

Aching emptiness filled him as he contemplated being without her. How could he bear it?

Someone tapped on his trailer door. He'd stripped to change from his California costume so he hastily donned a pair of sweat pants before telling whoever it was to come in.

Marla opened the door and peered in. 'Everyone decent?' she asked coyly.

'Yeah,' he said warily, wondering what she wanted.

'It occurred to me,' she said as she sat on his bed, 'that we might be able to console each other after we leave here.' She slanted him a sultry glance. 'At the very least, we could be friends. I have a couple weeks before I fly to Hawaii for my next picture. How about you?'

'I'm not scheduled to go to Jamaica for a month,' he admitted cautiously.

'You're the new guy in town; I could show you around.'

One of the most attractive and desirable women in the world sat on his bed telling him she was available for fun and games, no strings attached, and what was going through his mind? *Thanks, but no thanks.*

'I'll keep it in mind,' he hedged. 'As you say, we could be friends.'

'At least,' she amended, lounging back on his bed and smiling seductively up at him.

'But not at the moment,' he said lightly. 'I'd hate to be responsible for making Sawa give up her winnings.'

Marla sat up and frowned at him. 'What does she have to do with us?'

'She won a bet with three-to-one odds because I didn't climb into bed with you while the movie was being made.'

Springing up, Marla cried, 'What? Who had the nerve to make a bet like that?'

'The entire crew, as far as I can tell. Apparently you have a fearsome reputation for charming your leading men clean off their feet.'

Marla was obviously not pleased. 'How dare they!'

He shrugged. 'I didn't know a thing about it until after Sawa made her killing.'

Recovering, Marla essayed a smile. 'If I'd known earlier, I might have tried harder,' she told him. 'But I was preoccupied with Rich.' Her tone indicated he wouldn't have had a chance otherwise.

Because he wanted her to leave his trailer with her pride intact, he smiled as warmly as he could, hoping to imply she might be right. The truth was, once he'd met Carole, Marla hadn't interested him at all.

Once she was gone, he glanced at his watch. Time to get going if he expected to pick up Carole at a reasonable hour. And past time to make up his mind what he intended to do about her. He had to make some kind of decision.

When she heard the purr of Jerrold's Jag, Carole underwent an acute attack of stage fright. This was actually their first planned date – the barbecue had been more of a casual agreement. Everything else that had happened between them had been spontaneous and irresistible, as well as wonderful. Considering how intimate they'd been, tonight shouldn't have her on edge – but it did.

She answered the door when he rang and invited him in. Jerrold hesitated. 'If it's all right with you, I'd just as soon we take off now.'

'I'm ready,' she told him, picking up her bag and the mohair sweater.

Once he'd settled her in the Jag, he asked, 'Where are we having dinner? Since you know the area, I thought you should choose.'

'The Shepherd's Crook in Bakersfield,' she said without hesitation. 'The food is divine.'

'Bakersfield it is, then,' he said, swinging the Jag out of the circular drive.

The plump dark-haired hostess in the the Shepherd's Crook beamed at Carol and Jerrold when they entered. 'Carole!' she exclaimed. 'How lovely you look tonight. I'm so glad to see you.'

'I'm sorry we didn't have a chance to call for reservations,' Carole said, gazing at the many occupied tables.

The hostess waved a hand. 'No problem. There's always room for you.' Her gaze flicked to Jerrold. 'And any friend of yours.'

Remembering how autograph seekers and fans had trailed Jerrold in Las Vegas, Carole had tried to choose a quiet place for dinner. The Ardaizes Basque restaurant met the criteria, besides serving the best food around. The Shepherd's Crook had seemed ideal but, apparently, others had discovered it since she'd last been here. She'd also forgotten Mrs Ardaiz's friendly curiosity.

Since there was nothing for it but to introduce him, she did.

'Jerrold Telford.' Mrs Ardaiz rolled the syllables on her tongue. 'Why is that name familiar?'

To Carole's relief the Basque woman didn't wait for an answer but bustled through the small dining-room, leading them to a secluded table for two in the rear. She whisked the reserved sign away, saying archly, 'So you and Mr Telford can be private. Your grandmother, she is well?'

Carole assured her Theda was fine, but didn't mention her grandmother's marriage. That would wait until Theda herself announced it.

Mrs Ardaiz began to recite what they had to serve tonight – there were no menus – but Jerrold held up his hand. 'Carole tells me every item in your restaurant is out of this world. Why don't we let you'd decide what to serve us?'

Mrs Ardaiz beamed her approval. 'Ah, a man with good sense as well as good taste. I guarantee a meal you will never forget.'

'She'll adore you forever,' Carole told him after the hostess left them. 'And we're sure to have a fantastic dinner. You always seem to know the right buttons to push.'

'Not with you. Every time I think we've reached an understanding, I find I'm wrong.' His gaze held Carole's. 'Tonight we're going to straighten things out between us once and for all.'

She took a deep breath and eased it out. 'You make it sound so final.'

'Finality's exactly what I have in mind.' He leaned across the table toward her. 'I've given a lot of thought to what I'm going to say, so don't interrupt.'

She hoped he didn't mean to launch into a long, drawn-out farewell speech because she didn't think she could take it and she'd hate to make a scene by doing something idiotic like rushing out.

'By marrying your grandmother, my father has fouled your life up inexcusably,' he continued. 'I'm damned well going to put things right.' He leaned back. 'First of all –'

He paused when a waiter appeared with a wine bottle and two glasses. The man went into the ritual of showing the label, uncorking, then pouring a small amount of red *chacoli* into Jerrold's glass for his tasting and approval. At his go-ahead nod, the waiter filled both glasses, handing the untasted one to Carole.

'I'm not really a wine maven,' Jerrold said when the waiter was gone. 'I hope you like this.'

Carole sipped and said, 'The wine's lovely.'

'You're lovely, too.' The glow of desire in his dark eyes made her heart pound. Maybe it wasn't a farewell speech he had in mind. At least not this evening.

'I'm wearing Theda's blouse,' she admitted, regretting her words almost immediately. If he hadn't already realized her clothes fell short of being fashionable, she ought to have the sense not to give him clues. Would she ever learn to think before she spoke?

'It's not what you wear, it's you,' he said. 'I noticed that from the beginning.'

Carole laughed. 'If I recall, I looked like a drowned rat the day we met.'

He grinned. 'And an angry one. You read me off good and proper for taking advantage of your grandmother.' His smile faded. 'I'd never do that. But my father's a different story.' He sighed. 'I feel responsible for what's happened.'

'You're not responsible for what your father does.'

'You're wrong. I've been responsible for him for years, obligated to pay off his gambling debts. And the old perisher is a high-roller, no Mickey Mouse stakes for him. I've no intention of telling you how much money he's lost, but keeping up with his debts is no piece of cake. His most recent escapade took more than half of what I made on my last film.'

Carole stared at him, appalled. 'But he promised Theda he'd quit gambling for good. Don't you believe him?'

He shrugged. 'I've tried every damn method ever invented to get Calvin to stop gambling. Nothing worked. This last time I warned him I was going public with his problem. Calvin's a proud old sod and I knew he'd hate the exposure. I swore that the next time he left a trail of markers behind him I was going to let it all hang out with a press interview about my father's compulsive addiction to gambling.'

Carole cringed inwardly. Making Calvin's

problem public would be as humiliating for Jerrold as it would be for his father.

'Would you have, really?' she asked.

Jerrold shrugged. 'I don't know. Let's hope I never have to make the decision.'

'But if he promised Theda –?'

'Why would he go to Las Vegas if not to gamble? He did pay for the second trip and for the suites at the hotel so I figure he's been on a roll. Gamblers do have lucky streaks, you know. Sooner or later, though, Lady Luck bows out, just like Sinatra warns in that old song. She's a very fickle lady.'

'My grandmother will hold him to his promise,' she said.

'He's broken promises before.' Jerrold's voice was bleak.

The waiter arrived with appetizers, tiny split-open anchovies fried in batter and grilled sardines seasoned to perfection, but Carole only gave the food half her attention, her mind on how she might find ways to protect her grandmother from Calvin's excesses if he should break his promise to her, as Jerrold seemed sure he would. She failed to come up with any ideas.

'I'm not saying marriage will solve all the problems,' Jerrold said, 'but it'll help.'

Carole put down her fork and stared at him in confusion. Calvin's and Theda's marriage solving problems? Hadn't he said just the opposite only moments ago?

'I fail to see what you mean,' she said. 'Theda's and Calvin's marriage has created new problems, not solved any. My grandmother was certainly better off before . . .' She paused. 'Except for love, of course. She does love him.'

'I'm not talking about their marriage,' Jerrold said. 'I mean ours.'

Words deserted Carole as, shocked, she struggled to gather her confused thoughts.

'Don't look so surprised,' he said. 'If you'll think about it for a minute or two, you'll see marriage is your best solution.'

'*My* best solution?' she echoed, trying to gather her wits so she could make sense of what he was saying. 'What about you?'

'The point is, my agent got me a good contract for *Bandido* and also my next American film, so you won't have to worry about –'

Carole held up her hand. 'Jerrold, wait, go slower,' she pleaded, a whirlwind of confusion eddying in her mind. 'I haven't caught up to your reasoning. I must have missed something along the way. Are you asking me to marry you?'

'Why shouldn't you?' he demanded.

'That doesn't answer my question.'

He frowned. 'I'm asking you, yes.'

From his expression anyone would have thought he was waiting to see his dentist, Carole told herself bitterly. He hadn't mentioned love. Not once. Not when they made love and not

347

now. If he didn't love her, why offer to marry her? Because he felt obligated to out of guilt for what his father had done to Theda? Or because he'd decided that was the only way to get her to accept his financial aid? Tears pricked her eyes and she blinked them back desperately, not wanting to cry in front of him.

'I realize this is abrupt,' he went on, 'but we don't have much time.'

Anger temporarily short-circuited her tears. How dare he assume she'd marry him – or any man – for financial security?

'Think it over,' he advised. 'I think you'll agree it's the only practical solution to our problems.'

That did it! Carole sprang to her feet, her sudden move spilling the dregs in her wine glass on to the white tablecloth, making a stain as red as blood. As red as her heart's blood.

'No!' she cried. Not trusting herself to say another word without bursting into tears, she fled from the restaurant and into the street. She didn't know where she was going and she didn't care. All she wanted was to put as much distance as possible between her and Jerrold.

Her chest ached as she ran along the sidewalk, not from exertion but from heartbreak. Nothing in her life had ever hurt her as much as Jerrold's offer of a loveless marriage. Aware he'd come after her, Carole swerved into the first side street, then turned at the next corner and again at the next.

She knew Bakersfield and Jerrold did not, so chances were she'd be able to elude him. Breathing heavily, she slowed to consider her options. If she called home, someone would come and pick her up. She wouldn't disturb Theda or Calvin but she could ask José.

But would that be fair, asking an old man to drive to Bakersfield at night just because she was upset? She shook her head. What then? Not any of her girl friends, they'd nag for an explanation.

Rich? The more she considered him, the more logical the choice seemed. Rich was the one person who'd understand. Ducking into a small side-street café, she found a pay phone and dug a coin from her bag. She picked up the receiver, poised the coin over the slot and then stopped.

Back at the restaurant, Jerrold rushed out after Carole but she was nowhere in sight. He was about to get in the Jag to search for her, even though he had no idea where she might be headed, when Mrs Ardaiz hailed him.

'I left money on the table –' he began.

'No, no, never mind the money. I can see you and Carole have had a lover's quarrel and she's run off in a snit. I understand, for I did the same as a girl. Men have such difficulty understanding us women. My advice is not to run after her.'

'But she might be in danger,' he protested.

'I don't think so here on this side of town. Besides, you don't know where she's gone, do you?' When he shook his head, she asked, 'So how can you find her?' Not waiting for an answer, she went on.

'Listen to the advice of a woman who's gotten a bit wiser as she grew older. What I say is, Carole will eventually decide she's caused enough trouble. She knows you must be worrying about her and that will bother her. She's aware that if she doesn't return here, she'll have to find another way home. To do that, she has to call someone for a ride. If she calls someone, they'll expect some kind of explanation and she won't want to give them a truthful one. Which means she has to lie. I don't believe Carole is a good liar.'

'I can't argue with your logic,' Jerrold said impatiently, 'but I *am* worried about her alone on the night streets. If I drive around, I might spot her.'

'Never!' Mrs Ardaiz shook her finger at him. 'She'll hide from you – that car's a dead giveaway. I tell you she's too proud to admit the truth – that she quarreled with you – to anyone she knows and she hates to lie. Wait and she'll return, still on her high horse, no doubt, but ready to be taken home. In silence, probably.'

Jerrold hesitated. He wasn't accustomed to passivity, he tended toward action. But rushing off in all directions just to be moving wasn't necessarily the best choice. What if Mrs Ardaiz was right and Carole returned here to find him gone?

'I don't even know what upset her,' he confessed.

'Men often don't. And, quite possibly, she won't tell you.' Mrs Ardaiz spread her hands. 'We women are like that, especially when we're young. We expect the man we're fond of to be able to read our minds – or at least our moods. I've known Carole since she was a child. Listen to me when I tell you she'll come back. She may even apologize for causing you distress by running off. But don't expect her to be repentant. Whatever you said or did hurt her deeply, remember that.'

'I haven't one bloody idea what it could be.'

'Go over what was said, you may find a clue. Do come back inside to wait, Mr Telford. She'll know you're here when she sees the Jaguar is still parked in the lot.'

Jerrold, admitting to himself that his anxiety about Carole was mixed with anger, decided to follow her advice. It wasn't every day he asked a woman to marry him – in fact, this was only the second time in his life he'd ever uttered those fateful words. Was the idea so repulsive to Carole? What else could he deduce from her behavior? She'd glared at him as though he was some kind of monster, shouted 'No!' at him and bolted.

'Thank you for taking all this trouble,' he said to Mrs Ardaiz. 'I'm sorry you were inconvenienced.'

'Be assured she must be in love with you or you wouldn't have upset her so,' Mrs Ardaiz told him. 'I must go back in, I'm needed there.'

He watched her re-enter the restaurant, debating whether to follow her. He shook his head. If he must wait, he'd do so in the Jag. He still wasn't certain waiting was the right course, but he had to admit it was practical. He wondered how long he could stand the suspense.

Across the street, Carole held back when she saw Jerrold unlocking the driver's door of the Jag. She'd been almost positive she wouldn't find him still here; she'd pictured him driving frantically around the streets of Bakersfield. Well, maybe he'd be more angry than frantic. She certainly would be furious if someone walked out on her.

Not that she didn't have every right to walk out on him – although fleeing was a more accurate description. But it had done some good – at least she no longer felt like crying.

Maybe she should have called Rich after all. But how could she explain to a man who was crushed by being dumped by the woman he was infatuated with that she was upset because Jerrold asked her to marry him for the wrong reason? Far from understanding, Rich would think she was crazy – he'd be ready to take Marla on any terms.

Anyway, the fair thing was to return, acknowledge that she shouldn't have reacted so childishly and ride home with Jerrold. Hadn't Theda drummed into her head when she was younger that courtesy demanded you come home with the man who brought you unless he was under the influence or had behaved inexcusably, in which case you called home or a taxi?

She could have called a taxi, but she hadn't wanted to ride all those expensive miles with a stranger. Or could it be she knew all along she'd have to return? Fair was fair. But fairness didn't mean forgiveness.

Taking a deep breath, she marched across the street, her gaze fixed on Jerrold.

He'd started to slide into the car but, as though he felt her presence, he paused and turned his head. 'Carole!' he cried and strode toward her.

She evaded his attempt to put his arms around her. 'It was rude of me to run off,' she said stiffly. 'I believe I'm ready to go home now.'

'I'll be double-didgeridooed,' he muttered. 'Right on cue. How did she know?'

Carole didn't have the slightest idea what he was talking about. Nor did she care. She'd done her part and, on the drive home, she didn't intend to say one more word unless she had to.

'I don't suppose you'll speak to me in the car,

either,' he said, seemingly as much to himself as to her.

He was correct but she didn't bother to tell him so. He'd find out soon enough.

Once in the car, refusing to so much as glance at him, she stared straight ahead. If he was waiting for an explanation he'd have to wait until the sun went nova – in which case, it wouldn't matter, mothing would matter. If he had any feeling for her at all, he ought to be able to figure out what was wrong.

She kept expecting him to speak, to ask why she'd run off, to inquire if she was all right. He said not a word. After a time, she wrapped her arms about herself, feeling chilled to the heart.

CHAPTER 19

There were all kinds of silences, Carole thought morbidly as she and Jerrold drove toward the ranch. Actually, they didn't ride in complete silence if you wanted to count the faint rush of the tires speeding along the blacktop – he was driving far too fast – or the clink of one key against another in the ignition when the Jag hit a rough spot.

But the fact neither of them had uttered a word made it a silence of sorts. And a hostile silence at that – the worst kind – though what he had to be hostile about was beyond her. Hadn't she more or less apologized for running off? Of course he could be angry because she'd refused his marriage offer. Maybe his pride was hurt. She hoped so. She hoped he'd never recover from the injury.

If she hadn't made up her mind not to speak to him at all, she'd say something terse and tart about his excessive speed. The Jag might have been designed as a race car, but he didn't have to prove it. She almost hoped to see the revolving gumball lights of a patrol car behind them. Serve him right to get a ticket.

Marry me so I can save the ranch. How dared he!

The slowing of the car caught her attention. They weren't that close to the ranch turnoff – what was he up to? He wrenched the wheel and the Jag skidded into a turn as he left the main road.

'What do you think you're doing?' she demanded as they drove down a bumpy dirt trail. 'You're miles short of the turn to Harte's Way.'

'I'm aware of that.' He clipped each word in a very British, very annoying manner.

'Then why did you take this rabbit track?'

'I have my reasons.'

He obviously didn't intend to share them with her. She shot him a suspicious glance, the first she'd really looked at him since she got in the car. His expression, in the dim glow of the dash lights, was unreadable.

Peering from the window didn't help; the night was dark, with no visible moon, and there were no outside lights. In the headlights she finally made out what the trees crowding close to either side were.

'We're in somebody's orange grove!' she exclaimed.

At that moment he stopped the car and killed

the motor. 'I thought you'd feel more at home among the nematodes,' he said.

She glared at him. 'You won't be thanked for trespassing.'

'I'm considering buying a grove,' he said. 'What do you think of this one?'

She made a sound of exasperation. 'Are you crazy? It's pitch dark out there.'

'So it is. As dark as what's going on in my head. I don't expect enlightenment, not after Mrs Ardaiz's lecture on the insurmountable differences between men and women, but whatever I said to you at the restaurant that brought on your precipitate flight, I didn't intend to be inflammatory. Or insulting. Or whatever else you might have conceived it to be.'

What did Mrs Ardaiz have to do with this? she wondered. 'I don't care to discuss it,' she said.

He sighed. 'She warned me you wouldn't. All I did was mention marriage. Do you find me that disgusting?'

She? Mrs Ardaiz? How dare he talk about her to anyone! 'You know perfectly well I don't find you disgusting,' she snapped.

'I didn't think so. Not after Vegas and our night on the hill.'

For a moment she almost melted, remembering the magic they'd made together; then she decided he was a rat to bring it up under the circumstances. Firming her lips, she said, 'I don't care to be reminded.'

He flung out his hands. 'OK, I give up. I hoped we could solve this by trying to recover what we found on the hill but I was mistaken. It's clear you'd probably scream if I tried to kiss you or else clout me with the first available weapon. Or both. Apparently we're not going to resolve anything tonight, but don't forget – I always get what I go after. This is far from over.'

She could have made several snide replies, but she rejected them all for the dignified ambiguousness of silence. The nerve of him thinking he could placate her with a kiss or two!

'And to think I turned down a very generous offer earlier,' he muttered as he started the Jag. At least that's what she thought he said and she didn't much like the sound of it. Not that she planned to comment.

He swung around and bumped back to the highway. It seemed to take hours before they finally arrived at the ranch. In silence.

She flung herself from the Jag before he could open his door, much less get out. Moments later she was inside the house with the door slammed behind her. Hearing the car drive off, she told herself she was glad he'd finally realized she didn't want anything more to do with him. The sooner he left Harte's Way the better.

Standing in the entry, she felt a terrible letdown. At the same time she was still too agitated to even consider sleeping. Actually, the house seemed confining – she needed to be out in the fresh air. Take a walk? Not in these clothes. Discarding her skirt and Theda's blouse, she kicked off the black heels she'd worn, pulled on jeans and a sweatshirt and found an old pair of sneakers.

Letting herself out through the music-room door, she saw a light shining through the trees. Who was at the stable at this late hour? Had José forgotten and left a light burning?

To her surprise she found him in the stable checking the hind hoof of his gray.

He glanced up at her approach and went back to work. Moments later he said, 'Ah,' and a pebble dropped on to the dirt. 'He was favoring this leg,' José told her. 'I couldn't let it go.'

He set the gray's leg down, rose from the stool and led the horse into a stall. 'I look at him again in the morning,' he said. Coming out, he narrowed his eyes. 'You don't look happy.'

She shrugged. 'Just restless.'

'Restless.' José repeated the word, rolling it on his tongue. 'Me, I think restless happens when you're in love and you and him don't agree.'

'I'm not in love!'

José paid no attention to her denial. 'Love makes for fights. Me, I think you and Mr Jerrold don't agree, you have a fight.'

'He's insufferable,' she muttered, giving up on

denial. She might as well admit she'd quarreled with Jerrold since José wouldn't listen to her.

'Tomorrow you make up. I know. When *mi esposa* still live, we fight, make up, fight, make up.' José grinned. 'Man and woman, they don't get along so good sometimes but if they love they got to be together. Can't be apart, that makes it worse.'

'I'll never forgive Jerrold. Never!'

He shrugged. 'If you don't love him, you don't fight. You fight, so you love him. You love him so you make up sooner than never. I know.'

'I can see there's no point in arguing with you.'

'When you live as long as me, you learn what is true and what is not. Me, I know you from a tiny *niña*. You work hard and I think you love hard. He's a good man. So you make up soon. Me, I go to bed now. *Buenos noches*.'

Carole murmured goodnight and watched José limp toward his cottage tucked between two tall pines. He was like a second father to her. He meant well but, even though he might have known her from the moment of her birth, he didn't understand.

Turning away from the stable, she drifted along the path she and Jerrold had taken not long after she first met him. He'd kissed her for the first time that night. She sighed, remembering. She could almost taste his essence as she relived that moment. The kiss had rocked her back on her heels, it had changed her whole world . . .

Enough of that, she warned herself after a moment. Whatever happened then, it's over. Everything between you and Jerrold is over.

If her walk was only going to lead her into disturbed reminiscing, then she may as well go back inside, she decided. Maybe she could read herself to sleep.

In her bedroom, she undressed and pulled on a sleep-T bearing a logo she scowled at, then sat cross-legged on her bed, brushing her hair furiously.

Make up with Jerrold? Not until apples grew on orange trees. Not until water ran uphill. Not until horses grew claws instead of hooves.

When her scalp began to tingle she ceased brushing and slid off the bed. What she needed was a book. Choosing a paperback at random from a stack Kitty had given her, she settled herself among the pillows before glancing at the title.

Down Under: Passion and Greed in Victorian Australia.

She flung the book across the room. She'd had more than she wanted of Australia in the person of Jerrold Telford. She'd had her fill of passion, too.

I'll forget the times I spent in his arms, she vowed. I won't cry over him, either. Not one tear. Once I thought he was my knight in a shining white Jaguar but no longer. I'll stop loving him, he isn't worth loving.

I'll begin by – She broke off her thought, listening, hearing the low growl of a car. Jerrold's Jag? If he thought she'd let him into the house, he had another think coming!

The motor shut off and a car door slammed. From her room she wouldn't be able to hear if he rang the doorbell and that wouldn't do. She could picture him lying on the bell and then banging on the door, which might wake up Theda and Calvin. She couldn't permit that to happen. Springing up, she grabbed a robe in case of a confrontation and shrugged into it as she sped toward the front door, reaching it just as it opened.

To her consternation Calvin walked in, shutting the door behind him. When had he gone out? She was sure his Caddy had been parked under the *porte-cochère* when Jerrold dropped her off. Actually, it must have been after she arrived because he was wearing slippers and a brown silk dressing-robe over matching pajamas. Where would he have gone dressed like that? And why?

'There you are, then,' he said.

She stared at him, unsure what to say. Finally she asked, 'Is Theda all right?'

He nodded. 'Sleeping like a lamb. I heard the Jag, then the front door slammed and I knew something was amiss. Ordinarily you're quiet as a cat. Too early for her to be back, I told myself. I was awake anyway so I came out to see what was wrong. Found you'd disappeared, did the next best thing – drove over to Jerrold's trailer. Waste of time, he wouldn't talk. But I could see he was distraught.'

'We had a disagreement,' she said reluctantly.

Before she could add that she preferred not to discuss it, Calvin said, 'He needs you, Carole.'

She stiffened. 'If you mean Jerrold, I'm sorry but I never want to see him again.'

Calvin motioned toward the living room. 'Could we sit down? I'd like to talk to you.'

Not wanting to be discourteous – she wasn't angry at Calvin – Carol nodded.

After she curled herself warily into a corner of the couch, he sat at the opposite end. 'You've heard the boy go on about me, haven't you?' he said. 'Jerrold makes no secret of the fact he has no use for me. You believe he despises the very ground I walk on, don't you?'

She moved her shoulders uncomfortably, unsure how to respond. He'd pretty well described Jerrold's reaction to him, but she hesitated to say so.

'That's Jerrold for you,' Calvin went on. 'The boy never could admit caring for a living soul. But I know in my heart he loves me, no matter how much of a prize ratbag I've been. That's behind me now. Falling in love with your grandmother's given me a reason to shape up. Love, that's the ticket – you must remember that and take it to heart. Never mind what your set-to tonight was about, I'm sure he loves you.'

Despite her resolution not to cry, tears filled Carole's eyes, How could Jerrold love her and yet propose marriage in such a cold-blooded way?

Calvin reached over and patted her knee. 'It'll be right, love.'

Still fighting her tears, she didn't respond. How could anything between her and Jerrold ever be right? In the silence that followed, she grew conscious of hearing music. Was a radio on somewhere? The melody was minor-keyed, sounding as mournful as she felt.

'I wish you'd agree to see Jerrold,' Calvin said. 'The boy's beside himself.'

'I thought he wouldn't talk to you,' she said, wiping the remnants of tears from her eyes.

'He didn't have to. The look on his face told me all I needed to know. Can't you hear his sadness in the music?'

Carole sat up. What did the music have to do with Jerrold?

'At least say a few words to him,' Calvin urged, 'even if it's merely a polite goodnight. The boy's beside himself.'

Finally realizing the music was from the piano, she made the connection. 'Jerrold's here?'

'I persuaded him to ride back with me, told

him to come in through the side door. He's in the music room.'

How devious the Telfords, father and son, could be! About to refuse, Carole paused. The last thing she wanted was for Theda to wake up and come out to see what was going on. If she didn't make a token appearance, Jerrold might keep right on playing his mournful music until lord only knew when.

Slowly she nodded.

'Atta girl.' Calvin stood, reached his hand to her and, when she was on her feet, put his arm around her shoulders and gave her a quick hug before letting her go.

The gesture warmed her. Whether it was an act or not, Calvin made her feel he cared about her. She thought he might accompany her to the music room but he didn't.

As she neared the door, she realized she'd never before heard whatever it was Jerrold was playing, an alien, haunting tune that threatened to bring back her tears. Catching her lower lip between her teeth, she opened the door.

Jerrold turned, saw her and dropped his hands from the keys. He rose and faced her. For a moment his expression showed the same sadness and pain she'd heard in the music and her heart went out to him. But then he frowned and her shield went up again.

'Your father –' she began.

A quick gesture of his hand banished his father. 'Are you all right?' he demanded.

'Perfectly all right,' she replied tartly. Why would he think otherwise? Had he expected her to melt into a puddle of tears?

'Are you sure?'

She blinked. 'Sure I'm all right? Of course.'

'No, sure of that.' He leveled a finger at her chest.

Carole glanced down and saw that her robe gaped open, revealing the heart-enclosed logo across the front of her sleep-T: *Someone in California loves me*. She flushed, angry that she'd worn the thing.

Before she could react further, he strode to her and caught her by the shoulders. 'Here's one someone,' he said before bending to her.

His kiss was surprisingly tentative. She could easily have pulled away from him and she told herself she would. In a moment. She needed to steal an instant to savor the warmth of his lips and his seductive taste one last time.

But then the tip of his tongue flicked along her lips and, before she knew what she was doing, she'd parted them so he could enter. With a groan he pulled her closer and his kiss grew heated, melting all of Carole's resolutions and turning her resentment to ashes.

She belonged in his arms, Jerrold told himself. The Aboriginal tune he'd been playing told of a lost time and lost chances. It described how he'd felt before she came into the room. Without Carole he'd be forever lonely and lost, going into a spreading decline like a diseased orange tree.

'I didn't mean to insult you by asking you to marry me,' he murmured into her ear. He felt her stiffen and pull back and he muttered a curse under his breath.

Refusing to release her completely, he said, 'Call me an arrogant sod, but I love you so much it didn't occur to me you might not feel the same way about me.'

Carole stared at him, the shock in her beautiful golden eyes slowly changing to a warm glow. If that wasn't love he saw in them, what the hell was it?

'Is that what you thought?' she whispered. 'That I didn't love you?'

'I ask you to marry me, you get this stricken look on your face, leap to your feet shouting, "No!" and run away from me. What am I supposed to believe?'

'Oh, Jerrold,' she cried, laughing while tears brightened her eyes. 'I've been in love with you ever since we met.'

Mrs Ardaiz was right – women were inexplicable. He'd never understand them, not if he lived to a hundred and fifty. 'If you love me,' he growled, 'then why the hell won't you marry me?'

She lowered her eyelashes, seductively shadowing her gaze. 'It wasn't an unconditional no. Ask me again. Maybe I've changed my mind.'

'I certainly hope so, dear.' Theda's voice, coming from the doorway, startled Jerrold. He turned, one arm still around Carole.

Both Theda and Calvin stood looking at them. 'I missed having my wedding here,' Theda said, 'and I'll be considerably upset if I'm cheated out of yours. Calvin and I have decided to exchange our second vows in a private ceremony with just the family present, but I've been looking forward to a lovely big wedding for you. Do say yes, dear, so I can begin planning.'

Jerrold glanced down at Carole's flushed face, a face he'd never tire of looking at, and smiled. 'You're clearly outnumbered, love, so here we go again and let's hope I get it right this time. I adore you beyond all reason, you're the only one in the world for me. Will you be my wife?'

Gazing at him, her eyes dreamy with happiness, she whispered, 'Yes.'

He captured the word with his lips as he kissed her, a long kiss that promised love and passion as long as he lived. Caught in the magic of their love, he forgot the onlookers until he heard Calvin's, 'Bravo!'

Releasing her reluctantly, keeping one arm around her, he glanced toward the newlyweds.

'I hope you two will be very happy here,' Calvin said.

Jerrold raised an eyebrow. 'Here?'

'You've always insisted you're a rancher at heart,' his father said. 'You'll have the chance to prove it.'

'You see, dears,' Theda put in, 'Harte's Way belongs to Carole as her father always intended it should. I signed the ranch over to her before Calvin and I married.'

'And, knowing that,' Calvin said, looking squarely at Jerrold, 'I married Theda anyway. It must be true love, wouldn't you say, mate?'

Jerrold was speechless. Carole pulled away from him and ran to throw her arms around her grandmother, then Calvin. Slowly, reluctantly, Jerrold crossed to his father and held out his hand.

Calvin clasped it. 'Never think an old leopard can't change his spots,' he said. 'I've even got myself a job of sorts.'

'Australian accents are the "in" thing,' Theda told them. 'On our first trip to Las Vegas, Calvin attracted a good deal of attention when he talked to people. The result turned out to be most lucrative. He signed a contract to do commercials for an auto company – something about four-wheel-drives, I believe. They shot the first one in Las Vegas, that's why we had to go back the second time. I wanted to tell you right away, but Calvin insisted on keeping it a surprise.'

It *was* a surprise, Jerrold admitted. 'You fell into a bed of roses, then,' he said to his father.

'About time, wouldn't you say?' Calvin asked.

Theda smiled at him. 'I expect other contracts to pop up once people see you on TV. You're really very good.'

'But where will you and Calvin live?' Carole asked her grandmother.

'Somewhere in the LA area, I expect,' Theda said. 'I've always had a yearning to go back to my old stomping ground. The ranch holds many pleasant memories, but I've never been really committed to it like a proper Harte, even after all these years. And there's another thing – Herwin wants me for a supporting role in his next film. Isn't that exciting? I'm so thrilled!'

'Marvelous news,' Carole agreed. 'I know how much that means to you. You certainly proved to me you're a born actress.'

Carole turned her attention to Jerrold. 'Speaking of acting – how about yours? Do you really want to live here? To take on Harte's Way?'

He grinned. 'As my father said, ranching's my first love. Acting has always been only a way to support myself. I've been tossing hints at you ever since I first saw this place, but you never caught them. I finally figured you really didn't want me to come here and live with you.'

She crossed to him and reached up to touch her lips to his. 'Nothing would make me happier. I just didn't understand you meant it.'

'Love, between you and this ranch, all my dreams have come true,' he told her warmly, aching to kiss her thoroughly, to hold her close, to begin their own private dance of desire.

'Speaking of dreams,' Calvin said, 'it's after midnight. 'I, for one, am ready to say goodnight and save the celebrating for tomorrow. With all this fuss settled, tomorrow can't help but be a right beauty.'

Jerrold still didn't entirely trust his father but, gazing at Carole's glowing eyes, he had to agree with him. Tomorrow and all the rest of the tomorrows waiting to be spent with Carole — beauties, right enough.

'So goodnight, dears,' Theda said, threading her arm through Calvin's. 'Sweet dreams.'

Jerrold joined his murmur of goodnight with Carole's. When the door closed behind their elders, he wrapped his arms around her and said, 'I suppose we should call it a night, too, but I'm not quite ready to let you go.'

'Never let me go,' she whispered, snuggling closer.

'Not if I can help it,' he said, covering her mouth with his.

After the fiasco in the restaurant, not in her wildest imaginings had Carole expected this night to end with her in Jerrold's arms. In fact, she'd expected never to be held close to him again, to feel the hard strength of his body pressed against hers, to feel the pleasurable escalation of desire as it raced like wildfire through her.

I can tell him the truth now, she thought with joy. I can tell him I love him.

She still couldn't quite believe he loved her in return, that she was, by his own confession, the only one in the world for him and that he adored her.

'Is it real?' she murmured against his lips.

'No dream could feel this good,' he assured her. 'And as the old man said, speaking of dreams, perhaps we'd better stop here and retire to our separate beds before it's too late.'

Reluctance to have him leave warred with her own feeling that she'd rather not carry their lovemaking any further tonight, not here in the house, not until they were alone here.

With a thrill of excitement, she realized the house actually *was* hers now and would be hers and Jerrold's home. Since they were speaking of dreams, hers had all come true.

'Remember,' Jerrold whispered into her ear, his warm breath an erotic tickle, 'I always finish what I start. If not tonight, soon, maybe sooner than you think.'

His lips captured hers again in a kiss that left her weak-kneed. He let her go, struck a pose and intoned, ' "Parting is such sweet sorrow." '

'Goodnight, Romeo,' she said, smiling.

It wasn't until he'd turned away that she realized he hadn't answered one of her questions. What about his acting?

'How is it going to work out?' she blurted.

He whirled to face her. 'What do you mean?'

'Your career. How does it fit in with the ranch?'

He shrugged. 'I take off when I have a film I need to do – not any more than two a year and, I hope, only one – and leave you pining away at Harte's Way and me frustrated wherever I am. When we get the place in shape and enough money ahead, I'll retire with relief to pure ranch work.'

She chuckled. 'Nothing's pure about ranch work.'

'That's the way I like it. No artificiality. I was born to be a grubber, you know. Now I'd better be off before I have second thoughts about leaving at all.'

'Wait,' she said. 'One more thing. What was that you muttered at me when we trespassed in that orange grove? Something about turning down some wonderful offer. Whose offer?'

He blinked. 'You weren't supposed to hear that.'

'Marla. Am I right?'

He ran a hand through his hair, looking harassed. 'It's not easy to explain.'

'I don't see why. Apparently she came on to you and you rejected her generous offer. With some later regrets.'

He reached out and grabbed her, drawing her close. 'No regrets. I was somewhat irked at you –

that's an understatement, you stubborn wench – or I wouldn't have mentioned it. On second thoughts, maybe I did want you to hear what I said.'

'And get jealous so I'd come to my senses?'

He nuzzled her nose with his. 'Something like that. I'm sure Mrs Ardaiz would understand. She seems to have a good handle on the communication gap between men and women. Marla's pitch didn't even didn't tempt me, love. You're the only woman I want.'

'I hope so.'

'Know it. No one compares to you – or ever will. I'm a one-woman man who's finally found the right one.'

'What about your vow never to marry again?' She teased. trying to tamp down her need to press closer to him.

'Once we tie the knot, I never *will* marry again,' he assured her. 'So there.' He kissed her, cutting off any comment she might have made.

But she had nothing more to say, except with her passionate response to his kiss. When they finally broke apart, they both were breathing heavily. 'Go or stay?' he asked, the words rough with desire.

She wanted him to stay and yet . . .

He touched her lips with his finger. 'I recognize a face full of indecision when I see one. Undecided means we shut it down for tonight.'

He bestowed a quick kiss on the tip of her nose, released her, turned and left the house.

As she walked slowly toward her bedroom, she smiled with anticipation. Sooner or later Jerrold always *did* finish what he started.

CHAPTER 20

The setting sun held no warmth and the wind cut through Carole's suede jacket as she viewed Harte's Way from the top of her favorite hill. The same hill where she and Jerrold had made love, where maybe they would again when spring came to the Valley. Winter was setting in with a vengeance but the cold came only from the outside. Her heart was warm with love.

Except for the snow-capped peaks in the distance, wherever she looked, she saw Harte land. Her land. And now Jerrold's.

Without glancing at her watch, she knew it must be close to four, when Theda's farewell party for the cast would begin. *From 4.00 p.m. on*, the invitations read. Believing the guests would trickle in, as usually happened, Carole wasn't eager to return to the house to dress. The person she waited for wouldn't be there yet.

Sombrita snorted and shifted underneath her, the mare's way of telling her to get going.

'In a minute,' Carole soothed, her gaze on the

country road where a plume of dust came closer by the second.

When she was able to identify the white Jag as the dust-raiser, Carole clucked Sombrita into motion. Her knight in his shiny white Jaguar had returned.

With Sombrita as eager as she to reach the corral, they made record time. Since José was nowhere in sight, she tended to the mare herself. As she turned Sombrita into the corral, the sound of metal striking metal alerted her to José's whereabouts – he was in the repair shed next to the garage. On her way to the house, she detoured to glance inside the shed.

'Aren't you coming to the party?' she asked him.

José looked up from the dirt bike he was trying to fix. 'Later, after I finish this one thing.'

He meant the bike's front fender, which had been bent out of recognition by the impact. He'd almost gotten the curve back to the original shape.

Alex, she'd heard, had been released from the local hospital with a cast on his leg and had gone back to LA with Brad. Apparently his concussion had not been serious.

'I keep telling you guys that wrecked or not, technically that dirt bike still belongs to Alex,' she said. 'What if you manage to get it fixed and he comes back to claim it?'

José shook his head. 'That *hombre*, he's bad

but he's no fool. He don't come back. He know if he do come back, we – how you say? – press charges. Sawa wants the bike, so I fix it for her.'

The whole idea had blown Carole's mind. Sawa had insisted the bike be retrieved from Alcatraz Hill, so Jerrold had rounded up an ATV belonging to Horizon and brought the wrecked machine to the repair shed. Envisioning Sawa riding the dirt bike caused Carole to shake her head in disbelief.

'They give it to me, the ghosts,' Sawa had insisted. 'I give back the gold, they send me a gift. Now I don't have to walk everywhere I go.'

When Carole had pointed out that Sawa had never ridden a dirt bike, the old woman had grinned at her. 'I can learn. José, he'll teach me after he fixes it.'

Maybe she should chalk it up as good coming from evil, Carole told herself. She told José she'd see him later and headed for the house.

Jerrold's Jag wasn't parked nearby, meaning he'd gone to his trailer to change for the party. Relieved – she didn't want him to see her until she was wearing her new dress, a pre-wedding present from Theda – she slipped in through the side door and hurried to her bedroom. The clock on her bedside stand told her it was exactly four.

She opened the closet, pulled out the dress, laid it across the bed and stood back to admire the color and the design. The dress was deep red, a color she wouldn't have thought to choose for herself, but she loved the shade and the way the bodice dipped into a V, much like the gowns of the early 1900s.

Shedding her work clothes, she washed quickly and donned her fanciest lingerie, obeying Theda's dictate that what one wore underneath should match what was on top. This dress deserved the best.

Once she had her makeup fixed and the dress on, she stood in front of the mirror and clasped the garnet pendant around her neck. The deep glowing red of the stone was striking with the dress and, if she could believe what she saw in the mirror, she was striking, too.

When she eased into the living room, she was surprised at the crowd already gathered there. People were arriving earlier than she'd expected. Calvin, she noticed, was circulating, busy introducing Horizon people to the locals and charming everybody in the process. To her disappointment, Jerrold wasn't in sight. Deciding that Theda would expect her to act as a secondary hostess, Carole began the routine of greetings and introductions.

'A ripper night, Carole girl,' Calvin said, appearing at her elbow. 'You look as gorgeous as your grandmother. She's certainly a world class party-thrower. And hostess. Makes everyone feel she's their best friend. Picked me a winner, I did.'

'Theda's fantastic,' Carole agreed, smiling at him. 'But you're no slouch as a host yourself.'

He threw an arm over her shoulders and hugged her. 'When you find Jerrold,' he said, 'do me a favor. Bring him into Theda's memory room, will you? And keep him occupied until your grandmother and I get there.' Calvin winked at her. 'I'm sure you'll be able to. Now, if you'll excuse me, I've been requested to play.' He flexed his fingers and sauntered toward the music room.

Theda fluttered over to her. 'Isn't this marvelous?' she asked. Not waiting for Carole's nod, she said, 'You look like your great-grandmother in that dress, and she was a real beauty who always dressed well, or so I understood from your grandfather. Clothes may not make the woman, but good clothes do add a certain flair.'

'I'm beginning to understand what you mean.' She smiled at Theda. 'Just when you were ready to give up on me, I'm finally being converted.'

'Dear, you should know by now, I never give up.' Theda turned to examine her guests. 'Look, there's José. My, how elegant!'

Carole stared at a José transformed by his Californio outfit, complete with silver decorations. Leaving her grandmother, who was already talking to someone else, Carole intercepted him.

'A true Spanish don,' she said admiringly.

'Do you plan to give up ranching for the movies?'

He grinned at her. 'The little boss, he give me these clothes, say I fit them better than his actors. Maybe so, maybe not. Me, I ride a horse in one scene and those cameras, they make me so nervous I almost fall off. *Una vez, nada mas* – once is enough, no more. But the clothes, these I keep.'

'They do become you. Have you seen Sawa?'

He shook his head. 'She'll come when she's ready, like always. I hear something, though. I hear because she win *mucho* money on her bets on account of you, she weave you a special wedding basket.'

Carole flushed. 'I had nothing to do with her winning.'

'She thinks you did. Me, I think you did. Mr Jerrold, he think you did.'

'What's all this about winning?' Marla's voice came from behind Carole. 'Are you referring to that perfectly dreadful bet?'

'What bet?' Carole said quickly, turning to look at Marla, gorgeous in green, with her admirers in tow. Rich was not among them. 'Actually, we were discussing *Bandido* and we agreed it's sure to be a winner,' Carole added. 'Right, José?'

'Righto, mate,' José confirmed, his grin widening.

Marla's look told Carole she didn't for a

381

moment believe them. She started to say something, shook her head and smiled instead, obviously dismissing the matter. 'I have marvelous
news,' she said. 'After finishing the Hawaiian
film, I'm scheduled for the lead role of Princess
Ahes in a TV mini series to be filmed in
Brittany. The money's great, the exposure
won't hurt and I just love France!'

'You'll make a perfect princess,' Carole told
her, meaning every word. Marla already had the
proper imperial attitude. 'Congratulations.'

'Congrats to you, as well,' Marla said. 'You've
come up with your own prize, haven't you? I
hope he knows he's getting the genuine article
this time around.'

'Thank you,' Carole said, deciding to take
Marla's words as a compliment.

Marla's attention was distracted and she
drifted away. Wondering if Rich had even bothered to show up, Carole glanced around the
room. Not here. On her way to the music
room, to look for him there, she met Sawa,
dressed in the loveliest white buckskin dress
Carole had ever seen. The beadwork alone
made it a museum piece.

'How beautiful,' she breathed.

'I guess you don't mean me,' Sawa said,
chuckling. 'This dress I get married in, I put
away for a long time, now I wear it. Already
three people, they want to buy it.' She shook her
head. 'I sell them baskets, not my dress.'

'I hope you don't intend to ride that dirt bike in it,' Carole teased.

Sawa grinned at her. 'I show you how I can ride, you wait and see.'

A member of the cast came up and stood back to stare at Sawa. 'Fantastic beadwork,' she said. 'I suppose you don't want to sell.'

'Not the dress,' Sawa told her. 'But I make Miwok baskets to sell.'

'Handwoven,' Carole put in. 'True museum pieces.'

Leaving them discussing when the baskets could be seen, Carole edged into the music room, finally spotting Rich more or less hiding behind the piano. Calvin was playing and singing in a pleasant tenor an old-time sentimental ballad about walking alone and Carole shook her head. Apparently Rich was taking the words to heart. This wouldn't do, not at all. But how was she to rescue him from what Theda called 'the dismals'?

Then she saw Kitty Knowles standing on the far side of the piano, staring wistfully at Rich, who hadn't a clue she was anywhere around. Caught up in his misery over Marla, he probably had forgotten Kitty even existed, whereas Carole saw her friend as an answer to his problem. The trick was to make him aware of Kitty. Without a concrete plan, she'd have to play it by ear.

Carole moved purposefully toward Rich. 'Stop skulking in the shadows,' she scolded him. 'The least you could do is pretend to be having a good time.'

'Why?' he asked bleakly.

'To show Marla you really don't care,' she said bluntly, figuring nothing else might work.

Rich eyed her warily. 'How am I supposed to do that? I'm no actor.'

'We're all actors when we have to be. And right now you have to be. I insist.' Taking his hand, Carole led him from behind the piano. 'What you're going to do is meet the new, giggleless Kitty, who's trying to recover from her own mismatched affair. If you both pretend to have fun, actually you'll be helping each other.'

'Kitty?' he said, wincing.

'I told you, she's totally changed. No giggles, no rattling on. You won't know her. And, should you decide to take the trouble to give her a unprejudiced once-over, you'll notice she's one of the prettiest girls here.'

Kitty's red hair set off her understated black dress in a rather spectacular way. Carole suspected Theda had a hand in the dress selection because Kitty tended to choose fussier clothes. The simpler dress flattered her slender curves.

'Okay, so I admit she's not bad-looking,' Rich muttered. 'But –'

'Shh. I don't want to hear any excuses.'

Sighing in resignation, Rich let her lead him to Kitty. On the way, Carole tried to figure out how she was going to pull this off. Kitty didn't have a clue about the story she'd made up for Rich. Talk fast, she told herself, and hope for the best.

'Kitty,' she said, when they reached her, 'I've brought Rich over to cheer you up. I hope you won't mind that I've broken my word to keep it secret and told him about how you were forced to give your man the heave-ho and then wound up suffering an acute case of regret.'

Kitty stared at her in stupefaction until Carole stepped hard on her toe. 'Oh!' she gasped.

Taking advantage of Kitty's momentary wince of pain, Carole hurried on. 'I'm sorry if my sharing your confidence with Rich upsets you,' she said. 'But there's no need to suffer alone. Is there, Rich?' She jabbed him surreptitiously in the ribs.

'Uh, no,' he muttered. 'That is, I –' he floundered.

'Do you mean you know what I'm going through?' Kitty asked him, to Carole's relief. Her friend had finally picked up her cue. 'From your own experience? Oh, how sad. But please do tell me about it. Maybe it'll make us both feel better.'

'Well, I –' Rich broke off and glanced around. 'Let's look for a more private corner somewhere.'

Smiling with satisfaction – she'd got them together and misery loved company – Carole watched them walk away. Nothing might come of it but at least Rich wasn't brooding alone at the moment. Now it was up to Kitty to carry the ball and she wished her all the luck in the world.

Strong arms wrapped around her from behind and Jerrold's voice murmured in her ear, 'Whose canary has the cat eaten this time?'

'I'm trying to make a match,' she told him, leaning against his strength, feeling the tingle of desire begin inside her.

'Not for yourself, I hope – you're already taken. Permanently and totally.' He let her go, adding, 'Any more cuddling and we're out of here.'

She slanted him an intimate look, trying to convey that she wished they were alone. Recalling Calvin's words, she realized they could be – for a few moments, anyway – and she murmured, 'How about an assignation?'

'Reading my mind again?'

Taking his hand, she drew Jerrold with her through the crowd, smiling greetings as she went but not pausing. When they were inside Theda's memory room, a place her grandmother closed off for her parties as being too special for a crowd, Jerrold said, 'Alone at last.' He pulled Carole into his arms and kissed her enthusiastically. She responded with fervor.

His caresses grew more intimate, escalating her desire so that she clung to him, the rest of the world vanishing. There was only Jerrold and their love for one another.

Eventually, he eased her away, saying, 'If you don't want to be stripped out of that gorgeous red dress, we'd better take a breather. Holding her at arm's length, he added, 'How beautiful you are.'

Her heart sang with joy. 'I missed you,' she confessed.

'I feel like I've been gone for a year instead of a couple of days. I thought about you all the time and I brought you something special.'

Carole was exclaiming over earrings of garnet nestled in lacy antique gold that matched her great-grandmother's pendant, when the door opened and Calvin ushered Theda into the room. He was carrying what looked to be a large framed painting wrapped in brown paper.

Jerrold glanced at Carole. 'Planned?' he asked.

She nodded.

'I asked her to,' Calvin said, 'because I have a pre-wedding present for you, my boy.' He tore off the paper and held up a portrait done in oils.

As Carole stared in fascination at the portrait, she heard Jerrold draw in his breath sharply. From a gilded frame, a craggy-faced Scotsman in green-on-green kilt with a matching plaid over his shoulder, gazed sternly at them. A white terrier sat at his feet and a sheathed dagger was thrust into the top of the left knee-sock.

'There's no way of tracing the original,' Calvin said, offering the painting to Jerrold. 'Fortunately I found some old photographs of The McLeod in my trunk and a painter friend of Theda's used them, along with my description of the original, to create this.'

Jerrold, holding the portrait, stared at his father without speaking.

'Ugly old sod, wasn't he?' Calvin said. 'Still, I know he loved you as much as he hated me. Recreating his portrait for you doesn't make up for the past but it's the best I could do, son.'

Jerrold set the painting down very carefully, leaning it against the wall. He took a deep breath and, reaching for his father, threw his arms around him. 'Of all the perishing old sods,' he said huskily, 'you're the worst.'

'I told you he loved me,' Calvin said triumphantly after Jerrold released him, his voice as choked with emotion as Jerrold's.

Carole and Theda looked at one another and smiled, sharing their own moment of closeness.

Clearing his throat, Calvin added, 'It's a bloody beaut of a life, isn't it?'

Carole knew he spoke for them all. Life had never been so beautiful.

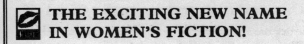

THE EXCITING NEW NAME
IN WOMEN'S FICTION!

PLEASE HELP ME TO HELP YOU!

Dear *Scarlet* Reader,

As Editor of *Scarlet* Books I want to make sure that the
books I offer you every month are up to the high standards
Scarlet readers expect. And to do that I need to know a
little more about you and your reading likes and dislikes. So
please spare a few minutes to fill in the short questionnaire
on the following pages and send it to me.

Looking forward to hearing from you,

Sally Cooper

Editor-in-Chief, *Scarlet*

QUESTIONNAIRE

Please tick the appropriate boxes to indicate your answers

1 Where did you get this Scarlet title?
Bought in supermarket ☐
Bought at my local bookstore ☐ Bought at chain bookstore ☐
Bought at book exchange or used bookstore ☐
Borrowed from a friend ☐
Other (please indicate) _____

2 Did you enjoy reading it?
A lot ☐   A little ☐   Not at all ☐

3 What did you particularly like about this book?
Believable characters ☐   Easy to read ☐
Good value for money ☐   Enjoyable locations ☐
Interesting story ☐   Modern setting ☐
Other _____

4 What did you particularly dislike about this book?
_____

5 Would you buy another Scarlet book?
Yes ☐   No ☐

6 What other kinds of book do you enjoy reading?
Horror ☐   Puzzle books ☐   Historical fiction ☐
General fiction ☐   Crime/Detective ☐   Cookery ☐
Other (please indicate) _____

7 Which magazines do you enjoy reading?
1. _____
2. _____
3. _____

And now a little about you –
8 How old are you?
Under 25 ☐   25–34 ☐   35–44 ☐
45–54 ☐   55–64 ☐   over 65 ☐

cont.

9 What is your marital status?
Single ☐   Married/living with partner ☐
Widowed ☐   Separated/divorced ☐

10 What is your current occupation?
Employed full-time ☐   Employed part-time ☐
Student ☐   Housewife full-time ☐
Unemployed ☐   Retired ☐

11 Do you have children? If so, how many and how old are they?
_____
_____

12 What is your annual household income?
under $15,000	☐	or	£10,000	☐
$15–25,000	☐	or	£10–20,000	☐
$25–35,000	☐	or	£20–30,000	☐
$35–50,000	☐	or	£30–40,000	☐
over $50,000	☐	or	£40,000	☐

Miss/Mrs/Ms _____

Address _____
_____
_____

Thank you for completing this questionnaire. Now tear it out – put it in an envelope and send it, before 30 June 1998, to:

Sally Cooper, Editor-in-Chief

USA/Can. address
SCARLET c/o London Bridge
85 River Rock Drive
Suite 202
Buffalo
NY 14207
USA

UK address/No stamp required
SCARLET
FREEPOST LON 3335
LONDON W8 4BR
Please use block capitals for address

Scarlet titles coming next month:

MARRIAGE DANCE   Jillian James
Anni Ross is totally committed to her career in dance. She's positive that she's got no time to spare for falling in love! But attractive lawyer Steve Hunter has other plans for Anni's future . . .

SLOW DANCING   Elizabeth Smith
Hallie Prescott is plunged into the world of glitter and glamour when she accompanies her screenwriter husband to Hollywood. But it's not long before the dream goes sour. Can Grant Keeler help Hallie rebuild her life?

THAT CINDERELLA FEELING   Anne Styles
Out of work actress Casey Taylor will take any job she can find. Which is how she ends up delivering a kissagram to the offices of Alex Havilland, a businessman who has no time for frivolity and who is definitely *not* amused!

A DARKER SHADOW   Patricia Wilson
Amy Scott can handle any problem that the world of computers throws at her. But when it comes to coping with sudden and frightening events in her private life, she doesn't know where to turn. Until her arrogant and disapproving boss Luc Martell decides to intervene . . .